A Night on the Orient Express

A Night on the Orient Express

Veronica Henry

First published in Great Britain in 2013 by Orion Books,
an imprint of The Orion Publishing Group Ltd,
Orion House, 5 Upper St Martin's Lane,
London WC2H 9EA

An Hachette UK company

1 3 5 7 9 10 8 6 4 2

A CIP catalogue record for this book is
available from the British Library.

ISBN (Hardback) 978 1 4091 3094 9
ISBN (Ebook) 978 1 4091 3096 3

Typeset at The Spartan Press Ltd,
Lymington, Hants

Printed and bound in Great Britain by
Clays Ltd, St Ives plc

The Orion Publishing Group's policy is to use papers that
are natural, renewable and recyclable products and
made from wood grown in sustainable forests. The logging
and manufacturing processes are expected to conform to
the environmental regulations of the country of origin.

www.orionbooks.co.uk

In memory of Samuel George Bright
1927–2013

Acknowledgements

This book was a sheer delight to research and an utter joy to write, but it would not have been possible without the help of Anna Nash at the Venice Simplon-Orient-Express, whose support and generosity for the project knew no bounds. Thank you, Anna. Thank you also to her successor, Emma Wylde, for her help and enthusiasm. I raise a glass of champagne to you both.

Thanks are also due to Rupert Aarons, our steward, and Walter Nisi, the head barman, who looked after my husband and me whilst on board the train and made it a journey never to be forgotten. Also, the team at the Hotel Cipriani for a magical stay.

The book was only enhanced by the eagle eyes and whip-cracking of my agent Araminta Whitley and editor Kate Mills, who both made sure it stayed on track and arrived at the station on time. Their guidance is appreciated more than they can ever know.

Big thanks too for your input – and much laughter – to Peta Nightingale and Sophie Hughes at Lucas Alexander Whitley. Working with you both is a dream.

For advice on what to see and do and where to eat in Venice, I am grateful to Rebecca Watson of Valerie

Hoskins Associates and Mark Lucas of Lucas Alexander Whitley.

I am also grateful to Claire McLeish, Alice Wilson and Ilana Fox for being the most amazing friends over the past year. *Oscar-style tears and gushing*

Thanks also to my husband Peter for allowing me to drag him back to Venice on a second honeymoon – tough, but there was no other man for the job!

Finally, eternal gratitude to Susan Lamb for her vision and determination, but most importantly her kindness.

Prologue

*A*s the clock chimes midnight, in a siding just outside Calais a train sits waiting under a still sky. Above it the moon glimmers, bathing it in a silvery glow. The carriages are empty, but for the ghosts of passengers walking up and down the corridors, their fingertips gliding along the marquetry, their scent mingling in the stillness of the air. The faint trace of piano music floats away into the black velvet night, weaving its way amidst whispers and promises. For here a thousand stories have already unfolded, stories of love and hope, of passion and heartache, of reconciliation and parting.

There are eleven sleeping cars, three dining cars and a bar. In a few hours' time, these silent carriages will burst into life as the train is prepared for its journey. No surface will be left unpolished. The cutlery and glassware will shine. Not a speck of dust or a smear of grease will remain. The livery will be hosed down until the metal gleams. Every wish, every need, every possible whim is considered as the provisions are brought on board, from the tiniest pats of creamy butter to bottles of the finest champagne.

At last, the staff will stand to attention under the gaze of the train manager, their uniforms pristine, ready for the final inspection before it leaves for the station.

On the platform, the waiting passengers shiver slightly. Whether from the crispness of the air or the excitement of climbing on board the most famous train in the world, who can say? Either way, their stories are waiting to be told.

Here! Here it is. The first glimpse of the Orient Express as it slides regally towards the platform. The sun bounces off the mirror-bright glass of the windows as the station master strides forward. There is a satisfying whoosh as the brakes are applied, and the train comes to a halt, purring, resplendent, proud – yet somehow welcoming. Who can resist such an invitation?

Come. Gather up your belongings. Wind the scarf more tightly round your neck; pull on your gloves and your hat as you take your lover's arm.

Hurry – your seat is waiting . . .

NOT ON THE SHELF
Matches made in heaven for over twenty years

Sign up to our website for your chance to win the trip of a lifetime

---

Have you despaired of ever meeting the right person? Are you convinced there is no one out there for you? Are you tired of friends trying to set you up with someone, your cheeks aching as you smile away the evening, bored rigid?

If this sounds like you, Not On The Shelf is offering you the chance to win the trip of a lifetime with your dream date. All you have to do is sign up to our website and send in your profile and we will examine the entries using our renowned matchmaking expertise.

Each profile is individually assessed by a panel of experts who have years of experience in pairing the right partners. We don't use a computer because computers can't read between the lines and spot the spark that will make a relationship come alive.

We will match up the perfect couple from the entries, and they will go on the ultimate blind date: a night on the Orient Express from London to Venice.

Enjoy breathtaking scenery as the legendary train takes you on the journey of a lifetime. Sip cocktails in the bar while the grand piano serenades you, then have a sumptuous dinner in the dining car with the finest wines. You will each have your own luxury cabin, with a steward on hand to fulfil your every wish.

Even if you don't win, the chance of your dream coming true and you finding the perfect partner is high. Since we began we have matched up thousands of happy couples, been responsible for hundreds of weddings and dozens of Not On The Shelf babies.

What are you waiting for? Go to our website and fill out the profile questionnaire. You might just embark on a journey that will change your life.

NOT ON THE SHELF
Profile Questionnaire

EMMIE DIXON

AGE: 26
OCCUPATION: Milliner
LIVES: London

FAVOURITE QUOTE: The most important thing is to enjoy your life – to be happy – it's all that matters. (Audrey Hepburn)

WHO WOULD PLAY ME IN THE FILM OF MY LIFE: Maggie Gyllenhaal.

ME IN 50 WORDS: I like to work hard and play hard. I love dressing up. I think life is an adventure and I never want to stop learning. I'm a city girl but I love escaping to the country. I believe in making your own luck, which is why I've entered this competition.

A FEW OF MY FAVOURITE THINGS: Violet creams, fireworks, good manners, picnics, snowmen, Agatha Christie, log fires, strawberry daiquiris, Saturday-morning brunch, wrapping presents.

MY IDEAL PARTNER IN ONE SENTENCE: I want someone who will surprise me and make me laugh, who is kind, and who knows how to have fun.

NOT ON THE SHELF
Profile Questionnaire

ARCHIE HARBINSON

AGE: 28
OCCUPATION: Farmer
LIVES: Cotswolds

FAVOURITE QUOTE: Who let the dogs out?

WHO WOULD PLAY ME IN THE FILM OF MY LIFE: Colin Firth

ME IN 50 WORDS: I love my farm but I love the bright lights as well. I can't cook to save my life and I'm a bit of a scruff but I scrub up well. I value loyalty over everything. I might come across as shy but deep down I know how to party.

A FEW OF MY FAVOURITE THINGS: Walking the land with my border terriers Sid and Nancy, Sunday lunch in the local pub, my vintage Morgan, Billie Holliday, the West End at Christmas, sunrise, the first cup of tea of the day, mojitos, socks warmed on the Aga, dancing.

MY IDEAL PARTNER IN ONE SENTENCE: I want someone to take care of, to make me laugh, and to keep me warm at night (my cottage has no central heating).

Before
the Journey

One

Adele Russell didn't much care for telephones. They were, of course, a necessity. An integral part of daily life. She couldn't imagine being without one but, unlike many of her friends, she spent as little time on the phone as possible. She liked eye contact, and to be able to read body language, especially when she was doing business. There were so many opportunities to be misunderstood on the phone. It was harder to say the things you really wanted to say, and so much could be left unsaid. And one rarely allowed oneself the luxury of silence: a moment to ruminate before replying. Perhaps this was a hangover from the days when a telephone call was an indulgence, when one kept the imparting of information to a bare minimum, conscious of the cost?

Adele would have preferred to have today's conversation in person, but she didn't have that option. She had put the call off for long enough already. Adele had never been a procrastinator, but burying the past had taken such a supreme effort of will at the time, she was reluctant to unearth it again. As she picked up the phone, she told herself she wasn't being greedy or grabby or grasping. She was simply asking for what was rightly hers. And it wasn't as if she even wanted it for herself.

Imogen. Her granddaughter's image flickered in her mind for a moment. She felt a mixture of pride and guilt and worry. If it weren't for Imogen, she would be leaving Pandora's box firmly shut, she thought. Or would she? Once again, she reminded herself that she had every right to do what she was doing.

Her finger, with its brightly painted nail, hovered over the first zero for a moment before she pressed it. She might be eighty-four, but she still kept herself groomed and glamorous. She heard the long tone of an overseas ring. While she waited for it to be answered, she remembered how many times she had phoned him in secret all those years ago, heart pounding, nose filled with the telephone-box smell of stale smoke, pushing in the money as the pips sounded . . .

'Hello?' The voice was young, female, English. Confident.

Adele ran through the possibilities: daughter, lover, second wife, housekeeper . . . ? Wrong number?

'May I speak to Jack Molloy?'

'Sure.' The disinterest in the speaker's voice told Adele there was no emotional involvement. Probably a housekeeper, then. 'Who's calling, please?'

This was just a routine question, not paranoia.

'Tell him it's Adele Russell.'

'Will he know what it's about?' Again, routine, not interrogative.

'He will.' Of this she was certain.

'One moment.' Adele heard the speaker put the phone down. Footsteps. Voices.

Then Jack.

'Adele. How very lovely. It's been a long time.'

He sounded totally unfazed to hear from her. His tone was dry, amused, teasing. As ever. But all those years on, it did not have the same effect it once had. She had thought she was so grown up at the time, but she had been so very far from grown up. Every decision she had made had been immature and selfish, until the very end. That's when her journey into adulthood had really begun, with the realisation that the world didn't revolve around Adele Russell and her needs.

'I had to wait until the time was right,' she replied.

'I saw William's obituary. I'm sorry.'

Three lines in the newspaper. Beloved husband, father and grandfather. No flowers. Donations to his favourite charity. Adele spread her fingers out on the desktop and looked at her wedding and engagement rings. She still wore them. She was still William's wife.

'This isn't a social call,' she told him, sounding as businesslike as she could. 'I'm calling about *The Inamorata*.'

There was a pause while he processed the information.

'Of course,' he replied. His tone was light, but she sensed he was crestfallen by her briskness. 'Well, it's here. I've looked after it for you with the greatest of care. She's ready for you to collect. Any time you like.'

Adele felt almost deflated. She had been ready for a fight.

'Good. I shall send somebody over.'

'Oh.' There was genuine disappointment in his voice. 'I was hoping to see you. To take you for dinner at least. You'd like where I am. Giudecca . . .'

Had he forgotten that she'd already been there? He couldn't have. Surely.

'I'm sure I would. But I no longer fly, I'm afraid.' It was all too much for her these days. The waiting, the discomfort, the inevitable delays. She had seen enough of the world over the years. She didn't feel the need to see any more of it.

'There's always the train. The Orient Express . . . Remember?'

'Of course I do.' Her tone was sharper than she intended. She saw herself, standing on the platform at the Gare de l'Est in Paris, shivering in the yellow linen dress with the matching coat that she'd bought in the rue du Faubourg the day before. Shivering not from the cold, but from anticipation and anxiety and guilt.

Adele felt her throat tighten. The memory was so bittersweet. She had no room for it, what with everything else. She had enough emotions to deal with right now. Selling Bridge House, where her children had been born and brought up, selling the gallery that had been her life, contemplating her future – and Imogen's: it had all been most unsettling. Necessary, but unsettling.

'I'll send someone over in about three weeks,' she told him. 'Will that be convenient?'

There was no reply for a moment. Adele wondered if Jack was going to be difficult after all. There was no paperwork to support her claim. It had just been a promise.

'Venice in April, Adele. I would be the perfect host. The perfect gentleman. Think about it.'

She felt the old anxiety tug at her insides. Perhaps she wasn't as immune as she thought? He'd always done this to her – made her want to do things she shouldn't do. In her mind's eye, she was already at his door, curiosity having got the better of her.

Why would she want to put herself through the turmoil again? At her age? She shuddered at the thought. It was far better to keep it in the past. That way she was in control.

'No, Jack.'

She heard his sigh.

'Well, you know your own mind. Consider it an open invitation. I'd be delighted to see you again.'

Adele gazed out of the window that looked onto the river. A strong current, swollen by the March rain, rippled between the banks, sweeping along with a certainty she envied. Taking a step into the unknown was a risk. At her age, she preferred to know exactly where she was.

'Thank you, but I think perhaps . . . not.'

There was an awkward silence, which Jack finally broke.

'I suppose I don't need to tell you how much the painting's worth now.'

'It's not about that, Jack.'

His laugh was the same.

'I don't care if it is. It's yours to do with what you will. Though I hope you won't just be selling it to the highest bidder.'

'Don't worry,' she reassured him. 'It won't be going out of the family. I'm giving it to my granddaughter. For her thirtieth birthday.'

'Well, I hope it gives her as much pleasure as it's given me.' Jack sounded pleased.

'I'm sure.'

'She's thirty? Not much younger than you were—'

'Indeed.' She cut him off. She would have to be brisk.

They were straying into sentimentality. 'My assistant will telephone you to keep you informed of the arrangements.' She was about to end the conversation and ring off, but something made her soften. They were both old. Chances were they wouldn't live another decade. 'You're well, I hope?'

'All things considered, I can't complain at all. Although I'm not as . . . vigorous as I once was.'

Adele smothered a smile.

'How very lucky for Venice,' she replied, slightly tart.

'And you, Adele?'

She didn't want to speak to him anymore. She felt smothered by the strong sense of what might have been, the feeling she had fought to keep at bay for all those years.

'Very well. I've enjoyed my business, and my family is nearby. Life is good.' She wasn't going to show a chink or elaborate. 'In fact, I must go. I have a lunch appointment.'

She rang off as quickly as was polite.

Her hands were shaking as she put the telephone back in its cradle. He still had an effect on her. She had never quite buried the longing. It had wormed its way up to the surface every now and again, when she least expected it.

Why hadn't she accepted his invitation? What harm could it do?

'Don't be so ridiculous!' Her voice rang out in the stillness of the morning room.

She looked up. The seascape was still hanging there – the one she had bid for on the day she and Jack first met. She had kept it over her writing desk ever since. Not a brush-stroke had changed in the intervening years. That was the beauty of paintings. They captured a moment. They always stayed the same.

The thought brought her back to the task in hand. She had so much to organise: estate agents, accountants, lawyers were all waiting on her decisions. Many people had advised her not to make any drastic decisions until some time after bereavement, but she felt sure she'd left it long enough now. Bridge House was too big for one; the Russell Gallery was too much for her, even with Imogen pretty much running things. And Imogen had assured her, again and again, that she didn't want to take it over, that it was time for her to have a fresh challenge, that she had never intended to stay in Shallowford so long. Adele had offered to find a compromise, but Imogen had insisted that she wanted a clean break. Nevertheless, Adele felt guilty, which was why she was retrieving *The Inamorata*. It would be quite the most wonderful gift. She couldn't think of anyone in the world who would appreciate it more than Imogen, and it would go some way towards salving her conscience.

She thought back over the conversation she had just had. How would her life have turned out, if she hadn't had Jack in it? Would things have been different? She felt certain that she would never have had the drive and determination she had ended up with, if she hadn't known him. Yet would she, perhaps, have been happier?

'You couldn't have been happier,' she told herself crossly. 'Jack was an error of judgement. Everyone's allowed to make mistakes.'

This she believed firmly. You had to get things wrong, in order to get things right. And in the end, she *had* got things right . . .

15

She dragged her mind back to the present. That was enough self-flagellation. She had plans to put into place. She was going to make some big changes, all for the better. She looked around the morning room, the room where she had made most of her important decisions. She loved its high ceilings and the sash windows looking over the river. In fact, she loved every square inch of Bridge House. Perfectly symmetrical, in a soft red brick, it sat, not surprisingly, by the bridge in Shallowford, quite the prettiest house in the little market town. Nicky, the estate agent and Imogen's best friend, had told her it would be snapped up, probably before they had time to print the glossy brochures that showed off its perfect proportions, the walled garden, the dark-red front door with the arched fan light . . .

For a moment, Adele felt doubt in her plan. She would miss this house terribly. She suffered a stab of resentment at having to give it up. She reminded herself that it was better to make difficult decisions while you were still in control, and before events overtook you. Determined, she unscrewed the lid from her fountain pen and pulled a pad of paper towards her. Adele was far from computer-phobic, but she still found writing things down focused her mind so much better.

As she worked through her list, part of her conversation with Jack kept floating back.

The Orient Express. It still ran from London to Venice; she knew that. An iconic journey. Possibly the most famous journey in the world. A plan began to form in her mind. She did a search on her computer, found the website she wanted, and browsed through the information. Before she had time to change her mind, she picked up the phone.

'Hello? Yes, I'd like to book a ticket. A single to Venice, please . . .'

As she waited to be connected to the right person, her gaze fell once more on the painting that hung over her desk. Jack was right – she hadn't been much older than Imogen the day she'd bought it. The day it had all begun. It seemed like only yesterday . . .

Two

*B*ridge House was ominous with silence. A silence that
mocked and taunted, and made Adele turn on the wireless,
the gramophone, even the television, although the received
wisdom was that one only turned it on for the evening news, if
one had any standards. But none of the voices filled the gaping
hole left by two small but noisy boys who had been packed off to
prep school for the first time.

There was no thump of the football hitting the side of the
house. No thundering up the stairs. No flushing of the loo in
the downstairs cloakroom – not that they always remembered
to flush. No high-pitched gleeful voices, no sudden wails when
an injury or injustice occurred. No laughter.

Worse, there was no momentum to the day. For seven years
the twins had given her life traction. Not that she had spent
her days hovering over them, by any means, but they had
always been there. Even when they were at the village school,
they'd come tearing home for lunch, so Adele had never spent
any great amount of time on her own. She never resented their
presence for a moment, unlike so many of her friends, who
seemed to breathe a sigh of relief when their offspring were
despatched.

If Adele had had her way, the boys would have stayed on at

the village school and then gone on to the grammar in Filbury at eleven, but that was a battle she was never going to win. Tony and Tim were destined for the same schools their father William had been to, in the time-honoured tradition of the British upper-middle classes.

So, she had known the day was coming, she had dreaded it, and now it had been and gone it was even worse than she had thought it would be. She didn't spend the days lying on her bed sobbing, but her heart felt as empty as the house.

Added to which, the twins' departure had coincided with William leaving too. Just after they married, the Russells had bought Bridge House because of the coach house attached, which had served as William's surgery for over ten years. Although Adele hadn't been directly involved, her role as the doctor's wife had been one she had taken seriously, engaging on a daily basis with his patients and being concerned with their welfare.

But now William had joined three other GPs to set up a modern practice in Filbury, five miles away. It was part of the NHS drive to make medical care more accessible. It was exciting for him – revolutionary – but it involved so much decision-making, so much more responsibility. So much more time. She barely saw him, and when he did come home, he was burdened with paperwork and reports. When he'd practised from Bridge House, he'd had morning surgery from nine until midday, then again from two until four, and that had been it, apart from being on call to answer emergencies and deliver difficult babies.

And thus Adele felt lonely and useless and rather sad. And, if she was honest, a tiny bit resentful towards her husband. If she was feeling particularly self-pitying, she blamed him for sending the boys away and then abandoning her. What did he expect her to do with her time?

Yet Adele wasn't really the type to bear a grudge or bemoan her lot. She was a doer, which was presumably why William assumed she could cope. And which was why, at twenty past nine on a Tuesday morning, she had already done everything she needed. She'd walked up the high street to the butcher for tonight's supper, and bought a punnet of plums to make a crumble – that would take all of ten minutes. There was no housework to be done, for she had Mrs Morris, her daily help. There was a coffee morning up at the town hall but she had a horrible feeling that she might, just might, burst into tears if anyone asked her how the twins were getting on, and that would make her feel foolish. She'd had her dark curls washed and set the day before, and had welled up when the hairdresser had enquired as to their wellbeing.

She picked up the local weekly newspaper and leafed through it for inspiration, although what she imagined might be in there she didn't know. She noticed there was a country-house sale not too far away. She thought she would go: she was thinking of turning the abandoned surgery into an annexe for house guests, and there might be some furniture there. Without thinking too much about it, she fished in her handbag for a pale-pink Coty lipstick, dragged it across her lips, took her mac from the hook in the hallway and picked up her gloves. It was either that or go and swap her books at the mobile library. They were waiting in a pile on the hall table but the very thought made her faint with tedium.

She went out to her car. A pale-blue A35 saloon. She was, she knew, lucky to have a car to drive. She was lucky full stop. She had the most coveted house in Shallowford, right on the bridge by the river, with a pretty walled garden and a wrought-iron walkway to the door . . . so why did she feel so empty?

There was, of course, one good reason, but she didn't dwell on it very often because really – what was the point? If she felt it was ironic that her own husband, who had delivered so many of the babies in the town they lived in, hadn't been there to supervise the birth of her own sons and had therefore not been able to prevent the subsequent damage, she had never said so. William felt badly, of course he did, that he had been so far away on that day. If he'd been nearer then maybe there would be another little Russell to fill the void left by the twins' departure, or maybe even two. But there wasn't, so . . .

As she pulled out of the drive and onto the high street, a dreary September rain began to fall. Adele turned on the windscreen wipers, which dragged themselves reluctantly back and forth. It was going to be a long winter.

The country-house sale was about ten miles away, in Wiltshire: it was a rather small, insignificant house and there was nothing of any great value or note in the catalogue. Adele enjoyed buying things at auction – she always preferred to buy antiques, and she loved the drama and competitiveness. It was much more satisfying than going to a department store, for you never knew quite what you might find.

Today, it didn't take her long to assess the lots. There was a great deal of ugly furniture of an indeterminate age – all the good stuff must have gone to family – but amidst the cumbersome wardrobes and endless sets of china she spotted a painting. It was a seascape, rather wild and abandoned, and she loved the colours: the bruised purple and silver. It was sombre and foreboding, but she felt that it suited her mood, somehow. She could feel its brooding quality roll off the canvas. And she knew that the most important thing about a painting was that it should make you feel something. She loved it. She was pretty sure it would go for next to nothing so she decided to bid for it.

The auction itself was in a tent in the garden, as none of the rooms in the house was quite large enough. It was cold and windy and she was starting to think perhaps she wouldn't bother at all, but it started to pour with rain again and she decided she would get wetter going back to the car, which was parked in an adjoining field, than going into the tent. She held the auction catalogue over her head and ran in.

The chairs were terribly uncomfortable, not helped by the fact that the floor, covered in coconut matting, was uneven. She huddled inside her coat, clutching the now-sodden auction catalogue. She'd marked the picture she was interested in, and written the price she was prepared to go to beside it – not a great deal. After all, it would need cleaning, and reframing. She had mentally hung it over the desk in the morning room where she wrote her letters. She would be able to look at it and imagine herself breathing in the salt of sea air.

Her eyes wandered over the bidders while she waited for her lot. A man walked in, his expression a mixture of exasperation and annoyance with himself for being late. He scanned the room to see if he recognised any competitors. His eyes settled on Adele and he held her gaze for a moment.

A ripple of something ran through her. It was as if she recognised him, although she knew absolutely she'd never seen him before. She shivered, but not from the cold. His gaze slid away and she felt momentarily bereft. He sat down in a spare seat and studied the catalogue intently as the auctioneer raced through the lots. Nothing was achieving any great price.

Adele felt tense, poised, as still as a hare just before it takes flight. She was intrigued. The man stood out amidst the rest of the tweedy, shabby audience, who were mostly ruddy-cheeked and covered in dog hair. It wasn't a large enough sale to attract London buyers, but his was a singularly metropolitan presence. The cut of his coat with its fur collar, the cravat at his neck, the curl of his hair all marked him out as a city dweller. He was tall, his face rather severe, with dark eyebrows. You couldn't fail to notice him. He had presence.

Adele breathed in, imagining his scent. It would be sharp, manly, exotic – something fluttered inside her. She put her hand up to her curls – the rain would have done nothing to help them. She hadn't put a full face on when she left this morning, only the lipstick, and now she wished she had. At least her mac, which was relatively new, covered up the rather dull blue dress she was wearing: she hadn't bothered to change, not even her shoes – she had on the rather clumpy lace-ups she had put on to walk to the butcher earlier. She thought longingly of the emerald boat-neck sweater hanging in her wardrobe that brought out the green in her eyes . . .

Surreptitiously, she bent down and fished in her handbag to touch up her lipstick, then opened the bottle of Yardley's English Lavender she kept in there. She dabbed some on her wrists, then re-emerged. He was still there, lighting a cigarette, looking slightly bored, as if he were there out of duty, having to humour some aged aunt by accompanying her. Yet Adele could see no such companion.

The auctioneer raced through the furniture, then the cutlery and china, before finally arriving at the paintings. He ploughed through third-rate hunting scenes and dingy landscapes then came to a halt at the one Adele was waiting for. She felt the usual excitement that precedes entering into the bidding. If the other lots were anything to go by, she would have no competition.

'An attractive seascape, signed by Paul Maze and dated 1934. Who's going to start the bidding for me?'

He swept an experienced gaze around the room and Adele raised her catalogue. He acknowledged it by pointing his gavel at her, then gave a cursory glance to see if there were any counter-bidders. He clearly wasn't expecting any.

The object of her intrigue had not offered up a single bid on anything as yet, so she was surprised to see him look up for the first time and nod at the auctioneer, who smiled his acknowledgement.

Adele raised her bid accordingly. She didn't mind that she was in competition. It was good to know someone else was interested in her potential purchase. Her opponent nodded his raised bid to the auctioneer, and she could feel her blood warm as her competitive spirit kicked in. The bidding quickly turned into a battle. The rest of the room was agog: this was as spirited as the sale had got all morning. The auctioneer was enjoying himself. He'd had no real momentum until now. As sales went, it was lacklustre. Lots had been knocked down at ridiculous prices to whoever could be bothered to cart them away.

Until now. The bids flew back and forth, not a moment's hesitation, getting higher and higher. Something in Adele wanted the painting more than anything. She was determined that it should be hers. She felt almost murderously protective of it. Her heart was pounding and her cheeks were flushed.

Her counter-bidder sat on the other side of the tent, unperturbed, unruffled, his face showing no emotion. She wondered if he knew something that she didn't. What piece of inside *information did he have? Was the painting by some undiscovered genius? Was it a long-forgotten masterpiece? Or did he have a personal reason for wanting it? How high would he be prepared to go?*

She suddenly realised that the next bid was with her and she had gone more than four times over her original limit. She had several guineas in her handbag, for William had given her the housekeeping in cash the day before, but she didn't have enough money with her if she was successful. Nor did she have their chequebook – it was sitting in her writing desk. It would be terribly embarrassing to have to admit to the auctioneer she couldn't pay. She mustn't, simply mustn't, go any further.

'The bid is with you, madam.'

She waited. It seemed to take an age for her to say no. She desperately wanted to continue but she didn't have the means. Could she leave her wedding ring, she wondered? All eyes were on her, including the auctioneer's. Except, of course, her rival's. He was coolly leafing through the rest of the catalogue without a care in the world.

She would be utterly mad to carry on. In the end, all she'd be doing was paying far too much for a painting that was good, but not exceptional.

She shook her head. Seconds later, the gavel came down. Her rival didn't bother to look up from the catalogue. She was aggrieved that the painting that should have been hers had gone to such a bloodless buyer. She wasn't usually a bad loser, but she felt nettled. She gathered up her things and edged her way out of the row of seats, excusing herself as she stepped on countless toes.

Outside, the damp air clamped itself around her. She was far more unsettled than she should have been. It wasn't because of the painting itself. She couldn't help feeling that there had been something personal about the counter-bidding. That man hadn't wanted her to have it. The set of his shoulders had spoken volumes. He had ensured the painting was never going to be hers.

She decided to go and have something to eat in the nearby town, where she remembered there was a very nice hotel. She could lick her wounds over lunch, then take a leisurely drive home and try and forget the incident. It was only a painting, after all.

At the hotel, she shook out her rain-sodden mac, hung it in the cloakroom and checked her appearance in the mirror. She saw wide green eyes with pretty eyebrows, and a hairdo that yesterday had been sleek and bouffant but was now beyond hope. She smoothed down her dress, adjusted her stockings, and made her way into the dining room.

She took a table by the window that looked out onto the high street. The rain had stopped, and a persistent sun was trying to nudge its way through the cloud. She ordered her lunch and made a list of things she needed to do: send the boys a bulging bag of mint humbugs, their favourite sweets, then write them a long letter each to go with them. She had a couple of dresses she wanted re-worked by the local dressmaker: dresses she liked but that needed an update. And she wanted to send an invitation to their newest neighbours for supper. She and William were very sociable, and Adele jotted down the names of two other couples she thought the newcomers might enjoy meeting. In fact, maybe she would make it a cocktail party — that way the newcomers could meet as many people as possible in one go. Gradually her pique at the morning's outcome faded.

She looked up as the waitress arrived to bring her whisky and soda: she had needed something to warm her, as getting so damp had chilled her to the bone. But it wasn't the waitress.

It was the victor. The spoils were under his arm. The painting was wrapped in brown paper but she knew that was what it was. He pulled out the chair opposite her without asking and sat down. His face was impassive as he looked at her.

'You bid for the only painting worth buying in that room.'

Adele stopped writing her list and put down her pen. She raised one eyebrow to accompany her smile. She might have seemed the picture of cool, but inside she felt as if she were melting, bubbling, fizzing, like a pan of sugar as it caramelises.

'I know,' she replied. She wasn't going to give anything away. Largely because there was nothing for her to give away. She had no idea what the game was, what the rules were, or what she should do next.

He put the painting down on the table in front of her.

'I'd like you to have it,' he told her.

Her cool wavered. She hadn't anticipated this. She'd expected some sort of inquisition as to what she knew about the painting's provenance. A rather nervous laugh escaped her, and she hated the sound it made. It betrayed her discomfort.

'Why?' was all she managed in reply, trying to keep her voice low and steady.

He shrugged. Then grinned. 'You deserve it more than I do. I should have let you have it right from the start.' He leaned forwards suddenly and she got a hint of his cologne. It was exactly as she had imagined.

'What will you do with it?' he asked, his expression fierce.

She tried to look composed, to belie the caramel that was sliding around inside her, sweet and dark.

'I've a place in my morning room. I should like to look at it while I write my letters. To my boys. I have two boys. Twins . . .'

It seemed important to tell him that. But then she realised she'd gone from mysteriously monosyllabic to blithering, and so was probably in no danger. He just nodded, then looked at her again.

'Do you mind if I join you for lunch?'

'It rather looks as if you already have.' At last. A game riposte. She smiled her consent as the waitress came over. He didn't miss a beat.

'I'll have the same as my companion and a bottle of champagne. And two glasses.'

She looked at him. 'Champagne? On a Tuesday?' Her heart was tripping over itself. She couldn't remember the last time she'd had champagne.

He smiled, and when he smiled his features seemed less forbidding. There was warmth in his eyes.

'Always on a Tuesday. Tuesdays are so dreadfully dull otherwise.' He tapped his fingers on the brown paper. 'Paul Maze. They're calling him the Lost Impressionist. It's a very fine painting and you have an excellent eye.'

She considered him for a moment. 'Am I being patronised? For all you know, I'm the world's leading expert on . . . Lost Impressionists. Sent by a top dealer to procure that very painting.'

He sat back, hooking his arm over the chair. He was one of

those men who fill a room with their presence, who seem to own it.

'No,' he replied. 'If you were, you'd have bid until you'd won.'

He was smug, confident, infuriating. A combination of characteristics that should have been repellent, yet Adele found herself transfixed. He was as far from William as it was possible for a man to be, she realised. There was something rather louche about him – the way he threw aside his coat, ran his fingers through his slightly-too-long hair, leant his elbows on the table, threw back his champagne and drained his glass until it was empty, then filled it again.

He was staring at her.

'What?' she asked.

'Has anyone told you that you look like Liz Taylor?'

She sighed. 'Yes. Only I am far older and my eyes are green, not violet.'

'From a distance, you could be her.'

She tried not to feel flattered. She was surprised, in her current state, that he had made the comparison.

'Tell me about yourself,' he ordered, as their veal fricassee arrived.

She looked down at her food. She had been hungry when she ordered it, but she couldn't imagine eating it now.

'I'm married,' she began.

'Well, yes. That's obvious.' He looked pointedly at the rings on her left hand, then tucked into his food with relish.

'To a doctor. I've two boys, as I said.'

He held his fork in his right hand, American style. He waved it at her. 'And?'

She paused, thinking about what to say next.

'That's it.' Never had she felt so dull. What else could she say? She was a housewife and mother – and not even that anymore, not really.

'Well,' he carried on. 'You really ought to do something about that.'

She realised she didn't know so much as his name. And she felt angry. What right did he have to judge her like that?

'You've got a nerve, barging in on my lunch and passing judgement on me. Who are you, anyway?'

He grinned. Put his fork down. 'I'm sorry. You're right. Jack Molloy.'

He held out his hand.

She took it. 'Adele. Adele Russell.'

Her heart was doing overtime. She extracted her fingers, because touching his had sent a charge through her she had never felt before.

She hadn't felt like this when she met William. At the time, she had thought their courtship passionate. She'd woken up with that fizzing feeling, unable to wait until the next time she saw him. She'd felt overwhelmed with happiness on their wedding day. She had always gazed at him when they made love, and felt as if it was right.

William had never made her feel like this, though. She sensed danger, real danger.

Jack topped up their glasses, pouring with abandon, like a reckless king at a banquet.

'You're American,' she said to him. 'Aren't you?'

She couldn't be sure, but he spoke with a definite twang.

'I sure am,' he said. 'But I've married into a very English family. The Dulvertons. Do you know them? The "family seat" is in Ox-ford-shire.'

He deliberately pronounced it with an exaggerated accent.

'I don't,' she said.

'My wife is very wealthy. Lucky for me.'

'That's awful.'

'Why?'

'To marry someone for their money.'

'I never said I did that. I married Rosamund because she was ravishingly beautiful. And far cleverer than I am.'

Adele suddenly felt insufficient. She felt sure she would pale in comparison to Rosamund.

'So what do you bring to the party?' she riposted.

He laughed. 'My sparkling wit. And a touch of glamour. I'm an art dealer. I bring starving artists home for dinner and six months later they are fetching more money for their paintings than they could ever have dreamed of. Rosamund gets a kick out of being part of that.'

'So what are you doing here?'

'I was driving back from Cornwall. I had to go and give one of my protégés a pep talk. And I can never pass a sale without looking in, just in case.' He picked up his glass and looked at her. 'What were you doing there?'

She didn't know what to say. 'It was something to do.'

She looked down at her plate. She wanted to tell him how empty she felt, how useless, but she thought he already knew.

When she looked up, he was surveying her critically.

'I think what you need, Mrs Russell,' he told her, 'is either a job or a lover. Or both.'

She put down her knife and fork. This was too close to the bone. She stood up. 'I have to go.'

He feigned disappointment. 'Oh, now, don't be offended.'

'You're very rude.' She was scrabbling in her purse for a

31

pound note, to pay her share of the lunch. She pulled one out, her hand shaking.

'Why is it people think you're being rude, when you're just speaking the truth?' He looked up at her. His eyes were laughing.

She put the pound note on the table. 'Goodbye, Mr Molloy.'

He bent down to pick up the painting, which he'd propped against the table leg. 'Don't forget this.'

'I don't want it.'

'I bought it for you.'

'You can sell it.'

'I can indeed.' He pushed it towards her. 'I can sell it for ten times what I paid for it.'

Adele tried hard not to look surprised. 'Then do so.'

'But I want you to have it.' He frowned. 'I tell you what. Give me your final bid – the amount you went up to. That would make it an honest transaction. You can take it away with impunity then.'

Adele hesitated. 'I can't.'

'Come on. You can't say fairer than that.' He was puzzled.

She shook her head. 'I can't. I don't have the money.'

He looked at her in awe. 'You bid for it without having the money?'

She shrugged. 'Yes.'

He threw back his head and laughed. The other diners in the restaurant looked round, alarmed.

'That's fantastic. I admire your spirit. Please. Take the painting. I can't think of a better home for it.'

Adele stood for a moment. Actually, she thought, why shouldn't she take it? If he was so keen for her to have it? It was a beautiful painting. And she felt that taking it from him would prove something. What, she wasn't quite sure, but maybe that she wasn't the dull provincial housewife he obviously thought her to be. So she picked up it.

'Thank you,' she said. 'And goodbye.'

As soon as she got home, she threw off her coat, dropped her handbag and ran up the stairs to change. She put on a full-skirted dress with tight sleeves, in a coral that she knew suited her colouring. She added the string of pearls William had given her for her thirtieth birthday. She admired their lustre as she applied her make-up, making herself perfect. She dabbed Shalimar at her neck – the Yardley from her handbag had long since faded.

Then she went downstairs to put on the supper, pour two whisky and sodas, and wait for her husband to come back so she could tell him the day's curious events.

Only William was late. Six o'clock came and went, then seven, then eight . . . by which time she had drunk both whiskies and hung the painting in the place where she had envisaged it.

And when William finally strolled in at twenty past eight, with only the merest flicker of apology, she told him nothing about her day at all.

On Friday, she found a letter on her breakfast plate. A white vellum envelope with turquoise ink. She didn't recognise the writing and there was no return address on the back, only a London postmark. She took the paper-knife and slit open the envelope. It was a brief letter riddled with dashes and under-lining and exclamation marks.

Darling darling Adele

Can you believe? Thank goodness – after all this time we are back in London at long last! Nairobi had its good points but heavens it's wonderful to feel chilly again!! Anyway, I am longing to hear all your news and tell you mine. Do say you'll come and have lunch with me. What about next Wednesday at the Savoy? The dear Savoy! How I've missed London!! And you. I will see you there at 1 p.m. unless I hear otherwise.

Mad dash – Brenda xxxx

'Goodness,' Adele said. 'Look at this.'

She passed it over to William, who was reading the paper.

He read the letter in the same way he read everything these days: scanning the page from top to bottom in record time, picking out the information he needed, disregarding the rest. He smiled and handed it back, balancing it between his first and second finger as he turned back to the news.

'You'll enjoy yourself,' he told her. Then frowned. 'Brenda – do I know her?'

'We were at school together. She was at our wedding. Ill-chosen hat that made her look as if she had a chicken sitting on her head. I think we might have laughed at her, poor thing. But she's a darling.'

William shook his head. He didn't remember.

Which was hardly surprising.

Adele didn't have – and never had had – a friend called Brenda.

The letter lay on her writing desk for three days, underneath her unconventionally acquired painting.

She went about her daily life. She told herself that Jack Molloy was presumptuous, provocative, and toying with her for his own amusement. Of course she wasn't going to go to lunch at the Savoy. The whole idea was absurd.

On Sunday night, she crumpled up the letter and threw it in the bin.

Yet somehow it had got under her skin. The words came back to her at all hours of the day and night, worming their way into her brain no matter how hard she tried to resist them. And she couldn't deny that the letter was ingenious. Jack Molloy had summed her up so well — he had told her that he knew exactly who she was, and the sort of friends she would have. His construct, Brenda, was the perfect alibi.

Adele could picture Brenda quite clearly, waiting at the table in the Savoy, in her good coat and hat and her brown shoes and gloves, all slightly out of date after years abroad, but eager to dispense gossip and trivia . . .

In short, a reflection of Adele herself: provincial, slightly dull, conventional. In which case, what on earth did he see in her? Why was he enticing her up to lunch, if she was such a dreary, laughable creature? So . . . unsophisticated.

Because he saw something in her, a little voice told her. Jack Molloy had seen her potential. He could unlock something in her that would make her blossom and flourish. She thought back to the thrill she had felt when he spoke to her, the feeling she had desperately tried to hide, so much so that she had fled the table.

The feeling that she wanted to have again.

She suppressed it. Apart from being mischievous and capricious, she could tell he was dangerous. Yet she had to do something with her life. The episode had highlighted to her just how empty she felt.

On Monday evening, she waited until William had taken off his tie, read his post, drunk his first whisky and was tucking into his lamb chops.

'I was wondering,' she said to him, 'if there was anything I could do to help at the new surgery. I mean, I've got so much time on my hands now, with the boys gone. I thought I could be of some assistance.'

He put his knife and fork down and looked at her. 'In what way?'

'I'm not sure, but there must be something I can do. You seem under pressure. Maybe I could help with paperwork, or organise a group for new mothers, or . . .' She trailed off, realising she hadn't really thought it through. 'It's so deathly quiet here now.'

'It's not really how it works, darling,' William told her. 'We have all the staff we need, and we are working to a very tight budget, which is what makes it so difficult.'

'Well, I wouldn't necessarily want to be paid—'

'The best thing you can do,' William said with finality, 'is keep things ticking over here. It's important for me to come home and be able to relax. I can't help feeling that if you were involved in the surgery too, things would become very awkward. And what would you do when the boys came home? They need you.' He smiled. 'I know you're finding it hard because they've gone but you will get used to it, darling, I promise you.'

He picked up his knife and fork again.

Something boiled up inside Adele. It was more than indignation. She knew William wasn't deliberately trying to *patronise her, but she felt outrage. He had put her in her place. She was a wife and mother and that was all.*

On Wednesday morning she woke up. She went through a checklist in her head. It was bed-changing day. Not that she changed the linen; Mrs Morris saw to that. The fish van was coming to Shallowford – William loved his Dover sole. Tim had written to ask her for some new games socks and a French dictionary.

As she lay in bed, a black blanket of gloom settled upon her. What was the point in getting up? Who would care, or indeed even notice, if she didn't? William was always up at six, and went downstairs before she woke. He had the same thing for breakfast every morning. Tomato juice, a cup of very strong black coffee which he made on top of the stove in an enamel jug, and a poached egg on toast. He didn't expect Adele to make it for him. He didn't even need her for that. If she didn't appear, he wouldn't care. He would leave the house at seven thirty-five safe in the knowledge that she would be there when he got home.

She sat up. What harm would lunch do? She had an alibi. And the new shantung silk dress she had bought for the tennis club summer party. She examined her hair in the mirror – there would be no time to have it done properly, but she had rollers. She smoothed her eyebrows and looked at herself, trying to read the expression in her own eyes. What was she expecting? What was she capable of? What did she want?

She went downstairs in her dressing gown.

'I'm going to have lunch with Brenda today, remember. At the Savoy,' she told William, who was sprinkling white pepper on his egg.

He smiled at her.

'Good girl,' he told her. 'You see? There's plenty to do. Make sure you enjoy yourself. And anyway, I probably won't be back until late.'

Again? Adele sometimes wondered why he didn't sleep at the surgery. But she didn't say as much. She simply smiled, and hoped William couldn't hear the thumping of her heart.

She didn't know why it was thumping so. It was only lunch, she told herself, because she had an idea and she wanted Jack Molloy's advice. That was all.

Three

Riley loved Harrods. He had loved it since the day he'd been sent there as a young photographer's assistant, to collect a leopard-skin hat for a photo shoot. It had dazzled him then and it dazzled him still now. There'd been nothing like it in the grimy Northern town where he had grown up. When he'd first stepped over the threshold, something deep inside him had whispered that perhaps its flagrant opulence was wrong, when there were people struggling to earn a crust, but the seventeen-year-old Riley had already known he was entering a world that worshipped excess and consumption and glamour. He couldn't stop that. All he could do was work hard and pay his taxes. And send money back home to his mum, which he had done until the day she died.

Nowadays, he could afford to go to Harrods whenever he liked, which he did whenever he had a present to buy, like today.

He moved easily amidst the crowds of customers. No one recognised him these days. He was a slight man – puckish, almost – with dark eyes that missed nothing. A handsome man too, but he was at an age at which he was all too aware most people become invisible, no matter how famous they might once have been. Nevertheless, he carried himself well. He wore jeans with a collarless shirt and a dark-brown leather jacket, old and battered, which moulded itself to his wiry frame. His hair was a distinguished salt and pepper, left long to the collar but still cut by the Italian barber he had used for over forty years. Riley was a creature of habit, from the espresso he heated on top of his stove in the morning to the small glass of cognac he drank before falling asleep at night.

If Sylvie was with him, there would be whispers and nudges and glances. Even in her mid-sixties she stopped people in their tracks. She didn't just have It. She had Everything. An indefinable, inimitable aura that came at birth, a melding of beauty, confidence and style that tipped the balance between simple stardom and being an icon.

Riley had sensed it the first day he'd seen her, nearly fifty years ago now. He'd been commissioned to shoot the cover of a new magazine, a supplement to accompany one of the Sunday papers. It was a prestigious commission for a young photographer, and the pressure was on for a fresh and exciting look.

He'd seen her on the Tube, a sulky-looking baggage with a ragged pageboy haircut, wearing a schoolgirl tunic with a see-through blouse underneath and long white boots. She had her feet up on the chair in front of her, smoking a cigarette and reading a magazine, languid with insouciance. He had leant over and clicked his fingers in front of her face, and as she looked up he knew he had found a new star. Her glare had drilled right into him, framed by straight dark brows that made her expression even more thunderous.

'Can I take your picture?' he asked her. 'I'm a photographer.'

He indicated the Leica he always kept with him, even when he wasn't on a job.

One of the eyebrows had shot skywards.

'If you pay,' she replied, with her trademark shrug and pout. 'I'll do whatever you like for money.'

'French?' he asked, recognising her accent as he dug in his pocket and held out a ten-shilling note.

'Kissing?' She pocketed the money with a grin that lit her up like a flash bulb.

He gave a wry smile as he loaded his camera with film. '*Are* you French?'

'Oui,' she said, with exaggerated sarcasm.

'Stand on the seat,' he told her, and she jumped up onto it, leaning against the window, spread-eagling herself against the grimy glass. She tipped her head back, lifted one leg so she stood like a flamingo, then turned her face to him, pouting.

He felt his stomach turn over with a terrible thrill. He had never met a girl with such a lack of self-consciousness, such an innate knowledge of what he expected. Most models needed coaxing, relaxing, a bit of direction, before they were on his wavelength.

'What do you do?'

'I'm an actress,' she lied effortlessly, thereby proving her ability.

Despite this, Riley wasn't taken in. He knew almost every aspiring actress in London.

'There's no point in trying to fool me, sweetheart.' He

carried on taking pictures, deadpan. 'You might as well tell me the truth.'

She crossed her arms in defiance, then capitulated with a laugh.

'OK,' she said. 'You win.' She jumped back down onto the seat.

Her parents were diplomats. She was being polished at some terribly smart finishing school in Kensington, but she hated it. She spent most of the day on the Tube or in cafes, watching people, reading, drinking endless cups of coffee, smoking.

Riley shot a whole roll of film between Bayswater and the Embankment. She leapt around the carriage without a care in the world, improvising, experimenting, charming the other passengers as they got on and off. In every shot her face was different. Capricious, vivacious, sultry, impish . . . and when she lay stretched out on the seat with her arms over her head, her eyes half-closed, her bee-stung lips just slightly parted, Riley felt something inside that frightened him. This girl was going to define him in so many different ways. This girl was his future.

They got off and walked up to the Strand and he bought her oxtail soup in a grimy cafe and listened as she talked about the awful girls in her class and how all they were interested in was finding a rich husband.

'And you? What do you want?' asked Riley, thinking she could do whatever she wanted and wondering if she knew that.

She shrugged. 'I just want to be me. Forever.'

He frowned as he realised he didn't actually know her name. 'And who are you, anyway?'

'Sylvie. Sylvie Chagall.'

Sylvie Chagall. Riley told her, as they shared a pot of tea, that the whole world would soon know her name. She had nodded, completely unfazed.

He had taken just one photo to the magazine editor. It was Sylvie, sitting on the Tube, laughing, her legs sprawled in front of her, next to an upright gentleman in a bowler hat, his face impassive. The photo seemed to represent London past and London future: the dawning of a new era.

Three weeks later Sylvie was on the magazine's debut cover. Six months later the world was wooing her. A year later they were in Venice, shooting a film with an infamous Italian director who had cast Sylvie in *Fascination,* the story of a man's obsession with his daughter's best friend. Riley was the official photographer. He never felt himself to be her chaperone. If anyone could look after herself, it was Sylvie.

Late one night, in the vast and sumptuous palazzo rented to accommodate the upper echelons of the cast and crew, she had come to his room. It was her eighteenth birthday, and they had all celebrated in a tiny restaurant in the Dorsoduro, dish after dish and glass after glass brought to them by the staff until they were glazed with rich food and heavy red wine. Sylvie, so self-assured, so unruffled by her imminent stardom, had held court with an extraordinary poise despite being the youngest on set by several years. Riley had taken her photograph, blowing out the candles on the sweet honeyed cake the proprietor had made especially for her, and thought he had never seen anyone so beautiful.

Now here she was in his bed.

'I want it to be you the first time, Riley,' she whispered as she slid on top of him. She was naked. 'I know you will be kind.'

All that time, nearly five decades, they had been lovers. The two of them had parity in their respective success, so neither was threatened by the other. They were both independent. Their work took each of them all over the world, but at different times. It was impossible to co-ordinate their diaries so they could live a life together, so they had never bothered. He had a flat in London; she had settled in her native Paris. Throughout the year they met when it was convenient, often at house parties of mutual friends – a riad in Marrakech, a yacht in the South of France, a penthouse in New York.

They both had other lovers over the years. It was the time they had been brought up in. Neither of them saw it as a betrayal. They would never dream of hurting each other. They were always there for each other, whenever, wherever. When Sylvie caught double pneumonia, after filming in the snow in Prague one winter, Riley was at her bedside in a shot. When his mother died, Sylvie was there at the funeral, holding his hand all the way through, glamorous in a black coat and dark glasses, and he got through it because she was there. His Sylvie.

And now, they might be in their autumn years, but they both still worked. They were both heavily in demand. Their experience and their reputations overrode any prejudice about age. They could pick and choose whom they worked for, and when, but they were both monumentally busy at a time when most people were looking to kick back and relax. Neither of them could imagine a life without work. It defined them.

The one thing that was sacrosanct was their annual trip to Venice on Sylvie's birthday, returning to the location of the film that had cemented their relationship. Even now, *Fascination* was a cult classic amongst film buffs, and the story of their romance on set was a legend. And nowadays, because they loved the twenty-four-hour bubble that cocooned them and allowed them to be themselves, just themselves, they travelled there on the Orient Express. Riley got on in London and Sylvie joined the train in Paris, and they celebrated her birthday on board.

And this morning, Riley was in Harrods to buy Sylvie her birthday present. He bought her the same thing every year. A silk scarf. Sylvie was never without one – slung round her neck, knotted to her bag, tied around her head, always with that effortless French chic. Riley smiled as he remembered her sliding one around his eyes once, tying it in a knot at the back of his head. It had smelled of her. She had done nothing but kiss him while he wore it, her lips light as a feather on his ear-lobe, his collarbone, his ribcage . . .

He walked through the heady scents of the perfume department, then through the candy colours of the hand-bags until he reached the scarf counter. He could tell that the charming assistant had no idea who he was. The young never did these days, but he didn't care at all. He'd had his moment.

'Is it for someone special?' she asked. Riley found it a peculiar question. Did she have a drawer of scarves for people who weren't special?

'It absolutely is,' he told her. 'Someone very special.' She seemed pleased by this reply, and started to pull out a selection, spreading them out on the glass counter for his inspection.

He loved the feeling of the silk as it slithered through his fingers. He loved the colours and the patterns. Swiftly, his particular eye divided the scarves into yes and no, gradually whittling them down, pushing his rejections back to the assistant with a shake of his head. All the while he had Sylvie in his mind's eye, her face as she opened it. They had never believed in ridiculously extravagant gestures. A scarf was what she wanted and what she would expect and what she would get. Yet it had to be absolutely right.

'This one,' he nodded decisively. Sometimes the choice made itself, and today it was like that. Emilio Pucci. The colours were subtle but striking, the pattern bold but intricate. Swiftly he made the transaction, and watched with pleasure as the scarf was folded and wrapped in tissue then slid into a special box.

He never bought a card. He always found an old photo, one that meant something to both of them, then messed about with it on his computer, customising it, adding a slogan or a message. Then he would print it out, hand colour it, and sign it with a fine Rotring pen – Riley, and just one kiss. Sylvie kept his cards in a shoe-box. She had never thrown one away. From the very first, which had been decorated with Letraset. A pile of almost fifty, he imagined now.

He took his package and wandered back through the store, stopping in the Food Hall to buy a slice of game pie and some gooseberry chutney that would do for his lunch. He had never been a big eater, but what he did eat had to be good. He didn't see the point of burdening yourself with excess calories. So many of his friends now bore the consequence of hedonistic gourmandising. They would be unrecognisable from their twenty-year-old selves, but he was pretty certain that he had more than just a glimmer of his youthful self in his appearance.

He left the store, emerging into the bustle of the Brompton Road, pushing through the crowds on the pavement until he reached the kerb. Riley never drove anywhere these days. It wasn't worth the expense, or the hassle of keeping your eye on the speed limit or how much you had drunk, or fighting for a parking space. If it was good weather and within the Circle Line, he walked. He would happily walk as many as five or six miles to a meeting or a lunch and then back again. It kept him fit, and he mostly went through the parks, even if it meant his journey was a little longer. If the weather displeased him, however, he took a cab. Today was one such day. There was a light mizzle, fine but persistent, so he raised an arm. A minute later he was tucked in the back of a taxi, homeward bound.

They were hurtling at speed around Hyde Park Corner when Riley saw a car pull out in front of them. The driver was either an optimist or an idiot. There was no way the cab would be able to stop in time. He didn't see his life flash before him. He saw only her face, as it had been the very first time he glimpsed her, her brows furrowed as she read her magazine.

'Sylvie,' he said out loud, before he heard the terrible crunch of metal on metal, and the bag he was carrying slipped from his fingers.

Four

Hospital waiting rooms, no matter how calming the colour scheme or distracting the artwork, always left you feeling the same. Archie had been in enough now to know nothing could quell the anxiety, although Jay seemed to manage to stay quite cheerful while they were waiting. It was always Archie who watched the clock, who chewed his fingernails, who jumped when Jay's name was called.

Today's wait was interminable. The white board indicated that appointments were running thirty minutes behind. Not long enough to leave the hospital and go and do something useful. Of course not. You were trapped, just in case they caught up with themselves or there was a no-show and your appointment was moved up. It was a pity they didn't have time to go for a pint, although he supposed it wouldn't look good, Jay turning up to the consultant reeking of beer.

But at this stage of the game, did it really matter?

He looked over at his friend. Jay was flicking through a magazine, stopping every time something caught his eye. He seemed able to find plenty to keep his attention. Archie wasn't a great reader, and he certainly wouldn't have found anything to fascinate him in the pile of old *National*

*Geographic*s and women's magazines left out for patients. He was far too preoccupied to be distracted by photos of polar bears and recipes for blueberry cheesecake.

Jay looked up, sensing he was being watched.

'Tell me about your ideal woman, Archie.'

'What do you mean?' said Archie.

'Your ideal woman. Describe her to me.'

Archie rolled his eyes. 'You're not doing one of those awful quizzes? *If you score mostly Cs then you're a psychopath with narcissistic tendencies . . .*'

Jay shook his head.

'It's a competition. I'm going to enter you.' Jay squinted more closely. 'Only a week till the closing date.'

He was laughing in a way that made Archie suspicious. He tried to lean over Jay's shoulder to look at the page, but Jay moved the magazine away from him so he couldn't see.

'Go on – what do you look for in a girl?'

'Me?' Archie grinned. 'I'm not fussy, as long as she's clean and has all her own teeth.'

Jay looked at him thoughtfully. Archie felt uncomfortable. Jay had been doing this recently, going from jocular to serious in the blink of an eye. He found it unsettling. 'What?'

'You're never going to meet Miss Right, are you, hanging around hospital waiting rooms with me?'

'Miss Right can wait,' said Archie.

Jay carried on staring at him.

'You deserve someone special. You do know that?'

'Doesn't everyone?'

Jay tore the page carefully out of the magazine and folded it up.

'What sort of competition is it?' Archie was even more suspicious now.

'Never you mind.'

A nurse stepped out of a door. 'Jay Hampton.'

The two men looked at each other.

'Do you want me to come in with you?' asked Archie.

Jay shook his head. 'Nah. I won't be long.' He got up, stuffing the page he had torn out of the magazine into his pocket.

Archie looked down at the grey, institutional carpet, lining his feet up carefully inside one of the tiles. He didn't have a good feeling. Jay was defiantly optimistic; Archie was filled with dread.

The two of them had grown up on neighbouring farms in the heart of the Cotswolds. Jay's parents had recently sold up, weary of the tough times that farmers were facing and knowing their children didn't want to follow them into the business. Archie, conversely, was playing the dutiful son, helping his father run the family farm. They just managed to keep it afloat by selling prime organic lamb and beef, while his mother rented out the courtyard of barns they had converted into holiday lets. This venture had proved such a success that Archie started a business advising other farmers on how to do the same, and set up a farm holiday website through which all the bookings could be coordinated. A couple of girls helped him run it from the farm office, and it was ticking over very nicely. Archie might not be wealthy, but he had a tiny cottage on the farm, and a Morgan sports car, and two border terriers called Sid and Nancy – what more could he want?

Jay, meanwhile, was renting a house with a workshop in

the next village where he'd set up in business restoring and renovating old beds. The idea of getting a proper job horrified him, despite his first-class honours degree. He could have done anything, but he wanted to work for himself, to decide what time he got up in the morning, to choose his own hours.

'Everyone needs a bed,' he told Archie. 'And everyone loves their bed. And everyone loves *old* beds . . . brass beds, iron beds, wooden beds. Watch me. I'll make a fortune.'

Jay had the entrepreneurial spirit all right. He knew just how to market himself. His brochures were lush and stunningly photographed: just the right side of decent yet with an erotic allure. His good looks made him perfect interview fodder for the interiors magazines and the Sunday supplements, and he interviewed well. A Jay Hampton bed became a status symbol, the middle-class must-have to sit alongside the Jo Malone candles and the White Company bedding. The beds were selling as quickly as he could reclaim them from the scrapyard and then work his magic on them, sandblasting and powder-coating them back to perfection. And he was right – he was making a fortune. If Archie hadn't loved his friend so much, he could have gone right off him, but they were still as thick as thieves, years after leaving school. They suited each other down to the ground. They were wildly different, but they balanced each other out. Jay, maverick and spontaneous. Archie, solid and reliable.

Then Jay went on holiday to Thailand for two weeks of sun and adventure and felt ropey once he got back. Tired. Not his usual energetic self. He had a persistent cough and lost weight. Archie worried about the change in him. He

51

thought that perhaps he had taken things a step too far in Thailand. Jay was always a risk-taker and a thrill-seeker. He did bungee jumps, threw himself off cliffs into the sea, ate unidentifiable food with the natives. Archie wondered if he had picked up some virus on his holiday, and persuaded him to go to the doctor.

'They're not easy to get rid of, these bugs. You could do yourself serious damage if you don't get it seen to.'

Jay phoned him a week later. His voice was bright. 'You were right, Archie. There is something the matter. I've got leukaemia.'

Only the slightest tremble in Jay's voice indicated that he might be scared.

'Acute lymphoblastic leukaemia, to be precise. I'm in hospital right now. I need blood transfusions, tests, probably chemo . . .'

'Shit. Which hospital?'

Archie had needed no second telling. Within an hour he was at his friend's bedside. The doctors worked well and swiftly. Jay was, by all accounts, lucky to have come in when he did.

His body was no longer making enough healthy red blood cells and platelets and his white cells were unable to protect his body from infection. The condition was about as serious as conditions get. The prognosis wasn't good, but he was in the best place, with the best doctors. Jay was amazing throughout the whole ordeal. He was brave and optimistic and uncomplaining, without a trace of the bitterness Archie thought he deserved to feel.

The only thing Jay did that Archie didn't approve of was

to tell his current girlfriend that one night in Thailand he'd slept with another girl.

'You didn't,' said Archie. 'I know you didn't.'

'Unless she thinks I've betrayed her, she won't leave me.' Jay was adamant. 'And I don't want her to feel she has to stick with me because of this disease. I wouldn't want to stay with me. It's tedious. She needs to get out there and find someone else.'

And of course the girl did leave him, because she felt justified after his confession. And Archie felt he was the only person left who really understood Jay and his fears after that. He watched his friend grow weak and frail through the endless transfusions and chemotherapy, and was amazed at how his spirit was never crushed, how his eyes still danced even when they were heavy with drugs and painkillers.

For a while, Jay had seemed to bounce back, until just over a month ago. He had started feeling unwell again, and the cough that had been so persistent the first time around had returned. He was tired, too. Jay had insisted he was simply under the weather, and had refused to tell his parents anything was wrong. Archie admired his optimism, but knew there was a point at which optimism became foolishness. He had forcibly marched him to the GP. Jay had been fast-tracked, referred back to the consultant alarmingly quickly.

Now, Archie felt helpless as he waited for the verdict. The clock seemed to tick painfully slowly. If everything was OK, he would take Jay for a slap-up lunch to celebrate.

It felt like a lifetime, but it was only ten minutes when

Jay emerged from the consultant's office. His face was white against his shock of dark hair.

'Ok, Archie,' he said. 'I can't put it off any longer. It's time to tell Mum and Dad.'

'What is it?' Archie felt a terrible fear squeeze his heart as he looked at his friend.

'I've got to have a transplant,' Jay told him. He gave a tired, sad smile. 'A bone-marrow transplant. As soon as possible.'

A week later they were back at the hospital. By some miracle, a match had been found. Jay had deteriorated in the seven days since the news, but his spirits were still indomitable. He made Archie drive him to the hospital in his Morgan. The roof was down and the sun shone on them as they navigated their way through the gingerbread houses that had defined their youth. They passed so many landmarks. The village hall where they had first got drunk on local cider at the Pony Club disco. The fields that hosted the point-to-point where they learned the vagaries of betting, invariably losing. Their favourite pub, the Marlborough Arms, where they had enjoyed illegal lock-ins and games of darts and flirted ferociously with the local girls.

Archie was terrified. He wanted to tell Jay how much their friendship had meant to him, but he knew that would be admitting defeat, so he offered him an Extra Strong Mint out of the glove compartment instead. They were meeting Jay's parents at the hospital. Archie was like another son to them, just as Jay was to Archie's parents. He was dreading seeing them.

Jay was drumming on the dashboard, beating his fingers

along to Counting Crows. The music defined them. They'd been to see them so many times over the years. Every song reminded Archie of the road trips they'd spent together, the fun they'd had. He felt a lump in his throat. He stared at the road ahead as it snaked its way towards the next village.

Jay suddenly turned the music down.

'You've got to promise me one thing,' he said. 'If I don't make it.'

'You're going to make it,' Archie told him firmly.

Jay looked at the horizon for a moment. Winter was just starting to soften into spring: buds and shoots were springing in the fields and hedgerows.

'Yeah, well, if I don't, you're not to hole up in that cottage of yours. I know what you're like.'

'What? What am I like?' Archie felt indignant. It was true that he wasn't as much of a party animal as Jay – given the choice between a quiet night in and a wild night out, he was quite content with the former – but that didn't mean he couldn't enjoy himself.

'I have to prise you off that sofa sometimes and drag you out of the house kicking and screaming—'

'No, you don't. I'm just happier with my own company than you are.'

'I'm worried you won't budge without me to give you a kick up the arse. That you'll become a recluse.'

'Don't be daft. I can get myself out there. Anyway, I don't know why we're even having this conversation.'

Archie flicked a glance sideways at Jay. Jay was staring at the road ahead.

'There's something else.'

Archie's heart jumped. 'What?'

He looked at Jay again. There was a smile playing at the corner of his mouth.

'That jumper? The one with the holes?'

'My blue one?' Archie affected an injured air. 'What's wrong with it?'

'It's got to go.'

'I love that jumper.'

'You're never going to pull wearing it.'

'It's comfy. I feel comfy in it.'

'If I die knowing I've left you to roam the earth in that jumper, I won't have done my job properly. As your best mate, I've got to be the one to tell you . . .'

Archie didn't speak for a moment. It was the first time either of them had actually mentioned the possibility of Jay dying. He decided to follow Jay's lead and keep it light. Now wasn't the time for a deep philosophical discussion.

'If it makes you happy, I'll stick it in the dogs' basket. Sid and Nancy can sleep on it.' He thumped him on the arm affectionately. 'You win. OK?'

'Good.' Jay nodded, satisfied. 'And while I think about it, I entered you in that magazine competition. If you win, you've got to promise me to go.'

'Yeah, yeah, yeah, yeah.'

'Even if you're lambing, or haymaking . . . I know you. Any excuse.'

Whatever the competition was, Archie was certain he wouldn't win. He'd never won anything in his life.

'Course,' he laughed. 'I promise.'

Jay turned the music back up.

'Good.'

Nothing more was said.

Archie dropped the car down a gear and took the next corner at a terrifying speed. Fear was making him reckless. Fear of the terrible thing he felt certain was coming? He wasn't at all sure how he was going to face it.

Face it he did, for that was in Archie's nature.

Three weeks later, he stood in front of the altar at St Mary's, the tiny little church where both he and Jay had been christened, and had seen through any number of carol services and midnight masses and Easter Sundays over the years. He didn't need notes during his eulogy. He didn't need anything to remind him of what his friend had meant to him. Jay, who had been so alive and vibrant and immediate, and was now lying as still as stone in a coffin made of elm. For a fleeting moment, Archie wondered if the undertaker had remembered to put in the list of things Jay's family had agreed he couldn't be without, the things which were intrinsically Jay: his blood-red cashmere scarf, his Panama Jack boots, his Laguiole knife, his ancient iPod – he'd had one long before anyone else, but still had the original. Jay was an early adopter yet appreciated longevity over innovation.

Archie looked out at the congregation as he spoke, at all the friends and neighbours who had been part of their lives over the years. To his left was a gaggle of Jay's mates from university; to the right, almost the entire rugby club. He counted at least five ex-girlfriends, including the one Jay had dumped when he had first been diagnosed, her eyes red from a night-time of tears, her long fingers worrying at a shredded tissue. Then there were Jay's parents, his brother and two sisters, a rank of cousins, his elderly grandmother. And Archie's own parents, of course.

His mum was worried about him, and the fact he was taking Jay's death so hard. He had barely slept since that awful moment when the consultant had come out to tell them the transplant had failed. Something had died in him, too. Hope, trust, optimism, belief – a part of his soul had gone with his friend.

'You take all the time off you need,' said his dad. 'I can manage. Your mum can help me with the cattle. The cottages aren't booked up yet till after Easter. We'll cope.'

After the funeral, everyone went for drinks at the Marlborough Arms. The landlord had laid out a trestle table with sausage rolls and pork pie and local cheese, thickly buttered tea-loaf and fruitcake and Victoria sponge oozing jam and cream. Jay's parents stayed until five and then went home. Archie was torn between escorting them back to their house to make sure they were all right, and mixing with the hard core of friends who were going to carry on toasting Jay for the rest of the night.

'You stay here, love,' said Jay's mother. 'We'll be all right. To be honest, I just want to go to bed.'

He stayed, because he felt as if he were the host. It was like the party to end all parties. All night, he felt as if Jay was going to walk in at any moment, grab a pint from the bar and start flirting with the nearest pretty girl, but he didn't. Of course he didn't.

At one point, Archie went outside. He felt overwhelmed. There were too many faces from the past, too many memories, a mix of people who might only have come together had Jay ever got married – a wedding that was now never going to be. He sat at the table that had always been theirs when they drank outside in the sunshine, the one nearest the hatch that served the foaming pints of Honeycote, the local ale. He took out his phone and started checking his emails for something to do, something to take his mind off what was happening.

He frowned. There was one from an address he didn't recognise. Not On The Shelf? What was that? The subject read 'Congratulations'. Spam, no doubt. Some hard sell disguised as a win, probably.

His eyes flicked over the contents of the email. Then he frowned, and read it again slowly.

Dear Mr Harbinson,

    It is with great delight that we would like to inform you that you are one of the two winners of our competition to win a night on the Orient Express. Our team of highly experienced matchmakers chose you from a considerable number of entries, and your companion for the journey is Emmie Dixon, whose profile we enclose for your interest. All we ask is for you both to have your photograph taken on departure at Victoria Station for publicity purposes, then the rest of this journey of a lifetime is yours to enjoy in total privacy . . .

The letter went on, detailing dates, times and travel arrangements.

Archie was mystified at first. He hadn't entered a competition. It must be a scam – no doubt they would ask him for his credit-card details at some point. Then, as he read through it again, he remembered that afternoon in the hospital – Jay snickering over something in a magazine.

Jay had set him up. Jay had entered him into a competition for the ultimate blind date. And now, Archie remembered their conversation on that final car journey, when he had promised Jay that, if he won, he would go. He'd taken little notice of the promise at the time. It had seemed irrelevant.

Despite his despair, despite his heavy heart, despite his grief, a slow smile spread itself across Archie's face.

'You bugger,' he said to the sky. 'You absolute bugger . . .'

Five

'Happy birthday dear Imoooooo . . .'

Imogen looked round at the smiling faces of her closest friends. They were all serenading her as Alfredo came in bearing the chocolate and chestnut gateau he had made and laid it reverently in front of her. Every year she came here for her birthday. It was the tradition. Nothing ever changed. Well, she didn't. Her friends sometimes did – sporting engagement rings, then wedding rings, then baby bumps. But somehow Imogen always remained the same. Except this year. This year she was just the tiniest bit different, not that anyone seemed to have noticed.

Not yet, anyway. It would be all too evident the moment he walked through the door. She had hoped he would be here in time for the cake. Somehow that was important to her. But the door to Alfredo's Trattoria on Shallowford high street remained firmly shut.

Meanwhile, thirty candles flickered in front of her eyes. Together with the spinach and ricotta cannelloni and several glasses of Gavi de Gavi, it made her feel slightly woozy.

She bent and blew out the candles.

'Make a wish! Make a wish!' ordered her friend Nicky as she passed her a knife to make the first incision.

Imogen hesitated. Making a wish wouldn't have any bearing whatsoever on whether Danny McVeigh came through that door in the next ten minutes. It was up to him entirely.

'Please, please, let that door open and let him walk in,' she thought as the knife cut through the sweet chocolate icing.

Earlier in the evening, she had been buoyant with optimism that he would grant her the one thing she'd asked of him on her birthday: to come to her celebratory dinner. Even though he'd told her, categorically, that very afternoon, as she lay curled into him, that he didn't think it was a good idea. 'I won't fit in with all your posh mates. They won't want a bit of rough at the dinner table.'

'I don't care.' Imogen grinned at him. A little bit of her wanted to shock her friends. Imogen Russell and Danny McVeigh – the scandal would ricochet round Shallowford in minutes. They had kept their relationship secret so far. It was early days, for a start, and it gave it more of an edge to keep it clandestine. His family would be just as horrified as hers to hear they had been seeing each other. The McVeighs didn't mix with the likes of the Russells.

But now Imogen felt ready to bring it all out into the open. It was always far better to be in control of people finding out your secrets. And somehow her birthday seemed the right time to do it.

'Please,' she had begged him, snaking herself around him, entwining her arms and legs around his until they were as one. 'It would mean a lot to me. It would be the best birthday present ever.'

'Even better than this?' He'd given her a wicked smile as he slid her hand down to feel him.

Foolishly, she'd taken that as agreement. She had convinced herself that he'd turn up. Now, the clock on the wall told her it was twenty past ten. It seemed very unlikely.

'So? What did you wish?' Nicky nudged her with a sharp elbow.

Imogen longed to tell her. She could picture Nicky's jaw dropping in astonishment. Nicky, who had married the local solicitor and drove around in her pristine four-by-four with her two immaculate children and worked in the estate agency to stop her getting bored but who didn't need to work at all if she didn't want to . . .

That was, Imo supposed, the sort of life she should have. By now she should have married well and be set up in her own home and at least be thinking about starting a family. That's what you did if you stayed in Shallowford. Somehow, though, she had missed the boat and now all the eligible men had been snapped up.

Leaving only the likes of Danny McVeigh . . .

Alfredo brought out a tray of tiny liqueur glasses filled with Limoncello. Just as he did every year. They were complimentary. Imogen suddenly found it an empty gesture. What was a quarter of a bottle of sickly Italian liqueur when she and her friends had spent several hundred quid on food and wine? Was she supposed to fall over herself with gratitude?

She knocked back a glass nevertheless. It wasn't like her to be so bitter and cynical. Not at all. But she wanted to numb the disappointment she felt.

How could she have imagined that Danny would come?

Because he was right – he wouldn't fit in with all her friends, with their perfect hair-dos and their tasteful little floral dresses and fitted cardigans. He must have sensed that she wanted him to turn up just to get a reaction. She couldn't deny that she'd been looking forward to the expressions on their faces when he walked in, lean and mean in his jeans and leather jacket. She'd wanted to show him off, to shock them. He knew that. And to punish her he hadn't turned up. Besides, why would he care what she wanted? Men like Danny weren't programmed to please women. They pleased themselves.

She got up from the table and walked to the cloakroom. She looked at herself in the mirror and saw unshed tears at the back of her green eyes. It wouldn't work in a million years. It was a game, that was all. Danny McVeigh was just a toy for a bored thirty-year-old; she was just another notch on his bedpost: a conquest. Yes, they had chemistry – her head spun at the memory of what they had done in bed over the past few months – but that was no basis for a serious relationship.

She re-applied her lipstick, ruffled her shoulder-length curls and gave herself a stern look in the mirror.

'Walk away, Imo,' she told herself. 'You knew you were playing with fire when you started this.'

She thought back to the day Danny had walked back into her life. The sleepy Berkshire town of Shallowford still followed the tradition of early closing on a Wednesday afternoon, which most people found irritating but Imogen was eternally grateful for. It was the day she rearranged paintings in the gallery, keeping the sign on the door saying 'Closed', but beckoning people in if they pressed their nose to the window. It was surprising how many customers bought something when they thought they had been given preferential treatment.

When she saw the man outside staring intently at the Ruskin Spear on the easel in the window, she gave him a wave to say 'Come on in.'

He pushed the door open. 'You're not closed, then?'

Imogen smothered a gasp. Now he was standing in front of her she recognised him, one hand in the pocket of his jeans, his dark hair falling across his eyes. He was so tall, well over six foot. And broad. She felt a tiny flicker of fear.

Danny had been two years above Imogen at school. Broodingly handsome, surly, rebellious, he'd been a source of fascination to the girls in Imogen's class, who'd held endless breathless conversations about his attractions. He always had a girl in tow, but rarely the same one. There were rumours about him drug-dealing, having an affair with the Latin teacher (not that he studied Latin, but it seems his charms beguiled even the cerebral), shoplifting, fighting . . . He was suspended twice before finally walking out the week before his GCSEs. The school was a duller place without him. He was something to look at during assembly.

Imogen had never really come into contact with Danny at school, but he had given her a lift home from a party once, when she had missed the last bus back from Filbury to Shallowford. The cheap wine she had drunk was swirling in her stomach. Her high heels were killing her. She couldn't work out whether to hobble along with them pinching her toes and rubbing her heels, or to take them off and walk in bare feet on the freezing tarmac. The night air gripped her in an icy cloak that took her breath away. She thought about curling up in a barn, or even knocking on a door to ask for help. She was an idiot. How could she have missed the bus?

He'd pulled up next to her on his motorbike. 'Wanna lift?'

'I haven't got a helmet.' She realised how prim she sounded.

He looked at her, then took off his own and handed it to her.

She took it and put it on, feeling awkward. It was heavy and unfamiliar. As it closed over her head, she realised it was still warm from him. She breathed in the smell of burnt orange. She walked unsteadily towards the bike and hitched up her dress. It was so tight she would almost have to have it up round her knickers if she was going to get on. She shimmied onto the seat behind him, anxious about burning her legs on the hot metal, then found the footrests with her feet. She didn't want to think about what would happen if they had an accident. She wouldn't have a hope.

'Hold on tight,' he told her, and she grabbed two handfuls of his jacket. 'Properly,' he commanded. 'Put your arms around my waist.'

She hunkered right into him. The leather of his jacket was rough on her cheek, and he was warm against her. The next minute the bike had started with a roar, and she felt as if her stomach was left behind as he accelerated off into the darkness of the night.

The journey was terrifying. The cold night air sliced at her legs. She had never travelled so fast. As they took each corner she shut her eyes in terror and clung on even tighter as the bike leant over. She was sure he was exaggerating every manoeuvre just to frighten her. She was convinced she was going to be killed.

At last, the lights of Shallowford were up ahead. She wanted to tell him to drop her at the top of the town so she could walk home alone. She didn't want to be seen with him. But there was no way to communicate this as she didn't dare let go. The bike roared up the high street. It must have woken every inhabitant.

At last he pulled up outside Bridge House. She climbed off. Her legs were weak with the tension and could hardly hold her up. She pulled her dress down as quickly as she could to cover her thighs, which were mottled almost blue in the lamplight. She tried to put her shoes back on but her feet were so cold it was painful.

'You want to get in a warm bath,' he told her. 'And have a hot drink. Maybe some brandy.'

She blushed at his concern. They eyed each other for a moment as she wondered about asking him in. Adele would be fast asleep. She could make them cocoa in the kitchen. She imagined him sitting at the table, laughing inwardly at the bone china cups and the sugar tongs.

And realising that the kitchen window would be easy to smash. And that no one in the house would hear someone breaking in.

There was a long moment of silence. Expectation hung in the air, shrouded in the icy clouds from their breath. Imogen decided that she didn't have the nerve.

'Thank you,' she managed eventually, handing back his helmet.

'Any time.' His eyes flickered over her for a moment, and

she wondered what he was thinking. Before she could say anything else, he was gone, in a thunderous roar and a cloud of heady exhaust fumes.

A few weeks later, she heard he'd been arrested for handling stolen goods and was put away, and she was thankful for her caution. If she'd let him in, goodness knows what she would have unleashed. Nevertheless, in her quieter moments she relived the scene, wondering what might have happened, letting her mind wander, imagining his hands on her cold skin, the warmth of him under that leather jacket.

And now, here he was, wanting to browse around the gallery. She'd glimpsed him occasionally in the intervening years once he'd been released, roaring up the high street on his bike that was even bigger and better than the one she'd been given a lift on. No doubt purchased through ill-gotten gains.

'Was there something particular you wanted help with?' she asked him as politely as she could.

'I like that painting in the window,' he told her. 'How much is it?'

She swallowed. She didn't want to tell him. It was one of the most valuable pieces they had. She had agonised over putting it in the window, and now she wished she hadn't.

'I'm awfully sorry,' she said. 'I'm afraid it's sold. We sold it at the weekend.'

He frowned. 'Oh. All right if I have a look round at the rest?'

She could hardly say no. 'Of course. Let me know if you have any questions.'

He nodded, and began to walk around, the heels of his

boots loud on the oak floorboards. Imogen began to feel nervous. He must be casing the joint. She imagined him and a bevy of his brothers sitting in some seedy pub making a plan to do the gallery over. They'd never get what the paintings were worth, unless they had contacts with some dodgy art dealer. Of course these existed, and she supposed it wouldn't be beyond the wit of the McVeighs to find one. Or maybe they'd been commissioned to steal to order?

Her eyes flicked up to the camera in the corner of the gallery. She prayed it was working. She didn't always check it every day. She felt sweat trickling down her neck. Could she sneak away and call the police? What would she say?

Maybe she should pick up the phone and call her grand-mother? The gallery adjoined Bridge House. Adele was probably at home: if Imogen could drop a hint, she could get the police around. Why hadn't they figured out some sort of code word for when they were in trouble?

Imogen flicked a glance over to Danny again. Age hadn't troubled him in the least – if anything he was better-looking than when he was eighteen. More . . . manly. But still pretty. It was a devastating combination. He was staring at a still life of a wine bottle on a table.

'I like this.' His voice made her jump.

Imogen dragged her eyes away from his shoulders under the black leather of his jacket. It looked more expensive than the one she had pressed herself against on that treacherous journey home. Softer, more supple . . .

'It's by Mary Fedden,' she managed. 'It's very collectable. It's one of my favourites, actually.'

He glanced at her and for a moment she felt complicity

between them. He seemed pleased by the fact that she liked it too.

'How much?'

Imogen had no idea if he knew what ballpark they were in price-wise. He would either throw up his hands in horror and walk out, or prove something by buying it. Or come back later tonight and nick it.

'It's four thousand pounds,' she told him.

'Will you do a deal for cash?'

'We don't do *cash*.'

'Don't be ridiculous. Everyone does cash.'

His eyes crinkled in amusement as he looked at her. Imogen felt a little bit warm under his scrutiny. She smiled sweetly.

'If we do *cash* then I won't be able to give you a proper receipt and you might have trouble selling it on.'

'I don't want to sell it on. I just want to buy it. Come on – they're not exactly queuing up. You need a sale. You must have overheads.'

All this was certainly true. One of the many reasons Adele and she had agreed that selling up was the best option. 'I can do you a little bit of a discount.'

'Ten per cent?'

'Five.'

'Five?' He didn't seem impressed with this offer.

'Your money's safe in that painting. Mary Fedden's very popular. And she died quite recently, sadly. Which will make her more collectable.' Imogen reached out and touched the frame, adjusting it slightly so the picture was straight. 'She taught David Hockney.'

He looked at her, raising a sardonic eyebrow. She wasn't

sure what it meant. Whether he meant *you know damn well I don't know who David Hockney is.* Or *don't patronize me.*

'Can you deliver? Only I can't really take it home on the back of my bike.'

'Of course. Are you local?'

He looked at her again. She blushed. He remembered her.

'I've just rented Woodbine Cottage. On the Shallowford estate.'

Imogen was surprised. Shallowford Manor had a number of cottages on its land. Her friend Nicky organised the rentals, but Nicky hadn't mentioned Danny McVeigh renting one. Woodbine Cottage was gorgeous – totally unspoilt, nestling in its own little wood. It had once belonged to the gamekeeper, but there was no longer a shoot on the estate.

'Gosh,' Imogen heard herself saying. 'How lovely.'

Danny nodded. 'It's all right. But it needs a few bits and pieces to make it home.'

Imogen found it hard to imagine Danny McVeigh calling anywhere 'home'. Home was such a . . . homey word. It spoke of soft cushions and drawn curtains and flickering candles. She could only imagine Danny dossing. Sprawled on a sofa somewhere, his longs legs stretched out, a bottle of beer on the floor somewhere. Although he didn't smell like a dosser. Now he was near to her, he smelled of fresh clean laundry and woodsmoke and still that trace of burnt orange.

Imogen looked in astonishment as he pulled a wad of fifty-pound notes out of his pocket.

'Um – there are money-laundering issues with that kind

of cash, I'm afraid. I have to notify the relevant authorities—'

He stopped counting the money for a moment with a sigh.

'Anyone would think you didn't want to sell anything.'

'I'm just saying.'

'Notify whom you like. I haven't got a guilty conscience. This isn't dirty money. I've earned it with my own fair hands.'

Imogen looked down at his hands. Large, a little rough. Workman's hands, but clearly used to counting money, his long fingers deftly sifting through the notes until there was a substantial pile on the table. 'Do you charge extra for delivery?' He held another fifty over the pile.

Imogen flinched. 'No. No, of course not.'

He nodded and put the rest of the wad back in his pocket.

'Will it be you bringing it?'

She wasn't sure why he was asking the question, or how it was relevant.

'Probably not. I have someone who handles that side of things.'

Well, she had Reg, her odd-job man, who did the odd bit of collecting and delivering for her, when she couldn't leave the gallery.

'Oh.' He seemed disappointed. 'Only I thought maybe you could tell me where to put it. I don't know much about these things.'

His gaze was intense. She felt rather awkward.

'That's a very personal decision.'

He was making her nervous. He shrugged.

'I just like the way you've made things look in here. It's like . . . there's nothing really in here but it feels . . .' he spread out his hands, searching for a description. 'Like somewhere you'd want to live.'

Despite her wariness, Imogen felt pleased. She'd worked hard to make the gallery inviting, while not distracting from the artwork. Neutral, but with a touch of warmth and a few details that lifted it from sterile to a place that held your interest.

'Well, it's mainly about choosing the right paint. That dictates the atmosphere. And lighting. Lighting is very important.'

'I've just got a naked lightbulb swinging from the ceiling at the moment.' For some reason hearing him say 'naked' made her blush. 'So you wouldn't mind giving me some advice? I can pay.'

'I'm not an interior designer.'

'No. But you've got an eye. You know what to do. I can see that.'

Imogen gazed at him, puzzled. Was this all part of the plan? To lure her away from the gallery so his dodgy relatives could break in?

'Don't worry,' he said. 'I'm not going to get my mates to do the place over while you're out.'

Her cheeks burned. 'I didn't think that!' she protested.

'I've got a house of my own for the first time in my life. I want it to look the part.' He looked at her, suddenly defiant. 'I've always wanted something from here. A real painting. A work of art. Something that someone has created.'

73

Imogen wasn't sure what to say. She was taken aback by his honesty. And rather touched.

'Well, you've definitely chosen well. I'm impressed.'

He held her gaze, frowning slightly.

'I'm surprised you're still in Shallowford. You always seemed like you had a future, when we were at school.'

She didn't even think he'd noticed her when they were at school.

'I'm not going to be here for much longer. My grandmother's selling the gallery.'

'So what are you going to do?'

'I've got plenty of options.'

'I bet you have. A girl like you must have a lot of contacts.'

She couldn't quite discern what he was implying. Whether he was being genuine or sarcastic. She busied herself with the paperwork. She didn't want to discuss her future, with him or anyone else. 'I'll bring some paint charts over with me when I bring the picture over, if you like.' Why on earth had she said that? She wanted to get rid of him. He was making her feel awkward, with his perspicacious remarks. His scrutiny that she didn't understand. Why start hitting on her now, twelve years later? If he was hitting on her. She simply couldn't tell what his game was. She wrote out the receipt, then put it in an envelope and handed it to him.

'How would tomorrow do? Some time in the afternoon?'

'Thanks,' he said. 'Here's my number. Call me if it changes.'

He handed her a card. Danny McVeigh, Security Solutions, it read. He grinned as she took in the irony.

'Classic poacher-turned-gamekeeper, eh?' he said. 'I'll give you a free consultation. Any time. Though I suppose it's too late. But just so you know, those cameras you've got are rubbish. Any burglar worth his salt would have them deactivated in a nanosecond.'

He left her staring from the card to the cameras, speechless. The door shut behind him. She felt unsettled. He'd left her with a funny feeling in the pit of her stomach that she couldn't identify – a mixture of nerves and fear and . . .

She turned away sharply. She knew what the feeling was. She remembered it from that night all those years ago, clinging onto him on the back of his bike.

It was desire.

In the end, decorating advice didn't really come into it, although Danny had by now, on Imogen's suggestion, painted his living room a deep greeny-grey and installed some halogen lamps, while Imogen had ended up as naked as his former lightbulb.

Now, however, after a few months together, it seemed as if that was all it was: a bit of decorating advice in return for a tumble or two. Imogen walked back into the restaurant. It was just a fling, she told herself. She didn't mean anything to Danny McVeigh. Of course he didn't want to come and join her friends for her birthday. That would indicate some kind of commitment. It would mean their relationship meant something. Appearing in public would rubber-stamp them. Conversely, there was no risk attached to a pleasurable but meaningless and clandestine romp on the rug in front of his fireplace.

She tried to block out the image, because it kindled something inside her. Lust, of course, but also something more lasting and pervasive. Hope, perhaps? Hope that their passion meant something more than simultaneous orgasms.

How could it? It was silly of her to read anything more into it than simple animal attraction. He was a McVeigh. That's all they understood. Even if he had done well for himself, with a business that was thriving and making good legitimate money, it was still McVeigh blood running through his veins beneath the veneer of respectability he had managed to achieve. She'd heard him on the phone to both clients and employees – a man who knew how to charm, how to give people what they wanted, and to get people to do what he wanted. She'd been impressed, captivated – but, she reminded herself, a leopard doesn't change its spots.

She sat back down at the table. Next to her place was the pile of presents her friends had bought her. Carefully chosen baubles and trinkets and luxuries that touched her heart. Danny had given her nothing, but that was no great surprise. He probably wasn't the kind of man who presented women with thoughtful tokens. And they'd hardly been an item long enough for her to merit so much as a card. Not that they were even an item, technically . . .

Everyone at the table was chilled out, drinking their Limoncello and lattes, gossiping, enjoying their midweek excursion. It was nearly eleven.

'I suppose I ought to go soon,' said Imogen to Nicky. 'I've got to get up at the crack of dawn.'

'Don't expect me to feel sorry for you,' Nicky replied. 'You jammy thing. A night on the Orient Express? Your grandmother is such a genius. What an amazing present.'

'I know,' said Imogen. 'Though it would be more fun if I was going with someone.'

'Don't knock it. I'd give anything for a couple of nights away on my own. I can't think of anything nicer. *And* you're staying at the Cipriani . . . total heaven.'

Imogen had to smile. 'Yes. I suppose you're right. I'm spoilt.'

She was. She knew she was. The train ticket and the night at the hotel weren't even her proper present. She was supposed to collect that when she got to Venice. A painting, called *The Inamorata*. One that someone had been keeping for Adele for the past fifty years. Imogen hadn't had time to think about it since her grandmother had sprung the surprise on her at breakfast.

Nicky was picking at the remains of cake on her plate. 'I think your grandmother feels guilty about selling the gallery. I think that's what it's all about.'

'She needn't feel guilty. I keep telling her that. I should have moved on years ago.'

'So what *are* you going to do?'

Imogen was quiet for a moment. Then she turned to her friend.

'I'm think I'm going to go to New York.'

Nicky's jaw dropped. 'What? Where did that come from?'

'I've got a long-standing job offer. From a gallery in Manhattan that specialises in British art. Oostermeyer and Sabol. They've told me any time I want to come over and work for them, I can. It's an open invitation.'

'Oh my God.' Nicky's eyes were round. 'You've got to be

kidding me. What's taken you so long? I would kill to go to New York. Anything to get away from Shallowford.'

Imogen was surprised. 'I thought you were happy with your lot?'

Nicky sighed. 'It's not all about the house of your dreams and a Range Rover Evoque, you know.'

'No,' said Imogen. 'I didn't think it was. But I thought you were content?'

'I'm never going to go anywhere or do anything, am I? I'm stuck doing the school run and making Nigel's supper for the next ten years, by which time it will be too late. Not like you. You've got the world at your feet. New York, Imo . . . I mean, wow.'

'You've got your job. You love your job!'

'What – writing up details for houses that no one in their right mind would want to live in? Breaking the news to people that their sale has fallen through? Telling people that their house is actually worth a hundred thousand pounds less than they think it is?'

Nicky slumped back in her chair. She looked slightly green, whether from envy or too much cake and wine Imogen couldn't be sure. She took a sip from her own glass. The wine was warm and slightly oily by now, but she needed it to take the edge off the shock of the decision she'd just made.

Because Nicky was right. Shallowford sucked you in and drained you of all your ambition. It was picture-postcard perfect on the surface, but when she looked around the table, there was something of the Stepford Wife in all her friends. If she didn't get out now, she never would. And if there was anything worse than being a Stepford Wife in Shallowford, it was being a spinster.

New York, however, would open up a whole new world. Imogen and Adele had done a lot of work with Oostermeyer and Sabol over the years, sourcing paintings for them and shipping them over. They'd visited them several times and built up a great working relationship. It was gratifying that they thought so much of her skills, thought Imogen. Although, as Danny had so shrewdly guessed, she had plenty of other contacts who would give her a lead, surely a spell in New York was the ultimate adventure for a thirty-year-old woman? Imogen wanted a new challenge. And in her heart of hearts, she thought it was probably best if she got far away from Danny McVeigh while she still could.

Determined that she had made the right decision, she drained her glass and stood up. She still hadn't packed. If she was going on the Orient Express, even if it was on her own, she wanted to look a million dollars.

The next morning, not long after dawn, Imogen's taxi crawled along the pitted track that led to Danny's cottage. In her hand she held an envelope. After sending an email to Oostermeyer and Sabol, she had stayed up until two composing a letter to him.

Dear Danny,

I'm writing this because a text seems a bit impersonal but I know if I see you in person my resolution will vanish.

Yesterday I was thirty, and I made a few decisions. It seemed the right time.

The most important of these is that I have decided to take up a position with a gallery in New York. I'll be leaving as soon as I get back from Venice. I should have left Shallowford a long time ago, and now I am it's terrifying. Terrifying but exciting.

I know we only have the tentative beginnings of a relationship, and I am not sure it would survive the distance, so I think it's probably better if we make a clean break. The past few weeks have been the most wonderful fun, and for that I thank you. I hope you understand.

Think of me in the Big Apple, a small town girl in the big city.

With lots of love
Imo

Wonderful fun? She laughed at her own understatement. Danny had made her feel like no man had ever done before, but she knew it was only a novelty, the thrill of being the gangster's moll, a sexual frisson with no real depth. How many times had she and her friends fantasised about him in the common room? Although at sixteen their imaginations hadn't stretched quite as far as what she and Danny had done . . .

She read the letter again. It sounded so stiff and stilted and uptight. She wondered what she could have done to soften it a bit, make it less formal. She sighed. She could spend the rest of her life writing and rewriting it. The important thing was to tell Danny it was over, because it wasn't fair to string him along. Not that he would care, probably.

She stared at his cottage for a moment. With its pointed

roof and gables and arched windows, it was like something out of a fairytale, just waiting for a princess or a woodcutter or a lost maiden to come along. There was nothing coming out of the chimney but she could still smell last night's woodsmoke in the chilly air. She got out of the car and picked her way along the moss-covered path in her high heels until she reached the door. For a moment she imagined him, naked and warm under his duvet. It was so tempting just to bang on the knocker. In five seconds flat she could be under the duvet with him, wrapping herself around him, feeling the warmth of his skin.

Better still, she could persuade him to come on the train. He could be packed and ready in ten minutes. The thought of it made her heart race. Danny McVeigh, pulling her towards him in the intimate confines of their cabin, those rough hands on her torso—

Stop it, Imo! she told herself. There was no room in her life for a rebel with a motorbike and a smile that could do untold damage to her heart and mind. She posted the letter through the letterbox, turned tail and fled.

Moments later, the cab made its way back down the rutted track. The motion made her feel a little sick. Imogen leaned back in the seat and shut her eyes. They felt gritty from lack of sleep, but it didn't matter. She could relax on the Orient Express – curl up in her cabin and go to sleep if she wanted.

Adele was absolutely right: she needed a couple of days to herself, in unashamed luxury, to recharge her batteries and consolidate her future. She had worked incredibly hard over the past few months in the run-up to the sale of the gallery, and she hadn't realised how exhausted she was. It was

81

amazing how her grandmother knew just the right thing to do. She was going to miss Adele being part of her everyday life, yet Imogen knew it was time for her to make her own way in the world.

She didn't look back. If she had, she might have seen Danny, still fuzzy with sleep, open the front door and gaze after her in bewilderment. In his right hand was her letter, the envelope ripped open and discarded. As the cab disappeared out of sight, he stepped back inside, crumpled the letter in his hand and threw it into the fireplace, where it sat amidst the cold grey ashes and the half-burned logs of the night before.

Six

Shut your eyes and count to ten, Stephanie told herself.

Simon was going to have a total fit if he saw his daughter. Stephanie realised she was going to have to deal with the situation, even though she tried to avoid disciplining the kids. They weren't exactly children anymore, and anyway it wasn't her place. Whether she would start to feel it was her place once the next few days were over was another thing. In the meantime, she hated interfering. Even more so when she was standing in her dressing gown and Velcro rollers and was supposed to be ready herself in less than fifteen minutes.

She looked in despair at the girl standing in front of her on the landing. Beth was dressed in a tight T-shirt, tiny cut-off denim shorts, fishnet tights and pink patent Dr Marten boots. Her blonde hair was backcombed and tied in a side ponytail.

Stephanie took a deep breath.

'Beth, you look amazing, but there's no way they'll let you on the train wearing that.' She kept her voice as casual as she could. 'The dress code is smart casual. And I know it's a pain but it's not fair on your dad. You know he'll freak.'

She felt she couldn't have been more conciliatory.

Nevertheless, Beth crossed her arms. 'It's all I've got.'

'No, it's not. You've got some lovely dresses.'

'They all make me look fat.'

Stephanie sighed.

'How could you look fat? You've got a great figure. Look at those amazing legs. I would kill for those legs.' Beth's legs were endless; Stephanie's were not. 'Come on, let's have a look and find something that isn't going to give your father a heart attack.'

She wasn't going to have time to do her hair properly now, but it was more important to get Beth sorted.

'I still don't get why he organised this trip. Who wants to be stuck on a train for all that time? Why couldn't we have gone to Dubai or somewhere? Or the Caribbean? That would have been cool.'

'There wasn't time to go that far.'

'Oh, yeah.' Beth looked at her knowingly. 'The café. Don't want to be leaving *that* alone for too long.'

Stephanie didn't rise. She guessed it was tough when your dad finally found a replacement for your mother and moved her into the family home, so she tried to excuse Beth's monstrous self-centredness. The girl was sweet underneath it all, but she was used to getting her own way and not thinking about anyone else. That's often how you turned out when you had divorcing parents, because their knee-jerk reaction was to spoil and indulge their kids to cover up the guilt – leaving other people to deal with the aftermath. She didn't want to bring Simon into the argument – he didn't deserve any more hassle; he got enough from his ex-wife Tanya – but she definitely needed to get Beth out of that outfit.

'Beth – babe – come on. Please?'

Beth rolled her eyes. Stephanie caught the scent of a recently smoked Marlboro Light mingled with some sweet and heavy pop-star-branded scent.

'I don't even know why you're bringing us with you,' said Beth. 'Surely you'd have more fun on your own?'

Stephanie looked down at the striped runner that ran the length of the corridor and counted to ten. Yep, she thought, at this rate they probably would. She wasn't going to say that, though.

'The whole trip is about us all having some fun together.'

'Oh yeah. Playing Happy Families. I'm missing two parties. Two.' Beth held up her fingers in case Stephanie hadn't got the message. Her nails were covered in chipped varnish in a lurid green.

'It won't kill you to miss them.' Stephanie knew this for certain. Every teenage party was the same. Cheap booze, vomiting, snogging and crying. She'd been to enough herself, and things hadn't changed that much. Yet she understood the angst Beth was going through. The fear that something monumental and life-changing would happen while your back was turned.

A door further down the corridor opened, and Jamie stepped out of his bedroom. In contrast to his sister, he was dressed appropriately: a striped blazer and red tie, skinny black trousers, his dark hair gelled in a tidy mess, the designer indie kid. He had the confident air of one who had never felt out of place in his life. Jamie had the perfect combination of attributes needed to get on in life: he was clever *and* cool.

'Creep,' said Beth.

Jamie looked her up and down, impassive. 'Dad's gonna wig.'

Beth pulled at the end of her ponytail. Despite her outward defiance, Stephanie could sense the girl's anxiety. She was running out of time.

'It's not as if anyone's even going to see you.' Even as she spoke, she knew how annoying she sounded. The voice of reason.

'I don't get why I can't wear what I want to wear.'

'Because it's not appropriate. Please, Beth.' Stephanie realised she was pleading. She wondered if bribery would help. Fifty quid? It would be worth it.

'She won't change,' Jamie chipped in. 'She loves winding people up.'

Beth glared at her brother, then threw up her hands.

'Fine. I'll change. As long as everyone *else* is happy, that's OK.'

She stormed back into her room. Stephanie looked at Jamie, who gave a false smile.

'Good times,' he said.

'I don't know why they can't be.' Stephanie leant against the wall. She felt drained.

'Because we're damaged,' Jamie told her. 'Terminally screwed up. Surely you figured that out on day one?'

Jamie was right – she *had* figured that out on day one. Although presumably hundreds of kids had been through what Jamie and Beth had been through. Broken homes were the norm. But she supposed that didn't make it any easier when your own parents split. Especially when it was your mother who left. It was so counter-intuitive, to walk out on your kids.

Mothers weren't supposed to do that. Ever.

And to be fair, Beth and Jamie had been pretty nice to her so far. She had been horribly self-conscious the first time she had come to spend the night at Simon's house, all too aware that she was stepping into Tanya's shoes, even though Tanya had long gone and she and Simon had been divorced for nearly two years. Simon insisted Stephanie had every right to be there, that he had every right to bring her back now they had been going out for nearly three months, but she had felt awkward nonetheless and still did, at times.

'I know they like you,' Simon told her. 'It's not as if they don't. Give it time. And try not to take it personally.'

That, thought Stephanie, was easy for Simon to say. And then he'd come up with the idea of the four of them going on the Orient Express, to spend some time together.

She walked back to the master bedroom. A billow of bergamot-scented steam came from the en-suite. The very essence of Simon. Her spirits lifted. He still made her heart leap with joy, even if she was finding it tough.

She got herself ready as quickly as she could, pulling the rollers out of her hair, putting on her make-up and sliding on her tights, her dress, her unfamiliar high heels. In just three months her life had changed so much. It had been a whirlwind romance – uplifting, exhilarating and wonderful. And now here she was, her evening dress hanging in a breathable linen dress carrier, her bag packed and ready to go on the Orient Express. She still wasn't sure she believed it.

It might be a fairytale, but there was still real life to deal with. She pulled her phone off its charger and held it in her hand for a moment. She had promised Simon she wouldn't call the café. They had made a pact with each other: four whole days without either of them contacting work. After all, it was obsession with work that had purportedly killed Simon's marriage and sent his wife Tanya running into the arms of another man. Keith, as a freelance architect who worked from home, had plenty of time to give Tanya the attention she craved.

Nevertheless Stephanie was desperate to check in. It was going to take all her strength to walk away without ringing. Her team had worked for her for over a year and were perfectly capable of dealing with any eventuality – fire, flood, food-poisoning – but Stephanie felt as anxious as a mother leaving her newborn for the first time. The café was everything to her. She had invested time, money, blood, sweat and tears *and* her previous relationship in it – which was why she had empathised so much with Simon when they met. Her ex-boyfriend had told her when they split that she worried more about the state of her muffins than she did him. At the time that had possibly been true, but the accusation had hurt.

Now, she had learnt that there was more to life than the consistency of your baked goods. Even so, she was hard-wired to worry.

She pressed speed dial, just as the door to the en-suite opened. Simon stepped out of the steam, a white towel wrapped around his waist. At fifty-two he still had a fine figure: broad shoulders tapering to a waist that showed only a hint of middle-age spread, and somehow that only added to the fact that he felt solid and safe. She cut off the call. She knew she looked guilty.

Simon raised an eyebrow. His eyebrows, dark and beautifully arched above his hazel eyes, were one of the things she loved best about him. She imagined he used them to great effect in court. A single twitch could speak volumes.

'Sorry, sorry . . .' Stephanie put the phone in her bag, then pulled the charger out of the wall. Simon dropped his towel to the floor and walked over to the wardrobe, looking over his shoulder with a grin.

'Go on. Call them back. Make sure the place hasn't been raided by hooligans overnight. Or razed to the ground . . .'

'I'm sure it's fine.' She felt foolish. Simon was a barrister, with umpteen vitally important cases piling up that he was managing not to check in on. And she was worrying about whether her two very able assistants had managed to unlock the door to the café and stick the coffee machine on.

He walked over to her, a pale-blue shirt in one hand, a striped tie in the other. 'Hey – I know it's hard. But you have to walk away. You're not indispensable. No one is.'

She knew he was speaking from experience. He'd retrained himself during his failed attempt to save his crumbling marriage.

'You look amazing, by the way,' he told her. 'That was definitely the right choice.'

'Makes a change from jeans and an apron.' She held out her arms for a more in-depth inspection.

'You know how that apron does it for me.'

'I can always pack it.'

He grinned. 'No. You'll do as you are.'

She had on a crocheted dress and a long, finely knit cardigan over the top: chic, understated and a million miles from her usual uniform. Simon had come with her to help choose her wardrobe for the journey, something he had never done with Tanya. Sometimes Stephanie felt guilty that she, rather than Simon's ex-wife, was benefiting from his decision to change, but it had been too late for Tanya.

'Anyway,' he had told her darkly, 'she didn't want me to change. Not really. It was just a convenient way of blaming me for her running off. It absolved her, didn't it? I was unreasonable. Married to my job. Never mind the fact that all that time she was the one putting pressure on me to earn the bloody money. I mean, you don't get all this,' he waved his hand around to indicate the four-storey house and all its luxury trappings, 'by being home for supper at six.'

Since they'd been together, the friends he'd introduced her to – there were only a couple who'd taken Tanya's side and refused to meet her – exclaimed about how Stephanie had changed him. But Stephanie hadn't deliberately changed Simon at all, far from it. If his habits had altered, it was perhaps because he had learned from his mistakes.

'Or maybe I actually want to be with you,' he told her. 'Coming home to Tanya inevitably meant being faced with a litany of what I hadn't done. She was very high-maintenance. Financially *and* emotionally.'

By all accounts Tanya had spent her days flitting between the gym, the hair salon and the beautician. Stephanie, by contrast, cut her own hair with the kitchen scissors and rarely painted her nails. When your hands were in a mixing bowl from dawn till dusk, there was little point.

Simon had also insisted on her finding time to go to the hairdresser and get a manicure before the trip.

'Don't worry – I'm not grooming you to be a trophy wife,' Simon teased her. 'Far from it. I just think you deserve pampering. You work bloody hard.'

After years of backbreaking work, getting up at dawn to

open the café and being the last to leave – but only after she had cashed up, wiped down every surface, washed the floor and cleaned every dish – Stephanie found she loved the attention and the luxury.

'I could get used to this,' she told Simon, swishing her shiny locks and showing him her coral-tipped fingers.

'Good,' he said.

And now here she was, done up to the nines, not a hair out of place, ready to go on the Orient Express to Venice. Helping a customer out with *The Times*' crossword was all part of the service at the café: Stephanie had never appreciated her extensive vocabulary before, but knowing the answer to seven across had definitely paid off. She looked at Simon, feeling a huge burst of glee and excitement and love. She took a step towards him and wound an arm around his neck.

He nuzzled into her. She could feel his lips on her skin.

'There's no time, I suppose . . . ?' he murmured.

She felt the familiar fizz seep into her. She hoped the feeling would never wear off. Out of the corner of her eye she saw the clock. She disengaged herself with extreme reluctance. Who knew when they'd next have the chance?

'Come on,' she said. 'Get dressed. The taxi's going to be here soon.'

Ten minutes later Stephanie, Simon and Jamie were waiting in the hall. It was huge, with a Minton tiled floor off which led the sweeping staircase. At the bottom of the stairs was the luggage.

Stephanie regarded their reflection in the mirror that took up most of the far wall. She would never have believed it if someone had told her she was going to find love with a middle-aged barrister with two teenage kids. Stephanie, the free spirit, so determined to make her own way in life, was astonished to find how much she enjoyed convention. A lot of her friends had been sceptical when she told them about their relationship, but as she revealed, 'Sometimes, you just know.'

And at last here was Beth, gliding down the stairs in a perfectly nice dress: navy-blue with swallows on it, and maybe a little short, but that was the deal these days – no one made a fuss about dress length anymore – and her tights had no holes and she wore low-heeled pumps which weren't at all scuffed and her hair was loose with a couple of sparkly slides and she looked . . . just right . . . Stephanie gave her an appreciative hug. 'You look lovely.'

Simon nodded. 'My gorgeous girl.'

Beth gave a wry smile. Her dad clearly had no idea of the earlier battle, and she was grateful to Stephanie for keeping quiet.

'Right, has everybody got everything?' asked Simon, poised to set the burglar alarm.

Just as everyone picked up their bags, the phone rang.

'Don't answer it. We haven't got time.' Simon began to punch in the code.

After four rings, the answer machine kicked in.

It was Tanya. Her voice was low and husky and sounded slightly slurred. As if she had just woken up. Or as if she was drunk.

'Darlings – I've probably missed you. I just wanted to say, have a wonderful time. I shall think of you. Oh – and Simon. Your prescription shades – the ones you take skiing?

I thought you might need them. Just in case you were wondering where they were, you left them here the other night. I'll keep them safe for you, shall I?'

There was absolutely no denying the smug triumph in her voice.

Simon looked thunderous as he reached out a finger and cut the message off.

Stephanie looked at him.

Jamie and Beth looked at each other.

Outside in the drive, the taxi beeped its arrival.

An awkward silence fell in the hall. The taxi driver eventually came and knocked on the door and could no longer be ignored, but at least his intervention galvanised everyone into action. Beth and Jamie started taking out the luggage. They could sense a crisis and went into helpful mode.

Simon cornered Stephanie in the doorway. He looked sheepish as he scratched his head and offered his explanation.

'Tanya wanted me to help her with her tax return. It's the first time she's had to do it on her own since the divorce, and honestly – she hasn't a clue. She's useless with figures. And I thought it was better for me to give her a hand than to face the fallout when she cocked it up.'

'You don't have to explain,' said Stephanie. She smiled a smile that belied the heaviness of her heart. She didn't want to overreact.

'I do. I don't want you to think that I sneak off and see Tanya behind your back.'

Stephanie didn't reply. That's exactly what he had done.

'I know that's what I did . . .' Simon looked shamefaced.

'But I didn't think it was worth mentioning. I didn't want to upset you. And it's just bloody typical of Tanya to dump me in it like that. When all I was trying to do was prevent an even bigger crisis . . .'

He trailed off.

'Honestly, it's OK,' said Stephanie. 'But next time, maybe mention it?'

'I know, I know. I made a mistake.'

Stephanie realised that it wasn't often that she saw Simon flustered. 'I understand if you have to see her. You can't wipe out twenty years of marriage. And she's still the children's mother.'

'You're amazing.' Simon leant in and kissed her. 'If it had been Tanya, I would never have heard the end of it. She'd have beaten me over the head with it for the rest of my life.'

'Maybe that's why you love me,' said Stephanie drily.

Simon touched her arm. 'I don't know what I'd do without you.'

He turned, and went to pick up her case. Stephanie watched him. She had no reason to disbelieve what he had told her, yet she couldn't help feeling the tiniest chink of doubt. Was that really why he had gone round? Or did he still have feelings for his wife, and had grabbed the opportunity to go and see her? Tanya was stunning, tempestuous, a handful. The sort of woman who broke men's hearts for a pastime. Although Simon protested that he had fallen out of love with her years and years ago, Stephanie knew that you could still love someone who treated you badly. Even when you'd found a replacement. And *I don't know what I'd do without you* wasn't the sort of thing you said to someone you'd lost your soul to. It was the sort of thing you said to a reliable cleaning lady.

Stop it, Stephanie told herself. Where on earth was this paranoia coming from? Of course Simon loved her. He'd said as much, hadn't he? And it was probably because she was nothing like Tanya. Tanya: who dressed provocatively and flirted outrageously and took cocaine in the loo at dinner parties even though she knew it would ruin Simon's career if it ever got out, because Tanya was, above all else, selfish.

Simon was probably relieved to have someone calm and sensible and trustworthy by his side. And she wasn't *that* boring, Stephanie chastised herself. Starting your own café and having people queue out of the door every lunchtime wasn't boring. She thought of her café window with pride – the giant pistachio-studded meringues, the raspberry tartlets, the legendary brownies – everything piled high, higgledy piggledy to the onlooker but actually just so, proportions and colours and amounts exactingly calculated so the display looked its absolute enticing best . . .

Tanya, Simon told her, was only good at spending money.

Besides, Stephanie thought with a minxy grin, she had fifteen years on Tanya. She might not be quite so glam, but she didn't need Botox.

She brushed her misgivings to one side. She wasn't going to sulk. Simon had given her an explanation, and an apology, and that was enough.

The Pullman
Victoria to Calais

Seven

It was the crispest of April mornings: still cold, but optimistically bright, the kind that filled your heart with joy at the thought of the warmer months to come. People blinked at the dazzling sun as they emerged from the Tube into Victoria Station and spilled out onto the concourse. Pigeons pecked for crumbs amidst the scurrying feet and litter. Train announcements boomed out over the heads of the commuters, the words floating up into the tiny puffs of white cloud in the blue sky, never to be heard again.

Archie strode under the departure board, past all the people with upturned faces waiting for their platform to be announced. He had a battered leather Gladstone in one hand, and an ancient Burberry mac that had belonged to his grandfather slung over his right shoulder. He was wearing a Tattersall check shirt and a silk tie and corduroys – he hoped he was smart enough. He didn't want to wear his dark suit. It had had enough wear over the past couple of weeks, what with all the trips to the solicitor and, of course, the funeral. He didn't care if he never saw it again.

Across the crowded platform, he could see the lounge where passengers waited for the English rake – the Pullman that would take them to Folkestone. There they would cross the Channel to Calais, where the Continental rake, comprising the historic wagons-lits, would await them. An elegant couple, arm in arm, were about to walk in. She was in golden, calf-length fur, while he was sporting an immaculately cut Savile Row suit. Archie watched as the door was opened for them by a uniformed steward, and they slipped inside.

He wasn't ready for this. He looked around to see if he could find a bar open. Just a quick Scotch, to give him some Dutch courage. Anyone would need a drink in this situation, surely? Although . . . did he really want to turn up with booze on his breath and start slurring? He'd had no breakfast, after all. He'd just get a coffee from one of the booths, take five minutes to gather himself.

He bought an espresso and felt the caffeine give him a jolt. Half of him wanted to laugh at the ludicrousness of the situation. The other half wanted to turn around and get a taxi straight back to Paddington to catch a train home.

It was so typical of his friend to set him up like this. Jay had been desperate to get Archie married off over the past couple of years, ever since his relationship with Kali had come to an end. Kali had been a feisty, robust Kiwi with a sense of fun and endless energy. After going out for five years, the plan had been for Archie and Kali to go and live in her native New Zealand and take over her parents' farm, but at the eleventh hour, Archie had bottled it. The love of his own family, his own farm, and his friends combined had been greater than his love for Kali. She had understood, because that's the sort of girl Kali was, and why he had loved her, but he simply didn't want to live on the other side of the world.

Ever since the split, Jay had thrown pretty girls his way. He inevitably had plenty to spare. Archie had dallied with some of them. Occasionally they had lasted more than a few weeks. But since Kali, he had never felt a real spark. They had all been interchangeable, as far as he was concerned, and he wasn't the type to string someone along if he didn't really feel anything.

'I'm quite happy as I am,' he used to insist, but Jay continued to set him up, regardless. Even from beyond the grave, it seemed. And so here he was, about to meet his blind date. He supposed it could have been worse. The prize could have been a trip to Alton Towers, or Blackpool. Then he really would have had to think about reneging on his promise. At the time, he hadn't believed there was a remote possibility that he would win, but he'd given his word.

Archie looked at the girl's profile again and sighed. Emmie Dixon. She sounded nice enough on paper, but apart from anything, this whole rigmarole wasn't fair on her. He hoped she wasn't pinning her hopes on some sort of romantic adventure with a happy ending. If she had any sense, she wouldn't. With any luck, she was just looking forward to the trip, and could see it for the public-relations exercise that it was.

The only good thing was that Not On The Shelf weren't filming the whole wretched thing. If that had been the case, he would definitely have put his foot down. As it was, he was dreading the photo-call that was the only requirement. Archie was quite self-contained and private and he didn't like attention.

He could only imagine how much Jay would have relished an opportunity like this. He would have milked it for all it was worth. He was a showman and an extrovert. Archie tried not to imagine him playing up to the cameras. Thinking about Jay was still too painful. He could feel the tension in the back of his neck creep up to the base of his skull. He hoped he wasn't going to get one of the headaches that had been plaguing him recently. He hadn't been eating or sleeping properly. His mother was driving him mad, sending him meals to warm up in the microwave. They sat in his fridge untouched, until he threw the contents in the bin and returned the dishes to her, pretending he'd eaten them. He'd lost half a stone in the past month.

He tossed his empty coffee cup into the bin, then headed for the Pullman Lounge. There was a red carpet outside, and two box trees flanking the arched glass door. Above it was a sign reading Venice-Simplon Orient Express.

He pushed the door open. Inside, the lounge was plush, with red walls and a gleaming parquet floor. He looked round at the other travellers as they checked in their luggage at the desk. Everyone was smiling, chattering, wrapped up in the romance and the glamour. They had all dressed for the occasion, and were groomed and coiffed and polished. The air was heavy with scent and cologne and expectation.

As he looked around, a woman in a grey suit surged forward, accompanied by a man with a camera slung around his neck. The woman wore red-rimmed glasses, a great deal of chunky jewellery and a rather predatory smile.

'Are you Archie Harbinson, by any chance?'

Archie felt cornered. He should deny it. Get away now.

'I recognise you from your photo.'

Jay was nothing if not thorough. Of course he'd sent a photo.

'Yes. I am,' Archie admitted, through gritted teeth.

Her smile grew even wider and she held out her hand. 'I'm Patricia, from Not On The Shelf. I'm so pleased to meet you. And congratulations. It was a really tough choice – we had hundreds and *hundreds* of entries.'

'Really?' All those desperate people out there. Most of whom deserved this trip more than he did.

'But your profile really stood out.'

'Did it?' Archie wondered what on earth Jay had written.

'It wasn't about finding a potential George Clooney,' Patricia went on to explain.

'Oh. Good. Well, you won't be disappointed, then.'

'It was about finding the perfect match. Two people who seemed made for each other.'

'I see . . .'

'You and Emmie seemed like dream partners. You were both very clear what you wanted, which always helps.'

What had Jay written? What had he said Archie wanted?

Patricia was nodding at him. 'We have high hopes of a happy future for you both. We at Not On The Shelf have a *feeling*.' To accentuate this feeling she balled her hand into a fist and prodded an area somewhere between her breasts and her stomach. 'And it's our *feeling* that makes us the success we are. No computer matching for us. Oh no. We go by *gut instinct*.'

Archie thought if her jewellery was anything to go by, he wouldn't trust her to pick out a tie for him, let alone a long-term partner. But he couldn't be bothered to argue.

Patricia took his arm. 'Let's not delay things a moment longer. I want you to meet your date.' She turned to the photographer. 'Are you ready? I think it's important to capture the moment they first set eyes on each other. It's what the other clients will want to see.'

The photographer held up his camera. 'Ready when you are.'

'*Love is in the air,*' warbled Patricia as she took Archie's arm.

Archie suddenly had an image of his blind date's disappointment when she saw him in the flesh. He steeled himself for the humiliation, inwardly cursing Jay, who he knew damn well was watching him from above. 'Don't even think about doing a runner, Harbinson,' he could hear him say. He let Patricia lead him over to a girl sitting on one of the plush banquettes that lined the lounge.

'Here we are,' said Patricia proudly. 'This is Emmie. Emmie Dixon – Archie Harbinson.'

The photographer began snapping away at the pair of them as the girl stood up. She was tiny, dainty, in a drop-waisted crepe de chine dress the colour of crushed mulberries. She wore it with strings of pearls and a matching cloche hat topped with a creamy, quivering ostrich feather. Beneath it her face was like a little doll's, with laughing brown eyes and the most kissable cherry-red lips. On the seat beside her was a pile of three hat boxes in pistachio green on which black spidery writing proclaimed: Emmie Dixon, Milliner.

She held out her hand.

'Hello,' she said shyly. 'I'm so pleased to meet you. I'm Emmie.'

'Archie. Very nice to meet you too.' It tripped off his tongue, for Archie's manners overrode his lack of enthusiasm. Besides, he was surprised. She was a million miles from what he had been expecting. He supposed he had watched too many episodes of *Blind Date*. He'd envisaged hair extensions and fake tan and a certain amount of leopardskin. Not someone who looked as if she had stepped out of another age.

As the photographer started snapping away, she leaned into him, talking in a low, confidential voice. 'I bet you've been dreading this. I know I have. I absolutely hate having my picture taken.'

'Me too. But then people don't often want to take mine.' Archie was deadpan.

'Smile for me, if you could, both of you?' said the photographer.

'Yes, remember you've just met the person of your dreams!' Patricia was beaming with the excitement.

The two of them turned to face the camera, obliging grins fixed to their faces.

'Perfect!' crowed the photographer.

'And it would be lovely if we could have one of you kissing the other,' added Patricia. 'Just on the cheek,' she added hastily. 'Just a little peck.'

Emmie bit her lip. Archie could see she was trying not to laugh. She leant in and brushed her cheek against his.

'This is awful,' she whispered. 'Everyone's staring.'

It was true. They were suddenly the centre of attention, as the other passengers surveyed them with curiosity, wondering if they were famous.

'Hopefully they'll let us have a drink in a minute,' replied Archie.

'And then let's have the two of you under the sign,' trilled Patricia. 'So we can get the picture into context. It's going to go up on the website as soon as possible. And on Facebook and Twitter and all of our social media. We might not use computers to matchmake but we are social-media savvy.'

'Oh joy,' muttered Archie. There was nothing like being plastered across the internet for posterity. He followed obediently as Patricia herded the three of them across the room. Emmie hooked her arm in Archie's.

'Say cheese,' said the photographer.

Archie grimaced in an approximation of a smile.

'Cheese!' said Emmie, and the flash went off.

From across the lounge, Riley observed the proceedings with interest, though he almost couldn't bear to watch. They were such an intriguing couple, but the photographer was making a terrible job of the shoot. He could just imagine what the pictures were going to be like. Awkward and badly lit and cheesy. The professional in him was desperate to shove the bloke out of the way and show him how it was done. But it would be rude and this was supposed to be his holiday. Riley had a camera with him – he always did; it would be like travelling without oxygen to go without one – but it was for personal use. Yet he still couldn't quell the urge to make the picture right. He could imagine exactly how he would set them up: the man in profile, gazing at the girl, who would be looking down with a half-smile. You had to find the story. And although there clearly *was* a story, it had been completely blown out of the water by lack of imagination. The two of them looked as if they wished they were anywhere else on the planet, which was the kiss of death for a photograph.

Instead of intruding, Riley sat down and enjoyed the tableau. The girl was exquisite. She'd never make a model – far too short, far too curvaceous – but she had a warmth and radiance that drew the eye. And the bloke was good-looking in a slightly dishevelled, Richard Curtis-movie sort of a way, with a mop of flyaway chestnut hair he kept pushing back from his eyes. His lack of vanity, of course, made him all the more attractive. Riley could see he was finding this pantomime torture. Many people hated being photographed, but this guy really loathed the limelight. Riley wondered why on earth he was putting up with being ordered around by that ghastly woman in the grey suit, and whether the two of them were actually going on the train. Maybe he'd find out more about them on the journey. He knew from experience that was half the fun of going on the Orient Express – the people-watching. He and Sylvie had spent years speculating, surmising, making up stories . . .

Sylvie. He looked at the clock. Less than twelve hours now until she was due to board the train in Paris. It was extraordinary, at his age, that he could feel so excited about seeing someone he had known for so long. Despite every-thing that had happened recently, he felt young. As young as the couple he'd been staring at, and as full of hope.

It took a brush with death, he thought, to make you realise how lucky you were. He'd been flung across the back of the taxi when it had hit the other car. Of course he hadn't been wearing his seatbelt. Had he been in a less sturdy vehicle, he might have come off far worse. He was lucky to get away with just damaging a kidney through the impact. It had been painful and debilitating, and he had felt helpless in the hospital during the two weeks it had taken to ascertain that it was still functioning and that he wasn't going to lose it. Day after day he had lain in excruciating agony while they drained the blood off, and only one thought had got him through it.

The moment he was released from hospital he got straight into another cab.

'Bond Street,' he told the driver.

It was time to do what he should have done years ago.

The Pullman, resplendent in chocolate and cream livery, basked in the April sunshine on Platform Two, smug in the knowledge that it was quite the most magnificent train at Victoria Station that day. People hurrying to and from the more prosaic commuter trains cast admiring glances, wondering if one day they might be lucky enough to pass through the glass turnstile, as a steady stream of passengers was now doing. The sense of occasion was palpable: everyone seemed to have a spring in their step, eager to get on board. In front of the train, white-jacketed waiters and gold-buttoned stewards awaited their passengers, confident in the knowledge that everything had been done to ensure the first leg of their journey was special, until they finally climbed on board the wagon-lits of the Orient Express in France.

Archie escorted Emmie, his arm in hers, along the platform. He was in too deep now, he thought. There was no escape. He'd put her straight as soon as he could, he thought, his eagle eye seeking out the carriage they had been allocated. There it was, flagged by a crested sign. Its name, Ibis, was emblazoned on the side. She was the oldest of the carriages, once used as part of the glamorous Deauville Express in the twenties, transporting decadently wealthy Parisians to the casino. Who knew what scandal and secrets lay inside her?

Inside, the dining car was like the most luxurious restaurant. The shining marquetry depicted medallions of Greek dancing girls. Tables of two or four were laid with pristine tablecloths, the chairs upholstered in pale-blue upholstery. Bone-china plates were flanked by gleaming silver cutlery, and a range of crystal glasses, etched with the Orient Express crest, stood to attention.

As the passengers were shown to their tables they were each handed a Bellini, a luscious concoction of fresh peach juice and Prosecco, a taste of Venice to come. They sank into their seats with sighs of satisfaction and anticipation. Bags were stowed overhead in the luggage racks, newspapers unfurled, excited texts with accompanying photographs were sent. It was another world, a step back in time and away from reality.

Archie and Emmie were shown into their own private compartment at the end of the carriage with an etched glass door that shut them off from the rest of the passengers. The two of them slid onto the cushioned banquettes, upholstered in cream and blue and complete with snow-white antimacassars.

'This is amazing. This is so amazing,' breathed Emmie, wide-eyed at her surroundings.

'Yes,' agreed Archie, despite his cynicism. It was impossible not to be impressed.

She stared around. 'You can just imagine what went on here years ago. Strangers on a train. Their eyes meeting across the compartment.' She looked around her, eyes shining. 'How many people have fallen in love in here, do you think?'

Archie was nonplussed. 'I have no idea.' In his head, people were using the train to get from A to B. He felt awkward. Emmie was obviously a girl who lived for romance. Maybe she really did have her hopes pinned on Archie? She'd filled out the application, after all. She was obviously looking for a partner. Why else had she entered the competition? His mouth went dry with panic. He'd have to come clean.

As he was about to speak, a steward appeared, immaculate in a crisp white shirt, black tie and black jacket, proffering a bottle of Bollinger.

'Compliments of Not On The Shelf, sir.'

'Thank you,' Archie said, and raised an eyebrow at Emmie. 'Might as well start the journey in style.'

He wasn't sure what the champagne would do for his headache, but it was kill or cure.

With perfect timing, the stationmaster blew his whistle. They sat back in their seats and looked out of the window as the train started up and slid graciously out of the station. On the platform, those left behind waved furiously until the track curved around and the engine was out of sight. The bottle opened with a satisfying pop, and the steward poured them each a glass of champagne with expert precision, the bubbles glowing golden in the sunshine as they headed over the Thames and past the towers of Battersea power station.

'Well,' said Archie. 'Here we are.'

The two of them clinked glasses. Emmie smiled, but Archie couldn't quite look her in the eye.

'Before we go any further,' he said, 'there is something I really ought to tell you.'

Eight

Danny didn't understand how anyone coped with London – the traffic, the congestion, the queues, the jams. Even on a motorbike, which meant he could weave in and out of the traffic, it was taking him far longer than he expected. The A4 had been chock-a-block. He thought his heart was going to burst with the frustration.

He wasn't usually given to dramatic gestures. The truth of it was, nothing had ever mattered to him before. Not like this. But after all this time, now he had come so close, he wasn't going to let her go.

He'd never told anyone, but he had been utterly captivated by Imogen when he was at school. She was so quietly confident, so sure of her way in the world. Not brazen, like so many of the girls. The ones who met his eye boldly and made it clear what they wanted from him weren't the ones he wanted. But Imogen, who had no real idea of her presence and the effect it had – he couldn't describe the feelings she awoke in him. Maybe if he'd paid more attention in English he could have found the words, but all he knew was that it was like a fire inside, a flame that he couldn't put out, no mattered how hard he tried.

He didn't think she even noticed him. He watched her

whenever he could. Bent over her hymn-book at assembly, one of the few who actually bothered to sing properly, her red lips mouthing the words. In the corridor, her regulation green jumper baggy, as was the fashion, yet still managing to cling to the curve of her breasts. In the cafeteria, where she unpacked her lunchbox with precision: sandwiches on granary bread, flapjack that looked home-made, a rosy red apple. Everything about her spoke of a life that was a million miles from his. She was cared for – not spoilt or pampered, but looked after and protected. He longed to be her protector, but the idea was laughable. He almost couldn't bear the torture, the daily knowledge that a girl like Imogen would never be interested in him as she brushed past him on the stairs, oblivious, leaving behind that clean, lemony scent.

Until he had found her on the road that night, after a party, drunk, bedraggled and abandoned, and it was the first time he'd ever felt in a position of strength, as if he had something to offer her. He had never forgotten the feeling of her warm body pressed against his back as he drove her home. He remembered the expectation, the moment when he thought she might have asked him in. He saw the desire in her eyes, but of course she didn't. He'd tried to be as chivalrous as he knew how, but he knew he'd never be invited over the threshold of Bridge House. That night he had accepted he would never be part of her life, and tried to erase her memory.

Ironically, it was being arrested that was the making of him, when a bungled job meant he ended up taking the rap for two of his brothers. They already had form and would have got much stiffer sentences, so he did the noble thing, but it was a shock when he got sent to a young offenders' institute. He supposed they were making an example of him. In the end, he only did a few months, but being inside was a real wake-up call. Danny realised that in the grand scheme of things he wasn't bad at all, and never wanted to spend any more time at her Majesty's pleasure – because next time round it would be a real prison. The institution was bad enough. He was able to look after himself, but you could never be off your guard. The worst thing was the boredom. Time dragged, and frustration gnawed at him until he thought he would scream. At which point he discovered the opportunities available to him and, with the help of a tutor, started a course in business studies.

Once he was let out, he didn't carry on. Danny wasn't interested in qualifications, but it had given him a taste for a legitimate business. Something wicked inside him saw the humour in becoming a security consultant. He didn't go back to Shallowford because he feared his reputation would go before him, so he settled in the Thames Valley, near Reading. He started small, knocking on doors and offering to install home systems. After five years he was in demand, specialising in pubs and restaurants, teaching landlords how to spot if their employees' fingers were in the till. His turnover doubled, tripled, quadrupled. And Annabel, a glamorous fifty-something landlady from a Thameside gastro-pub, let him into her heart. She was raucously posh, fearless, passionate, ruthless, and he learned from her, hungrily.

He was surprised how much simpler it was to be straight. There was no ducking and diving and bobbing and weaving. You did a day's work for a day's pay and that was it. When he visited his family – as infrequently as he could, though he wanted to make sure his mum was all right – they thought he was mad and had gone soft. They laughed at him for paying his taxes and not signing on, but at least he had a clear conscience. And actually, he was better off. He might have to work for the money he had in his bank account, but it was better than scamming and nicking and scrounging and constantly watching your back. And he found he got more pleasure from spending his own money than the ill-gotten gains he was used to.

And then Annabel had gently ended their relationship. She was selling up, moving to the South of France, and although she was very fond of Danny, she didn't think their bond would survive the move. He was sorry, but not devastated. Annabel had given him confidence, and if not a taste then at least a curiosity for the finer things, but he knew only too well she was far from being the love of his life.

Somehow the time seemed right for him to move back to his hometown. His mum was getting old. She suffered from lupus, and none of his siblings could be bothered to help. He had no intention of moving back into the heart of the rabble, but he wanted to be able to check on her on a regular basis.

A friend of a friend had told him about the cottage on the Shallowford Manor estate. He didn't think he would get it, as he had no references, but he'd struck a deal with the estate manager. It turned out that the manor house needed a security update. Danny got the contract, and a six-month renewable lease on Woodbine Cottage.

He couldn't believe how happy it made him. The peace was incredible. He stepped out of his front door at night and looked up at the stars above, breathing in the freezing air, and felt a glow of contentment. The only time in his life he had been alone like this was when he was in prison, in his cell. But that had been different. An imposed, enforced alone. Not the kind that made you feel free. He cut wood for his log burner, and bought a book that helped him recognise the stars. He got a scrappy ginger kitten because he was sure he'd heard mice in the roof. He called him Top Cat, after his favourite childhood cartoon. He cut down on his drinking, and felt better for it. He bought an acoustic guitar, and tried to play along with his favourite songs. He was no great musical talent, but he enjoyed it. Gradually, he felt as if the real Danny was emerging. He was no angel – he still had a wild streak, an urge for danger – but he felt as if his energies were being put to more constructive use.

And then, that afternoon, he had glimpsed Imogen through the window of the gallery and something told him this was his only chance. What was the worst that could happen? He knew she wasn't seeing anyone else. One of the few advantages of living in Shallowford was you could find out anything you wanted about anyone. He was a man now, not a callow schoolboy. He knew that if you didn't ask, you didn't get.

And he'd got her. By some miracle, he had got the girl of his dreams. She lit up his house with her warmth and her laughter. He felt safe when he woke up with her in his arms. Safe and sure and happy for the first time in his life. Optimistic that he had a meaningful future. He had thought she felt it too.

But then, mind-blowing sex did that to you: made you feel as if you had more of a connection with someone than you really did. It covered up the fact that deep down you had nothing in common. Imogen had obviously woken up to that sooner than he had. She was the one who had drawn the short straw, after all.

Danny felt filled with an impotent rage as he dropped down a gear and roared into the car park, startling passers-by. He was furious with himself. Somehow, he had dropped the ball and not paid her enough attention. Or not the right kind of attention.

In his gut, he knew it was because he hadn't been to her party. That was the kind of thing that was important to women, for some reason. But he knew it would have been a disaster if he had turned up. It was still too early on. That friend of hers, the estate agent – Nicky – would have looked right through him with her cold and calculating eyes, just as she had when he had come into the office about renting Woodbine Cottage. She'd looked at him as if to say *we don't rent to scum like you*, only he'd proved her wrong. Which would have given her all the more reason to pull Imogen aside in the toilets and ask if she was mad. Nicky, who'd bagged herself a rich man and who radiated dissatisfaction and unhappiness, wouldn't have understood what she was doing with him. And they hadn't been together long enough for Imogen to have confidence in their relationship. She would have seen him through her friends' eyes. She would have dropped him like a hot potato.

As it was, she had anyway. Even though he'd told her he wasn't going to go, she'd obviously expected him to. Maybe he should have made his feelings clearer, or outlined his fears? Danny wasn't used to expressing how he felt. He'd thought that the passion he and Imogen had in bed said it all, but of course, that wasn't how women worked. They liked it spelt out. They liked concrete evidence, tokens of affections, proof . . .

He should have turned up. He should have swallowed his pride and shown Nicky and the rest of them that he was worthy of Imogen, because he bloody well was. He had a successful business, his past was behind him, his future was . . . well, he could do anything he liked.

As he locked up his bike and ran through the car park, he prayed it wasn't too late. He pushed people out of the way as he hurtled through the entrance to the station, then through the crowds to Platform 2. He knew that was where the train departed. He saw the glass turnstile. And the train track beyond it.

Empty.

He grabbed a passing guard.

'The train for Venice – the Orient Express. Has it gone?'

He knew the answer.

'You've missed it by five minutes.' The guard looked at him. He pursed his lips. 'Sorry, mate.'

'Where's the next stop?'

The guard looked at his watch.

'Next stop for passengers is Paris. About nine o'clock tonight.'

Danny stared past him. He imagined getting back on his bike, tearing down the railway track after the train in some crazy James Bond stunt – Imogen looking out of the window, her face radiant with joy as she caught sight of him.

Not a chance. By the time he'd got his bike out of the car park, the train would be long gone.

Paris it was.

Nine

'The thing is,' said Archie. 'I'm here under false pretences, rather. My friend entered me in this competition. I think it was his idea of a joke. He filled out the profile and sent it in on my behalf. He had a rather warped sense of humour.'

The Pullman was winding its way through the outskirts of London, past bustling urban high streets and back gardens and allotments on its way to the east coast. From time to time, someone from the outside world waved at the train, excited by its glory, their envy palpable. It never failed to elicit a reaction.

Archie put his glass down on the snowy tablecloth and stared at the bubbles rising.

Emmie was silent for a moment. 'Had?'

Archie nodded. He cleared his throat. Suddenly it felt rather tight.

'Yes. He . . . died a couple of weeks ago.'

Emmie looked shocked. 'I'm so sorry.'

'It's OK. He'd been ill for a while, so in a way it was . . .'

Not unexpected? A relief? Archie looked out of the window, unable to find the words. He decided he didn't want to find them. He shook his head.

'Anyway, I promised him if I won this competition, I would go on the trip. But I'm not looking for . . .' He looked awkward. 'I'm not trying to find . . . um . . .'

God, this was embarrassing. He didn't want to offend her. She was staring at him, and he had no idea what she was thinking. Was she going to be angry? Tell him he'd broken the rules of the competition? Get him thrown off the train? Would he be escorted off by a security guard, only to find his story plastered across the newspapers? Not On The Shelf were very keen on publicity, he could see that, so he could imagine them leaking the whole sorry tale to get some coverage. He should have kept his mouth shut.

'I don't want a relationship,' he finally managed. 'And I'm terribly sorry if you feel cheated. I shouldn't have come at all, but as I said, I made a promise.'

To his bemusement, she burst into peals of laughter.

'You have no idea what a relief that is,' she told him. 'I'm in exactly the same situation. My sister entered me in this competition. I could have killed her when I found out what she'd done, but then when I won I couldn't resist. I couldn't afford a holiday otherwise. And certainly never a trip on the Orient Express.'

'Seriously?'

'Honestly. I just thought – what the hell? I'll go along for the ride. I prayed you wouldn't turn out to be too much of a monster.'

A monster? He certainly hadn't been a bundle of laughs. Archie began to feel guilty that he'd been so standoffish.

'I hope I'm not.'

'No! No, you're not. You're not at all.'

Archie looked at her. Was she just being polite? He really

should have the good grace to be a bit more forthcoming, now he knew she wasn't chasing some romantic notion. He topped up their champagne. It was doing the trick – taking the edge off his tension, and his headache had faded, rather than worsened.

He managed a smile.

'Well, that's certainly taken the pressure off. Maybe we can relax a bit, now we know we're not expecting to find true love. Or, heaven forbid, wedding bells. Which I think is what Patricia was hoping for.'

'I mean, really,' said Emmie. 'What are the chances? Of finding your true love on a website?'

'The whole idea's just awful,' said Archie.

'I agree,' said Emmie. 'But people can't help interfering. They don't understand how you can possibly be happy being single.'

'Quite.'

'I mean, I love my own company. I don't want to clutter up my life with another person.'

'Nor me.'

For a moment, there was an awkward silence as they smiled at each other, both of them keenly aware what a peculiar situation this was. Then Emmie looked down at her lap.

'Never again,' she said, her voice rather small.

Archie thought he caught the silvery glint of a tear in the corner of one eye.

'Oh hell.' Her voice was strained with the effort of not crying. 'I promised myself I wouldn't mention it.'

Emotional women always made Archie panicky. He was never sure what to say, and ended up making things worse, not better. He tended to be very practical, and never *quite* picked up on the nuances of whatever it was that had upset them. He tapped his fingers on the table and smiled politely, hoping she would change the subject.

Emmie picked up her glass. 'But the thing is,' she leaned forward, confidentially. 'You can never trust a gambler.'

Archie was slightly nonplussed. 'Well,' he said. 'I don't know. I mean, I like a flutter as much as the next man. On Derby Day. And the Cheltenham Gold Cup.'

'There's a flutter,' said Emmie darkly. 'And there's putting someone's life savings on a rank outsider.'

'Ah,' said Archie.

Before Emmie could divulge any more, the door to the compartment slid open and the steward came in with wild mushrooms on brioche. The two of them waited politely while he served them, and poured them each steaming cups of fresh coffee. By now, the untidy remnants of outer London had been left behind, and the train forged on through the chalk of the North Downs.

As the door slid shut again, Archie picked up the silver jug.

'Cream in your coffee?' he asked.

Emmie nodded.

'I wouldn't have minded so much,' she told him, 'if Charlie hadn't been such good fun.'

Archie poured a stream of cream into her cup. He was going to get her life story, whether he liked it or not.

'You'd better tell me everything,' he said. 'Right from the beginning.'

It was deepest, darkest November. The frosty ground was seeping upwards through the soles of Emmie's sheepskin boots, and her toes were starting to go numb. A stall at the biggest winter race meeting in the country had seemed like a good idea, but nothing had prepared her for the cold. Business was brisk – very brisk – which more than compensated for the cost of her tiny pitch. But a five-foot-by-ten-foot canvas tent with an open front did nothing to protect her from the elements. The commentator kept reminding everyone that the going was hard, even though the morning's frost was melting away, but standing still in near-freezing conditions was starting to become unbearable. Her fingers were so cold she could hardly count out the change.

Around her was a U-shaped arrangement of trestle tables covered in hats. Hats in every shape, size and colour which she had trimmed with feathers, ribbons, sequins, fur, lace, vintage brooches: anything she could lay her hands on. Race-goers were by their very nature an extrovert and hat-loving breed, it seemed, and the hats were going like hot cakes. She had sold more than twenty, and lots of people had taken her card offering a bespoke millinery service. These people were her target market, sure enough. Perhaps, after years of being a mere shop assistant, she was one step closer to realising her dream.

'Here. You look half-frozen. This might warm you up.' She turned to find a tall man in a navy cashmere coat with a velvet collar pressing a paper cup of hot chocolate into her hand. The scent of brandy pervaded the steam. She supposed it was unwise to accept a drink from a total stranger, but now she had smelt it she couldn't resist, and the warmth of the cup brought comfort to her numb fingers.

'Thank you,' she said. 'That's very kind. I'm so cold I don't think I'll ever feel warm again.'

'Your lips are almost blue,' he told her. 'Do you want me to take over for a few minutes while you go into the grandstand and warm up?'

She frowned. She could hardly waltz off and leave the stall in the hands of someone she had never met.

'Don't worry. I'm not going to run off with any of your hats. I'm not sure they'd suit me,' he grinned. He had smiling, twinkly eyes and a cheekiness to him that was immediately disarming. 'And you've got your takings with you.'

She had a moneybag tied round her waist stuffed with the cash she had taken so far. It wasn't a good look – she felt like a market trader – but there was only one of her, so she couldn't risk a till. She looked more closely at the man. Why was he offering to help her?

'Listen,' he said. 'I'm up on the last race. I want to quit while I'm ahead. The only way to stop myself putting another bet on and losing the lot is if I'm stuck here. You'd be doing me a favour.'

That should have told Emmie everything she needed to know. Yet there was something about the man she found trustworthy, and she desperately needed the loo. She smiled.

'Ten quid off if people buy two,' she told him. 'I'll be as quick as I can.'

'Take your time,' he told her. 'Grab something to eat. I can recommend the hot pork rolls.'

She pushed her way through the crowds into the grand-stand, wondering if she was mad, if she would come back to three empty tables. Somehow she thought not. He couldn't pack up all her hats and make off with them in ten minutes – it had taken her more than an hour to lug them from her car. And where would he sell them on?

She was surrounded by throngs of people, all slightly the worse for wear, milling from the bar to the totes and back again. She had to queue for ages in the bathroom, and by the time she got to the hot pork roll stand they had sold out, so she bought two hot sugary doughnuts instead and felt her strength return.

When she got back, her Good Samaritan was doing a spectacular sales patter, charming potential customers with his spiel. She stood by, impressed, while he sold a pair of green fedoras decorated with pheasant feathers to what was clearly a mother and daughter.

'I'm impressed,' she told him.

'I'm Charlie,' he told her, and she laughed.

'You really did do me a favour,' he went on. 'I was going to put my money on Dipsy, and he fell at the fourth fence. So I'm quids in – four hundred, to be precise. And I sold five hats.' He looked inordinately proud.

'I don't know how to thank you.'

'I know exactly how,' he said. 'Come out to dinner with me.'

She frowned. 'Why?'

'I've got a good feeling,' he told her, and her cheeks blushed rosier than the cold air had already made them. He was charming, there was no doubt about that, and he had that twinkle in his eye, and he was obviously well off – his cashmere coat and expensive suede brogues told her that. Not that Emmie was the type to go for money, necessarily, but she felt a little comforted by the fact he had a certain polish.

He helped her pack up all the hats she hadn't sold, and the trestle tables, and put them in the back of her car, then whisked her off to a thatched pub where he procured a table by the fireside. Emmie was conscious that she was only in jeans and layers of T-shirts and jumpers, but she'd managed to find a tube of lip-gloss in her handbag, and stolen a brooch off one of her hats to put on. Not the ideal outfit for a first date, but the best she could do, and he had seen her at her worst so he obviously didn't mind.

Charlie was a property surveyor – 'deeply dull; it means I run about all day with a tape measure looking for rising damp' – and he made her laugh. All evening he cossetted her, forcing her to finish all her chips and then have sticky toffee pudding, as it was the pub's speciality.

'Of course I fell for him,' Emmie told Archie at this point. 'It seemed too good to be true. He was my white knight. He was everything I needed. He was kind, loving, supportive, fun . . .'

'And a gambler,' said Archie.

'It's so easy to hide. It's not like being an alcoholic, when you can tell if someone's been drinking. Of course, I could sometimes tell by his moods whether he'd won or lost, but what I had no idea about was the amount of money he was putting on. Thousands. Thousands and thousands.'

'Ouch.' The most Archie had ever put on was fifty quid.

Emmie looked down at her lap. 'I didn't read the warning signs. I trusted him too much. He helped me with the business. Well, of course he did – he wanted to get his hands on ready cash. And to be fair, with his help, I did really well. He helped me to apply for a bank loan, and a grant, and found me a workshop, and did all my publicity – he had loads of posh contacts, and they started coming to me for hats. And he made me charge properly for them – hundreds of pounds – and they were happy to pay. And suddenly I was making a profit – a good one.'

'You've obviously got a talent.'

'Yes. But spotting a con man isn't one of them.' A bitterness had crept into Emmie's tone, which didn't suit her. 'One day he emptied my bank account. I'd been stupid enough to make him a signatory. Turns out he had a tip from a stable lad. A dead cert.'

'There's no such thing.'

'No. Especially in this case. The horse didn't even make it out of the starting gate.' Emmie paused. She was finding this part of the story hard to tell. 'And I lost eleven thousand pounds of hard-earned money that was going to be a deposit on a shop.'

'Oh dear.' That seemed like a massive underreaction, but Archie wasn't sure what else to say. 'I'm sure it wasn't premeditated. I'm sure it just happened. That one day he just couldn't help himself. That's what happens to addicts.'

He said this as if he had expert inside knowledge, which he didn't.

'Either way, I lost everything. My money. And him. Of course, he made me all sorts of promises, about it never happening again, but the trust was gone. I couldn't give him a second chance. Could I?'

'No.' Archie was very definite. 'It's too much responsibility for you and too much temptation for him. You did the right thing. He sounds a bit of a cad.'

A cad? Where did that word spring from? Why was he talking like Bertie Wooster all of a sudden? Because Emmie was sitting there as if she had stepped from the pages of PG Woodhouse, that's why. She looked as if she was off to spend the weekend at a house party in the country. He imagined a Silver Shadow Rolls Royce drawing up at the station, and an elegant friend jumping out to collect her, complete with a saluki on a lead.

'A cad?' She was laughing now, which was good. 'Anyway, listen – I'm sorry. I think I needed to get that off my chest.'

'It's fine. I understand. It passed the time.'

There was an awkward silence. Emmie cleared her throat.

'Are you . . . are you missing your friend?'

'Yes. Yes, I suppose I am.' Archie looked down. 'I'm sorry. I don't think I'm going to be very good company on this trip.'

'It doesn't matter.'

On impulse, Emmie leaned forward and laid her hands over his. Archie froze. He realised this was the first physical contact he'd had with anyone since Jay's death, apart from the occasional pat on the arm or handshake. As an executor to Jay's will, and the one to whom he had entrusted everything, it had been weeks of paperwork, solicitors, accountants, bureaucracy, decisions, signatures, formalities.

Yet Archie wasn't used to close contact and he felt a bit embarrassed. He disentangled his fingers, cleared his throat and picked up his glass.

'Anyway, I think we both owe it to ourselves to make sure we enjoy this journey. Even if neither of us is here under ideal circumstances.'

'Absolutely,' said Emmie. 'It's the journey of a lifetime. Let's forget the past for the time being and make the most of it.'

As the train wound its way through the Weald of Kent, where the blossom was just starting to unfurl and tiny lambs frolicked in the fields, the two of them chinked glasses over the table.

Ten

As the Pullman wound its way through the Garden of England towards the east coast, Imogen sat in the carriage named Zena, cocooned in the burnished glow of her art deco marquetry. The place setting opposite her had been tactfully removed, but in fact she didn't mind being on her own. She was quite used to travelling solo on business, and had perfected the art of dining alone without feeling self-conscious.

While she ate her brunch, she drew out her iPad, eager to re-read the email she had received just before her head had finally hit the pillow the night before.

Dearest Imogen,

We were so thrilled to get your email and learn of your decision. We have long felt that Sabol and Oostermeyer could be your spiritual home, and we know we can give as much back to you as you can give to us. Surely the perfect working relationship?

Why don't you get on a plane and come discuss it with us as soon as you can? There is a lot to talk about, and a lot we can help you with. We understand that this is a big change for you and we would like to do everything we can to make it a happy and stress-free change.

This is hugely exciting for us.
Let us know your plans.
With warmest regards
Kathy and Gina

This was the biggest decision she had ever made. It felt as if she were about to step off the edge of the world. She took a sip of her Bellini to quell her nerves. She was doing the right thing, she told herself. It wasn't as if she hadn't been to New York before. She and Adele went every other year. And Kathy Sabol and Gina Oostermeyer were almost like family. They would sweep her up and look after her in their inimitable way – she would be fussed over and paraded proudly and within two weeks she would feel like a native New Yorker. She imagined herself in an apartment in Manhattan, hailing a yellow cab, picking up her dinner from Dean and DeLuca, going out to the Hamptons with friends at the weekend, dressed for success, manicured and blow-dried, high heeled . . .

Exciting though the prospect was, it was also daunting. Imogen had lived in Shallowford all her life. She had always had her grandmother by her side. Not that she was in Adele's shadow, or couldn't make a decision without her, but Imogen recognised that perhaps her grandmother held too great an influence over her, even if it was subconscious on both of their parts.

There had never been any doubt in Imogen's mind that she would follow her grandmother into the business. She had known it right from the start. She had ended up virtually living at Bridge House with her grandparents as a child, because her parents worked abroad so often. She went with Adele to picture sales, auctions, public galleries, private views. She went to the picture restorers and the picture framers, and learnt how to bring a painting back from the dead. At eighteen, she insisted she didn't want to go to university. She wanted to start work in the gallery. But Adele had insisted equally forcefully that she should go and get some experience.

'Coming straight to work for me would be far too claustrophobic. I want you to spend time with other people your age, get some independence. Broaden your mind. The art world is very small and insular, and if you are to be a success in it you need to develop other skills. You need to be influenced by people other than me. You need to question yourself, and other people.'

So Imogen had dutifully gone to study fine art. And the day after her graduation, she had presented herself in her grandmother's gallery in Shallowford.

'You're not going to get rid of me that easily. I want to take over when you retire,' she told her. 'So I might as well start now.'

Adele had relented, with reluctance. 'I'll give you two years,' she said.

Those two years, however, had grown into nine. Only now it was time to move on. The timing was perfect. Except for one small thing . . .

She wasn't going to think about Danny. She wasn't going to think about them laughing in bed while Top Cat kneaded the duvet with his paws, mewing indignantly above them. She wasn't going to think about curling into him on the sofa with a glass of wine while they watched a movie. There was no point. They had no future together. It was just a fling. It had been breathtaking, but he didn't want to be part of her world.

She pulled her iPad towards her, suddenly terrified that she was going to cry. What was she crying for? Danny McVeigh had been to *prison*, for heaven's sake. How could she ever have imagined it would work? What they'd had was a temporary high. It was best to move on now, before the cracks appeared. At least this way they could preserve the memory.

Even if the memory made her feel unnaturally warm. Or was it the heating in the carriage that was making her cheeks pink? To distract herself, she pulled up her internet browser and typed *Jack Molloy* into the search engine. To her surprise, his name came up first on Wikipedia.

JACK WILLIAM MOLLOY (21 September 1924) is an Anglo-American art dealer, critic and curator.

Born in the United States, Molloy attended Trinity Pawling in Massachusetts and then the Ruskin School in Oxford. Whilst there he met the society heiress Rosamund Dulverton, whom he later married. He began work as an art dealer, and later became a respected curator. In the early 1960s he nurtured the young Reuben Zeale, putting together his first exhibition. He moved on to become an influential and respected, if sometimes savage, art critic, and made as many enemies as friends. He became a prominent media personality, and occupied a number of roles at the Arts Council as well as being a Trustee at the Tate Gallery. He was awarded a Golden Lion at the 1993 Venice Biennale for curating a retrospective of Reuben Zeale's work.

His wife Rosamund died in 2003. They have three daughters: Silvestra, Melinda and Cecily.

Jack Molloy now lives on the Venetian island of Giudecca.

Imogen was fascinated. She felt she should have been aware of Jack Molloy's existence. After all, Reuben Zeale was one of the most influential artists of the late twentieth century. His paintings – usually nudes or portraits – were extremely collectable. He had died in the early nineties, and the art world had considered his premature death a tragedy, though not surprising. Zeale's lifestyle had been gruesomely unsustainable and at odds with the beauty of his work. He was a drunk, volatile, bisexual, bipolar – and vodka and anti-depressants were not good bedfellows. If Jack Molloy had been Zeale's mentor, he hadn't done a very good job of looking after him.

Imogen clicked onto *Images*. There were plenty of photos of Jack Molloy. He was an arresting man, tall, with a shock of black hair and eyes that looked right through you. As he grew older, his eyes had become hooded, but he still had a hypnotic gaze as he stared at the camera with a rather world-weary smile. There were frequently women in the photographs with him. Powerful, but manipulative, Imogen decided. And attractive. Although he wasn't classically good-looking, she could sense his allure even from the photos.

He must be someone Adele had come across during her career. They were a similar age, after all. Were they friends? Business acquaintances? Or something more? And why had she been sent to collect the painting? Why didn't Adele go, or simply have it sent over? Imogen sensed a story: something she was being drawn into.

She searched for *The Inamorata*. There was nothing relevant in the results that sprang up. Only the dictionary definition.

'A woman with whom one is in love or has an intimate relationship.'

She closed down her browser, feeling slightly disconcerted, then leant her head back and shut her eyes. The late night combined with the Bellini was suddenly catching up with her. Who was Jack Molloy to Adele? And why did he have *The Inamorata*? She could feel herself drifting off as she wondered what the connection was.

Eleven

*A*dele stood on the platform at Filbury waiting for the train up to Paddington. She didn't want to wait in the café, drinking undrinkable tea, in case someone she knew caught sight of her and wanted to engage her in conversation, which would mean she would have to start equivocating. Besides, it reminded her too much of Brief Encounter, and she had always thought Celia Johnson the most awful drip. She would have cheerfully pushed her under that train, she thought.

In the end, after much deliberation, she had rejected the shantung and decided to wear a two-piece suit. It seemed more businesslike than a dress. And besides, she knew it thoroughly became her; in mustard wool, the jacket was very fitted and showed off her waist, and the large buttons made it chic. With cream high heels, and a matching bag and gloves, she felt as confident as she was ever going to feel.

The train pulled in and Adele hurried up to the first-class carriage. Again, there was less chance of seeing someone she knew in here. She settled into her seat, and as the train pulled away she breathed in the smell of burning coke that drifted in through the open window. Only half a mile away, William would be examining patients in his surgery, oblivious to her incipient treachery.

Only it didn't need to be treachery. Adele told herself that she didn't need to go anywhere near the Savoy once she arrived at Paddington. She could go to an exhibition, or a show, or shopping, or call on one of several friends who would be only too pleased to see her. It would be a perfectly pleasant day out.

She couldn't remember the last time William had taken her up to town. They used to go quite often, out for dinner and then maybe dancing, but their trips had dwindled of late, even though they should have increased now the boys were at school. Perhaps she should insist, or arrange it herself. But it was hard to know these days if he was going to be late home.

Just before midday she was at Paddington. She stood on the concourse for a moment, as men with bowler hats and young girls with cigarettes milled round her. Then she made her way out onto Praed Street. The traffic seemed heavier than ever — vans and Vespas jostled with taxis at the traffic lights. She found a cab with its light on and jumped in.

She alighted at Trafalgar Square. In the back of her mind, she thought she could go to the National Portrait Gallery. Gazing at all those faces had always fascinated and inspired her; she tried to imagine their thoughts and feelings, their true sense of self as they sat for the artist. No one, after all, is really what they portray to the outside world. Today, she certainly wasn't. She stood for a moment, watching the pigeons. On the surface she was nothing but a respectable, happily married mother of two who was treating herself to a day in town.

Had she turned left, she would have remained that person.

She looked calm and serene as she turned right to walk along the Strand, but on the inside her blood was simmering, like a pan of milk just before it comes to the boil. She walked into the Savoy as if she did so every week.

136

She glided into the restaurant, trying not to be intimidated by its glittering glamour – the chandeliers and the gold leaf and the sheer size of it. A white-aproned maître d' came forward with a smile. 'I'm dining with Mr Jack Molloy,' she told him, and hearing herself say his name made her quiver inside. The maître d' bowed, smiled, and indicated a table by the window.

Jack was sitting back in his chair, a glass of wine in his right hand. He was looking right at her and raised his glass. He had known all along she would come. She felt her cheeks catch fire. Her hands trembled. Why? she asked herself. She was, after all, only here to ask his advice. She felt her courage fail her.

She was always confident, in every social occasion. Was she going to make a fool of herself? Perhaps she already had, by turning up. Why hadn't she torn up the letter and stayed at home? She could be making a ham sandwich for Mrs Morris, her daily help, right now. Dull, perhaps, but safe.

How enticing dull and safe seemed as she walked past the other diners.

He stood up as she reached his table. His smile wasn't mocking, as she feared it might be. It showed genuine pleasure. He reached out and held her elbows in his hands as he kissed her on each cheek, a chivalrous gesture, not untoward. She sat, her tongue heavy in her mouth, not sure what to say.

'I'm so pleased you came,' he told her. 'London has been so dreary lately. And I have a notoriously short attention span. I need novelty.' He looked at her with delight, like a small boy who had just opened the birthday present of his dreams.

'Well, I'm sure you will tire of me before the meal is out. I don't know that I have much to say that would interest you.'

'Never mind,' he replied. 'You are very beautiful and that will do for now.'

Her cheeks flushed. She hated herself for falling for his patter – she felt sure compliments fell easily from his tongue when it suited him. She knew perfectly well he was preying on her vanity. She knew the pains she'd gone to that morning to make herself look her very best without, of course, making it look as if she had done so.

Still, she would have been irked if he hadn't commented on her appearance.

'Thank you,' she murmured, and took her seat opposite him, feeling his gaze drink her in. He poured her a glass of wine and she took it gratefully. Her mouth felt dry. She gathered up her nerve. She wanted to gain the upper hand. She wanted to make sure he knew she wasn't easy prey. She wanted to turn the tables on him.

'Actually,' she said, 'I want to pick your brain. I'm thinking of opening a gallery and I'd like your advice.'

She was secretly delighted at the surprise on his face. He hadn't expected that.

'A gallery,' he said eventually. 'Tell me more.'

'Well . . . the coach house adjoining our house used to be William's surgery, but it's empty now. I was thinking about what I could do with it. I was going to turn it into an annexe for guests, but that seemed terribly dull. So I thought – what about a gallery? Just a small one, nothing too ambitious . . .'

She trailed off, gauging his reaction. He nodded for her to go on.

'I think it would go down well in Shallowford. There are plenty of antique shops, lots of people with money. And it would give me something to do.' She gave an embarrassed shrug. 'With the boys away now, I'm bored. It would give me an interest. And I know William would be supportive.'

Somehow, she thought saying William's name at this point would protect her in some way.

'So,' said Jack. 'Does he know you're here today?'

Adele looked down at the tablecloth. It was pristine, brilliant white. To her horror, she found herself smiling. She looked up, looked Jack right in the eye.

'No,' she said. 'No, he doesn't.' Jack smirked, and she leant forward. 'Because I want to do my research thoroughly. I don't want to go to him with a half-baked plan that makes me look like a silly housewife playing shop. I want it to be a credible proposition.'

Jack nodded. 'So you want me to give you all my trade secrets? Is that what you're saying?'

Adele laughed. 'You needn't worry that I'm going to be any sort of threat to you. I'm not going to be dealing in grand masters and the next big thing. I just wondered . . . if you thought it was viable. Or if you think it's a silly idea.'

Jack picked up his glass. 'I think it sounds a perfectly respectable way for a bored housewife to keep herself out of trouble.' He took a sip of wine and locked his eyes with hers.

For a moment, she contemplated throwing the contents of her glass over him. He was infuriating. Patronising. Yet she knew this was how she was supposed to feel. She refused to rise to the bait.

'Of course, if you're too grand to share your wisdom, I apologise for being presumptuous. I'll merely have to learn by my own mistakes.'

There was silence for a moment. Adele recognised that she had outmanoeuvred him and he wasn't sure what to say or how to proceed.

'I would be absolutely delighted to give you any advice you need,' he said finally. 'Of course I would.'

'Thank you,' she replied. She picked up the menu and studied it so he couldn't see her smile. She felt rather elated, and wasn't quite sure what she had started. The idea of a gallery had started as a whim, a passing fancy, but suddenly, with Jack's validation, it became a bona fide proposition. She started to visualise it. The coach house was a lovely building. It would be easy to convert. It was near the high street, with good pedestrian access. The venture wouldn't have to interfere with their private life. It actually made sense. She felt a leap of excitement deep inside her as the possibility came one step closer to reality.

Lunch was sublime. They had lemon sole and iles flotants and drank far too much wine while they discussed the possibilities. Jack was inspirational and enthusiastic and full of ideas that Adele hadn't thought of. He told her of sales he would take her to, and contacts he would let her have, and promised to let her in on all the tricks of the trade – some of them scrupulous, some of them not so.

Adele warned herself not to get carried away, yet somehow nothing Jack suggested seemed impossible. Far from it. After all, she had the premises. She had a little bit of money – a legacy from an aged great aunt – and she felt fairly certain that William would give her some to invest. He shouldn't take long to talk round. He would be glad she had found something to keep her busy, as he seemed reluctant to let her get involved in the surgery.

By the time lunch drew to a close, she felt curiously light-headed and effervescent.

'I can't thank you enough,' she told Jack. 'This is going to be unbelievably thrilling.'

'Your eyes have gone all sparkly,' he observed.

She laughed. 'It must be the wine. I've had far too much.'

Jack signalled to the waiter to bring him the bill. The restaurant was beginning to empty – around them people were pushing back their chairs, looking slightly glazed from the food and drink.

Adele picked up her handbag and her gloves and looked round for the waiter to call her a taxi. They had been talking for hours. She couldn't remember the last time an afternoon had gone so quickly.

'We'll go to my club for coffee,' Jack said.

She hesitated. Coffee was probably just what she needed, she told herself. She felt a bit unsteady, if she was honest. She would have one cup. She could be back at Paddington for six o'clock. All perfectly respectable.

'Lovely,' she said. He slid his arm into hers. It felt quite natural.

It was a business meeting, she told herself. But she wasn't fooled. Not really.

They walked. Up through Covent Garden and along Shaftesbury Avenue and into the grimy, hectic mayhem of Soho, into the little maze of streets that were so hard to tell from one another. Snack bars and advertising hoardings and Coca Cola signs converged on one another. It smelled of coffee and cigarettes and decadence. Adele felt slightly bewildered. There was an air of people doing the wrong things at the wrong time of day: drinking when they should be sleeping, sleeping when they should be eating, eating when they should be working . . . A sleepily salacious girl in a red silk dressing *gown yawned in a doorway. A drunk rolled out into the road and narrowly missed being run over by a young boy on a moped. A cat on a windowsill seemed unperturbed by any of it. Adele clung onto Jack's arm, not sure whether to be afraid or beguiled. This was not her world. Far from it.*

They stopped outside a green door. Jack gave two sharp raps and it opened immediately. A rather dishevelled creature in a white ball dress fell out onto the steps in front of them, collapsing in a pile of taffeta. She stared up at the sky, her eyes blank, streams of flaxen hair falling over her shoulders, looking for all the world like a mermaid who had been washed up on the shore. It was three o'clock in the afternoon.

'Hello, Miranda,' said Jack mildly, and stepped over her. Adele followed him down a set of narrow stairs. She was no longer quite sure what to expect. When Jack had said 'club' she had imagined leather armchairs and a book-lined library where women were allowed by invitation only. The sort of place where William might go with one of his consultant cronies.

This club couldn't have been further from that. Inside, it was mayhem. A veritable bear garden.

Behind the bar was a black woman, over six feet tall, her hair piled high on top of her head, stunningly regal in a green dress with a man's jacket over the top, the sleeves rolled back, every one of her fingers jammed with gold rings. She was serving drinks as quickly as she could to the rabble. As far as Adele could see no money seemed to change hands, and the only drink on offer came from a dubious bottle with white liquid she sloshed into mismatched glasses.

Everywhere people were arguing, laughing, smoking, dancing. Miles Davis spilled out of a pair of loudspeakers. In the darkest corner, a lone woman sobbed. She was wearing a tangerine polo-neck sweater and black-rimmed glasses; occasionally somebody patted her on the shoulder or topped up her drink. Elsewhere, an enraged Irish girl was berating a trio of middle-aged men, who listened to her tirade agog.

In the midst of it all, a baby sat bolt upright in a pram, smiling and clapping, a rabbit-fur cape around her shoulders, gold hoops in her ears. It was anyone's guess to whom she belonged. Every now and then someone scooped her up and kissed her before plonking her back down.

'Welcome to Simone's,' Jack smiled.

'Is that Simone?' asked Adele, rather dazed, pointing to the giantess behind the bar. Jack just laughed.

Adele felt as if she had stepped into another world; as if, like Alice, she had fallen down a rabbit hole and entered a kingdom where nothing made sense. Yet she didn't feel an outsider, for there didn't seem to be any rules about the sort of person you needed to be to belong here. The only rule appeared to be that you had to be drunk, which she already was, a little. Jack gave her a stool, and a very dirty glass filled with some clear liquid that set her insides on fire. Within moments any discomfort she felt had evaporated and she felt part of the crowd. There was no stuffiness or standing on ceremony. No one judged or made assumptions or cared two hoots about who she was or where she was from. They seemed to take her on face value, which was very refreshing.

In Shallowford, she was the doctor's wife. This gave her a high social status, but no one was ever actually interested in what she had to say, not in the way they hung on to William's every word. She hadn't minded until now. She was used to her role. Suddenly, though, she was being asked for her opinion on *everything from the best way to eat artichokes to Che Guevara's antics in Cuba. The only subject on which she was any authority was the artichokes (with vinaigrette; she was very definite about this) but it didn't matter – her opinions were valued regardless. Everyone was in a pleasant state of inebriation. Relaxed and convivial.*

'This girl has got a simply wonderful eye for a masterpiece,' Jack told anyone who would listen. 'I'm going to train her up. I'll regret it, because the last thing I need is competition. But you watch . . .'

Adele felt a glow inside, unused to the attention and the flattery. She felt herself unfurling, becoming someone else: a sophisticated, metropolitan art dealer. She'd never felt the need to be someone else before, but now the desire had been awoken, she indulged it, playing the part, playing off Jack's vision, telling everyone the plans she had. But Simone's was like that. She sensed everyone in there was playing a part, living out a fantasy.

Lying to themselves.

She chain-smoked cigarettes all afternoon, which was unusual – she occasionally had one after dinner, but it seemed de rigueur to light the next before the one you were smoking was finished, and she was so caught up in the spirit of the place she joined in.

She felt glittery, languid. A sense of expectation throbbed inside her: her future unwound in front of her, shimmering like a silver thread, unlike the grey vacuum that had stretched in front of her until now. Never before had she felt as if she could do anything. She was elated.

Then suddenly she realised with a bump that it was past six o'clock. She was filled with panic. The last train was at ten to seven. There was no chance of her getting back home, and even if she made the train by some miracle – perhaps if it was running late – she couldn't arrive back three sheets to the wind. It would be totally out of character. She never usually got drunk, but for some reason that afternoon she had drunk whatever was given to her and the drink, as is its wont, had made her feel invincible and a little bit reckless.

She went into the tiny lavatory to contemplate her predicament. It was filthy, with a cracked sink and no soap or towel. She noticed too late that there was no paper either. The smell made her nauseous, although it was probably more likely to be the unaccustomed drinking and smoking mixed with panic that was turning her stomach.

She splashed cold water on her face to sober herself up. She sensed she would get no sympathy or sense from anyone in the club, least of all Jack. Nobody seemed to have any responsibility or conscience. She hadn't seen one of them look at a clock or a watch all afternoon. They had nowhere to be, no one to answer to.

She leant with her back against the cloakroom door, trying to gather her thoughts and be logical. She decided she would either have to get a taxi cab all the way home to Shallowford, or, safer and far less suspicious, stay away for the night. She couldn't face the thought of reeling in through the front door. It was far less incriminating for her to stay in London. She left the cloakroom, wormed her way through the crowds – the club was full to bursting by now – and went out into the dank evening to find a telephone box.

'Shallowford 753,' she told the operator.

'Brenda has asked me,' she told William when he answered,

very carefully so as not to reveal her state, 'to stay the night. She wants some help choosing wallpaper and things.'

'Of course, darling,' said William. 'Send her my best, will you?'

'Of course, darling,' she echoed.

'You sound strange.'

'It's a terrible line,' she told him, and pressed her finger down to cut off the call.

She put the phone back on the hook. She rested her head on the cool of the glass, wondering what on earth had come over her. She needed to gather herself together, find a small hotel . . . she looked in her purse to see how much cash she had. Not much. It would have to be somewhere modest. Or perhaps she could borrow some money from Jack . . .

She couldn't get back inside the green door. She knocked and knocked as Jack had done but no one could hear her. After ten minutes she began to panic. She felt a sense of outrage that Jack hadn't come out to find her. Surely any gentleman would? Surely if he cared he would? She was about to turn on her heel and find a taxi – she would have to run inside and find the money when she got home – when the door burst open and the Irish girl stormed out, eyes blazing.

She stopped for a moment and looked at Adele.

'You're with Jack Molloy.' It sounded like an accusation rather than a question.

Adele frowned, not sure if it was something she should admit or deny, but the evidence was against her. Her stomach turned over. Perhaps this girl was a friend of Jack's wife? It seemed unlikely – Rosamund sounded like the most fragrant of women, and this girl was rather blowsy, in a too-tight pencil skirt and very high heels.

'Yes,' she answered, then added, 'He's advising me on business.'

She sounded defensive. And guilty.

The girl surveyed her, suspicious eyes flicking up and down. 'He's a monster. You do know that?'

Adele shook her head. She had very little idea about him at all.

'He hasn't a caring bone in his body. He doesn't know how to give.' She tossed her head in indignation. 'Only take.'

'Oh.' This was all rather startling information.

For a moment the girl seemed to soften, and Adele saw something bordering on pity in her eyes. The girl touched her on the arm, her Kerry accent silky with concern.

'Just be careful, darling, is all. Don't expect anything from him and you won't be disappointed. In fact, if I were you, I'd get away now, while you can.'

And she was gone, off down Dean Street before Adele could ask her any more. She had no idea if her warning came from first-hand experience or mere observation. She felt as if the breath had been knocked out of her. The girl's parting shot had shown genuine concern. What had she meant? Was Jack some kind of con artist? Was he going to trick her into parting with money? Or something more sinister? Adele shivered in the cool of the evening air.

In retrospect, she should have gone and looked for a hotel then and there, but the door was still open and she felt she ought to say goodbye, at the very least. And anyway, the Irish girl had seemed a little unhinged. Perhaps Jack had rejected her advances once upon a time? She didn't look like a girl who took kindly to rejection.

Adele stumbled down the stairs. She was starting to feel

rather grim, in the way that you do when you've been drinking and you suddenly stop. The room seemed even darker and more crowded. The music was louder and the air was thick with smoke.

'I thought you'd run out on me.' There was a glitter in Jack's eye that hadn't been there at lunch, and Adele realised he was very drunk, more drunk than she was, though he was probably used to it. For a moment she panicked that he'd rather she had run out on him, that he didn't want her here, that now he was amongst his bohemian friends she was cramping his style. And it made her realise how much she wanted his approval, to matter, and to belong.

Then he seemed to relent, holding out an arm and pulling her into him. He looked down at her, and bent to brush his lips on hers.

If he hadn't done that, she might have found the sense to escape, but the whole world seemed to be in that kiss. She pulled herself into him, up against him, and he reached up a hand and tangled his fingers in her hair. No one took any notice.

Adele's whole world turned upside down but, it seemed, theirs all stayed the same.

Jack took Adele back to his flat, which was only two streets away, above an Italian coffee bar. Juke-box music spilled out of the door, and a clutch of young men in leather jackets loitered on the pavement, smoking and laughing. They greeted Jack as he walked past them.

Adele was surprised how restrained the flat was. She'd expected chaos and flamboyance, but it was remarkably austere. The living room had sash windows dressed with long velvet curtains. The only furniture was a sofa that took up the whole of one wall, a very low table covered in art books and auction catalogues, and Jack's campaign desk. Everything was very neat and organised; everything had its place.

'It's just somewhere to rest my head,' he told her, 'and to keep up with correspondence. I never bring clients here.'

What about women? she wondered, and he could see exactly what she was thinking because he laughed at her. The drink was wearing off and she was nervous, unsure of herself. What was she doing here, for heaven's sake? Coming back to his flat would only mean one thing to a man like Jack, and she was far from succumbing.

'I'm sorry,' she said. 'I have to go . . .'

'Rubbish,' he said. 'The last train will have long gone and it's too late to start ringing on people's doorbells – they will only suspect the worst.'

'I can find a hotel.'

She was in the West End, after all, and she was sure she could spin a yarn that would elicit sympathy rather than suspicion, as long as they didn't smell the drink on her breath. She looked like a respectable woman.

And then he reached out a hand and ran his finger along her collarbone.

'I want you,' he told her.

She tipped her head back. She felt the lightest of caresses on her throat; his thumb touched the place where her pulse pounded.

'I can't.'

'Why not?'

'It's wrong.'

'Who will know?'

Everyone, she thought. *Everyone who was in Simone's this afternoon. She had seen the knowing glances as they left. She thought of the Irish girl and her warning. 'Just be careful, darling, is all.'*

Jack moved in closer. His cologne wrapped itself around her.

'Unless they're actually in this room, watching us, no one can know. It's just supposition.'

He bent his head to kiss her neck. She felt iridescent, as if her skin was covered in shimmering scales. To her dismay, she let out a sound, something between a sigh and moan.

'It's what you want,' he whispered.

'I know . . .'

'You'll regret it if you don't. You'll always wonder . . .'

She knew he was manipulating her. She knew he understood women so well that he could home straight in on their weak spots, their innermost desires. She knew that to succumb would be foolish. But no one had ever made her feel like this before.

And then he stopped. Pulled away from her. Dropped his hands down by his sides.

'I'm not going to force you into anything you don't want to do.'

He walked over to a record player in the corner of the room. He picked up an LP, slid the black disc out of its cover.

A terrible feeling washed over her. A cold, desolate feeling.

She walked across the room and took the record out of his hands. She put her hand on the back of his neck and pulled his head forward to kiss him. And in that moment she felt her marriage vows break. Every word she had spoken on that day ten years ago, kneeling at the altar in white satin, meant nothing. She didn't think of William, lying in their bed in

Shallowford, or her boys, slumbering sweetly in their dormitory, and what her treachery might mean to them.

She thought only of herself.

When she woke early the next morning she was shivering, although it was warm in the room and she had been sufficiently covered by a pink silk eiderdown. She thought perhaps she was in shock, her body and mind traumatised by what she had done. The light creeping through the curtains told her it was a new day, the first day of her life as an adulteress. She felt sick, with fear and guilt and the surfeit of drink: its protective shield had worn off, leaving her vulnerable and exposed.

She looked at the sleeping body next to her and wondered how she could have risked everything so wilfully. Her marriage, her integrity, her sanity. Apart from anything, she knew nothing about this man except what he had chosen to tell her. She had no proof at all that what he claimed was true. For all she knew the flat wasn't even his. He could be a madman . . . a murderer. Perhaps he preyed on women like her, reeling them in with his undeniable charm, then blackmailing them? She imagined the eyes that she had found so bewitching turning hard as he asked her for money before she left, money to keep his silence. Blackmailing the respectable doctor's wife. How easy . . .

She scrabbled out from under the sheets, running to the bathroom, locking the door, putting her hands to her head and twisting her hair with anxiety as she looked in the mirror at the idiotic woman she now knew herself to be. Weak, shallow, vain, self-absorbed. Her forehead was peppered with perspiration; her skin looked greasy and sallow. There were black rings under her eyes. Not such an attractive proposition this morning, Mrs Russell, she thought, as the heat of panic danced over her.

She washed herself as quietly as she could, rubbing tooth-paste on her teeth with her finger. She didn't flush the lavatory. She didn't want to wake Jack. She crept back into the bedroom and found her clothes. He was still in a deep sleep as she got dressed and found her shoes and handbag. Compared to the bandbox-fresh woman who had arrived at the Savoy yesterday lunchtime, she was in a sorry state. Her clothes were crumpled, her stockings snagged. She had no scent to spray on – it was in her everyday handbag. She hadn't expected to need it.

She wondered if Jack was pretending to sleep to avoid an awkward farewell. She didn't care. She tiptoed out of the flat and down the stairs with her shoes in her hand. She opened the front door and stepped out into the street. The cold hit her, bit her. Cold always felt colder when you were tired. The café was closed up, shutters over the windows. A milk float rattled past, reminding her of how thirsty she was. She thought about stopping it, but she wanted to get away as quickly as she could.

A woman walked past and looked her up and down with distaste. She supposed she looked exactly like what she was: a fallen woman leaving her lover's lair. Never in her life had she felt so grubby or filled with self-loathing. She limped to Shaftesbury Avenue, raised her hand and called the first taxi she could find.

The journey home was endless.

She asked the taxi driver to stop at Fenwick's in Bond Street. It was full of normal, happy women who didn't feel guilty, women treating themselves to a new lipstick, or buying an out-fit for a special occasion. Adele bought a pair of stockings to replace the ones that had been torn the night before, and changed them in the Ladies'. She put the old pair in the bin, filled with shame at her attempt to cover up the evidence of her wrongdoing. Then she went back into the shop and randomly picked a pair of gloves, a hairbrush and a pot of cold cream. She needed none of them and could have bought them all in Filbury, but she couldn't think beyond the fact that she needed some proof of normality, if only to prove it to herself, and some form of alibi. Some meagre evidence to prove her activities had been only too innocent over the past twenty-four hours.

On the train, she sat with her handbag and her shopping on her lap, her head pressed against the window, her eyes burning with fatigue. Her body felt bruised. She couldn't think about why.

She was back by midday. William, thank goodness, wasn't lunching at home. She only had Mrs Morris to face and by one o'clock she had gone. She couldn't bear the thought of food, even though Mrs M had left her out some cold ham and a bowl of garden salad.

She went to run herself a deep, hot bath, imagining that she could somehow soak away her sins. She could still smell his cologne on her. She had seen the bottle in his bathroom. Zizonia, by Penhaligon's. It sent her into a turbulent, troubled reverie. For despite feeling the worst she had ever felt in her life, the memory of what he had done to her was intoxicating. She couldn't help but relive every dark, delicious moment.

By the time William came home, she felt cleansed but light-headed. She forced herself to eat supper with him. Each forkful was a challenge. She wondered if she would ever be able to enjoy food again. He seemed very pleased to see her, and asked solicitously after Brenda.

'She's a terrible fusspot and needs help choosing everything,' she told him. 'I think she feels left behind, having been in Kenya for so long, and doesn't know what she should be buying.'

'She should buy whatever she likes.' William could never understand why women agonised over things.

'Oh, it's not as easy as that and you know it isn't. Still, it's rather fun, helping someone else decorate. Anyway, while I was with her I had the most wonderful brainwave.' She might as well tell him now. 'I thought I would open an art gallery. In the old surgery. What do you think?'

Why on earth had she said that? Was she really going to go ahead with this plan? Why not? she thought. She could do it by herself. She didn't need Jack Molloy's help. She could start small, build it up gradually. It would give a purpose to her life. A glorified hobby, really, but it could be fun. And who knew where it might lead.

As far away from Soho as possible, with luck.

William put his head to one side as he considered her suggestion.

'That sounds rather a good idea,' he replied eventually. 'As long as we don't have hordes of people thundering about the place.'

Adele cleared the table, and brought over two bowls of peach melba.

'I'll put some figures together and see what it would cost.' Her hands were shaking with exhaustion. 'And ask a builder to come and see how easy it would be to convert. I don't think it would be too much work.'

Despite her fighting talk, she longed for her bed. If she could sleep, then she could escape the horror of what she had done.

'I think I'll get an early night,' she told William, as she

squirted Fairy Liquid into the washing-up bowl. 'Brenda's spare room looks out onto the road. I hardly got a wink.'

While he was out in the garden, having his evening cigar and looking at the roses, she dived into his doctor's bag and found a bottle of sleeping tablets. She couldn't guarantee that Jack Molloy wouldn't visit her in her dreams. He was already starting to flit around the edges of her consciousness – his dark eyes, his black hair, his ready smile . . . No matter how hard she tried to forget him and what they had done, the images were taunting her.

The next morning she felt better. More composed, and the guilt at what she had done had faded slightly. She decided that everyone was allowed one mistake. She'd had a moment of weakness. These things, she told herself, do happen – although she found it hard to imagine any of her friends in a similar situation. Why couldn't she be respectable and content, like they were? What on earth had got into her?

She determined to focus on her family. William and the boys. She was not going to lose them for the sake of a dose of excitement, a serving of flattery and a night of . . .

She didn't want to think about the night. If she thought about the night then her resolve would falter and her thoughts would stray.

That weekend, she and William were due to take the twins out for their first exeat – just an afternoon out, but Adele couldn't wait to see them. For the first time since her exploit, she woke thinking of them rather than Jack Molloy. As she dressed for the day, she prayed that Jack would have satisfied himself with her seduction, ticked her off as another conquest, and would move on to the next unsuspecting victim without another thought. Meanwhile she was going to bury his memory, pack it away in mothballs like an unsuitable dress she never wanted to wear again.

Adele and William drove the short journey to Ebberley Hall. She was in a state of excitement, and chattered all the way about her plans for the gallery.

'I had the carpenter in yesterday, to see about making the windows bigger so I can have a display. It'll be a bit of a mess but he says it can be done. And he'll put picture rails all around the room, so hanging will be easy. And he can make a proper sign over the front – I thought dark red with gold writing. What do you think?'

'What are you going to call it?'

'The Russell Gallery, of course. Don't you think that has a ring to it?'

'I absolutely do.' He looked sideways at her and smiled. 'I think it sounds just the job.'

At Ebberley Hall, they were greeted by two overexcited small boys who seemed to have grown at least two inches each since she'd seen them. She hugged them to her, with their freckled noses and their sticky-out ears and their pockets full of conkers. They were what mattered, these two little beings.

They took the boys to the tearooms in the nearby town where they gorged themselves on scones and cream and jam. After several days of not eating much Adele suddenly found her appetite had returned, and she felt stronger. She bought the boys a gingerbread man each to take back to school.

Leaving them again was torture. As they drove back up the drive she felt filled with dread. It would be four long weeks until half term. At least she knew they were happy there – they chattered non-stop about everything they had done and their new friends. As they put their arms around her and hugged her goodbye – they still hadn't reached that age where physical contact with your mother was repellent – she felt filled with resolve once again. They were her raison d'être, with their scabby knees and their angelic smiles.

'Why are you crying?' Tim asked her, concerned, and she realised that she had tears on her cheeks. She never usually allowed herself to cry when she said goodbye to the twins. She liked to set them a good example.

'Because I love you very much and you make me happy,' she told him. 'Tears don't always mean you're sad.'

On the way back to Shallowford, a dreadful emptiness gnawed at her. She couldn't face the silence of Bridge House.

'Let's go out for dinner,' she suggested to William. 'Oh, let's. We haven't gone out just the two of us, for ages.'

'I've got a heap of papers to look through,' he told her. 'I just want a quiet supper and to sit in the drawing room with a bit of Brahms, and look through them. Do you mind if we don't?'

She did mind. Awfully.

'No, of course. That's fine,' she replied. 'I'll do omelettes.'

She couldn't be bothered to do anything more elaborate, but William seemed perfectly happy with her suggestion.

That night William pulled her to him but she pretended to be asleep. She had never done that before, but she knew if they made love she would unravel. The memories she was trying to suppress were only just beneath the surface. Any physical contact would bring them rushing up again. She needed more time for the memory of the thrill to fade. Instead, she lay curled up with William's arms around her and prayed for sleep.

A few days further on and Adele's emotions had entirely recalibrated.

Guilt and shame had faded and the sick feeling that had plagued her went away. The memories re-emerged not as something to be ashamed of, but as a fantasy that she couldn't quite believe had happened. Her subconscious toyed with her, sending her images when she least expected them. She would be talking to the carpenter and suddenly recall Jack's warm lips on her collarbone, or the weight of him on her.

'I'm sorry,' she said, blushing, as the carpenter talked about different types of wood for the window frames. 'Could you explain that again?'

She began to wonder about Jack. She tried her best to put him out of her head, but somehow it wasn't the cold horror of the morning after she remembered, the wretchedness she had felt on creeping away, only the heat of the night before.

More than anything, she couldn't bear the thought of Jack moving on to his next conquest, of her having been of no consequence whatsoever. She wanted to be important to him. Or at least know what effect their night of passion had had on him. She wanted him to be plagued by dreams of her day and night, as she was by dreams of him.

Of course, she heard nothing from him. Which was absolutely for the best. And in the meantime, plans for the gallery were coming on apace. The conversion was proving successful. The coach house now sported two bow windows either side of the door. Inside, the space was much brighter as a result, and she had had it painted in a sunny pale yellow. She had revamped William's old office as well, and had a new telephone line fitted. No one had called the number yet, but she practised saying 'The Russell Gallery' when she picked it up.

She was a long way from opening yet. She had little stock – she was going to spend the next three months buying paintings. On the desk was a huge pile of auction catalogues that had been sent to her, as well as catalogues from other galleries so she could compare stock and prices.

Another week on and a catalogue arrived for a sale in Chelsea. It had an interesting variety of lots, and Adele thought she could probably pick up quite a few pictures at a reasonable price. She would go, she decided.

She was deluding only herself. She knew perfectly well Jack would be there. She had seen the catalogue on his desk herself. But she told herself she could cope with seeing him. She was a businesswoman now.

Nevertheless, she put on the red suit with the fur collar she had bought from Hepworths which made her look even more like Elizabeth Taylor than usual. She told herself it was because she wanted to look strong-minded and independent, but she knew it fitted her tiny waist to perfection, and her legs were shapely underneath it, and her breasts were creamily inviting beneath the fox fur.

She bid successfully for five paintings, and felt a sense of euphoria as the auctioneer took her details and arranged for delivery. As she signed the paperwork, she smelled a familiar scent. Zizonia. It was heady and enticing. She turned, and Jack looked down at her.

'Quite a spending spree,' he remarked.

'I'm opening the gallery,' she told him. 'I took your advice.'

'Then we should have lunch to celebrate.'

She didn't demur. They could discuss her new venture, she

told herself. There were still lots of things she wasn't clear about and he had years of experience.

By mid-afternoon she was in his arms, then his bed, then over her head.

The Orient Express
Calais to Venice

Twelve

Waiting for a new wave of passengers always gave the staff on board the Orient Express a frisson of stage-fright. It sent a crackle of electricity up and down the train that they all felt. Each time, there was a sense of anticipation that was just like waiting for the curtain to go up. Would everything run smoothly? How would the passengers react? Would the journey fulfil their expectations? There was also the camaraderie and pride, as well as an element of competition, since each steward on board the train wanted to feel that the passengers in their carriage were better looked after than the next.

The steward in charge of Sleeping Car 3473 checked his cabins one last time. She had been built in Birmingham in 1929, and started service in the Train Bleu, a luxurious train linking Paris with the Riviera. Anyone who was anyone flocked to the Casino in Monte Carlo on her, and to the playground that was the Cote d'Azur. The glamour of those days still lived on. Sometimes, he thought he could hear the laughter and the music, smell the scent of Chanel and Gauloises as the passengers racketed south to the sun.

Now she had been restored to her former splendour and had joined the Orient Express. From the tiny bunk where he slept at one end, to the bathroom at the other, all joined by an intricate garland of flowers in a marquetry frieze that entwined its way around the cabins and along the corridors, this was his domain.

He knew the cabins in his care were pristine, but he wanted to make sure. The day he stopped bothering was the day he would leave, for this job was all about perfectionism. He never tired of the routine. Each cabin was a stage of its own, waiting for a new drama to unfold. And for the next twenty-four hours, he would be embroiled in the passengers' stories. People could never resist pulling him into their lives. Over the years, he had dispensed advice, reassurance and hangover cures in equal measures. No story was ever the same.

Satisfied that everything was just as it should be, the steward slipped into his royal-blue frock coat with the gold buttons, set his cap carefully onto his curls, then checked his appearance in the mirror with pride. This was his world, his life, and he wouldn't change it for anything.

He stepped onto the platform and took his place next to the other stewards as they lined up to greet the newcomers in front of the long line of blue and gold cars, the Compagnie Internationale des Wagons-Lits. Happily, the sun was shining. As the first of the people destined for his carriage made their way forward, he stepped towards them with a smile.

'Hello, I'm Robert. I'm going to be looking after you on your journey. Welcome on board the Orient Express . . .'

Stephanie and Simon followed Robert onto the train, exchanging surreptitious grins of glee. The corridor stretched out before them, a row of windows to one side, and a row of identical doors in shining blonde wood inlaid with delicate marquetry on the other. Robert unlatched the door to their cabin and they stepped inside.

The cabin was tiny – not much bigger than their en-suite at home, Stephanie guessed – but it was perfectly appointed. The far wall was taken up by a picture window to gaze out of at the passing scenery. At right angles to it was a wide seat upholstered in rich tapestry and padded with cushions. Opposite that was a tiny table laid with crystal glasses and a bottle of champagne waiting in an ice-bucket. The carpet underfoot was soft; the walls were the same highly polished wood as the corridor, and their luggage was already stowed overhead in the art deco luggage rack.

'So – this is all yours for the journey. Your home from home,' smiled Robert proudly. He showed them a bell. 'Anything you want, just call me. I can bring you whatever you like. You're booked into the first sitting for dinner, which is at seven o'clock, so you can have drinks in the bar car beforehand – or I can bring cocktails to your cabin.'

He made his way over to a curved cabinet. He pulled open the doors with a flourish, revealing a tiny white porcelain sink surrounded by chrome accessories: soap dishes, tooth mugs, a towel rail adorned with bright white towels bearing the Orient Express crest, and a shining mirror.

'There's toothpaste, soap – everything you need. And these,' he held up two pairs of monogrammed slippers with a twinkle. 'Then while you are at dinner I'll transform your cabin into a bedchamber.' He patted the bench seat. 'This turns into two bunks – there's a ladder for whoever wants to take the top. They might look small but they are very comfy, though some people find the rocking motion of the train takes a bit of getting used to.'

'It'll be wonderful,' said Stephanie. 'It's so cosy.'

Simon nodded. 'It's such incredible craftsmanship.' He ran his fingers over the inlay on the bathroom cabinet. 'Made in the days when people really cared about what they were doing.'

Robert unfurled a map, laying it out on the table, then traced with his finger the route the train was going to take. 'We're travelling down towards Paris, which we'll reach later this evening. Then tonight we'll go through the rest of France and into Switzerland, reaching Lake Zurich first thing in the morning. We'll stop at Innsbruck tomorrow just before lunch, then down through Italy until we finally arrive in Venice.'

He laid the map on the table by the window, then went to open the bottle of champagne.

Simon took it out of his hands.

'Don't worry. I'll do that.'

'You're sure?'

'Absolutely.'

Robert knew he had been dismissed. He left the cabin with a bow and a smile. He had an instinct for when passengers wanted to be left alone.

Simon unpeeled the foil and eased the cork from the bottle. 'This is even more amazing than I thought it would be.'

'It's fantastic. Look at it. It's tiny, but they've thought of everything.' Stephanie's eyes were shining as she took a glass of champagne from Simon.

'Well, we're prisoners for the next twenty-four hours,'

said Simon. 'And rightly so. If I hadn't taken you away, you'd still be running round that café. And I'd still be at work reading through cases.'

Stephanie gave a contented sigh.

'A whole twenty-four hours being waited on for a change. It's going to be bliss.'

A whistle blew and the train started to move. Stephanie came to stand by Simon at the window as they drew out of the station.

'I still can't believe how lucky I am,' she murmured.

'Neither can I.' He slipped an arm round her waist.

'I don't know how I'm going to repay you.'

He frowned. 'Repay me?'

'All of this. I mean, what can I do in return? Supply you with a lifetime of flapjacks?'

'I wouldn't care if you never brought another cake, pie or biscuit into the house again,' said Simon. 'This isn't a *deal*. I did this because I wanted to. I love you for you. I don't want anything back.'

She took in his smiling eyes, the laughter lines by his mouth, the kindness of his face. She lifted a hand and smoothed back his hair. He looked at her questioningly.

'I suppose,' she said, 'there's one thing I could do . . .'

She slid a finger down his shirt-front, and with a wicked smile started to undo the buttons. Wordlessly, Simon stepped backwards and flipped the lock on the door, his eyes never leaving hers until he came back to her.

Next door, Jamie had chucked his bag into the luggage rack and was already lounging on his seat, feet up on a stool. The cabin was super-cool, he decided. He'd like a room like this:

everything hidden away. He leant his head back against the cushion and shut his eyes, trying to relax. But he couldn't.

The thorny issue hadn't gone away. It was sitting there, right in the middle of his brain, and he knew it wouldn't leave until he dealt with it. But when was going to be the right time to approach Dad?

He looked up as the interconnecting door to the next cabin opened and Beth's face peered in at him. His instinct was to tell her to go away and leave him alone, but actually, he quite fancied some company to take his mind off his problem.

'Hey,' he said. 'You OK?'

She lifted her shoulder in an apathetic gesture. Honestly, Beth wouldn't be happy anywhere. You could stick her in a penthouse suite at the best hotel in the world and she'd still find something to moan about. She stood in the doorway, glaring at him moodily.

'Aren't you drinking your champagne?' He lifted up his glass. Maybe he'd just get quietly trolleyed.

She shook her head. 'I don't fancy it.'

Beth? Who could tank down seven WKDs in a row without blinking?

Jamie shrugged. 'I'll have yours then.' He looked at his watch. 'We won't be able to have a cigarette till we get to Paris. Unless we hang out of the window?'

'We can't do that. They'd probably stop the train.'

Jamie levered off his shoes with his toes, and swung his feet up onto the seat so he was stretched out. He put his hands behind his head and gazed out of the window. Beth came and sat over his legs, bending her knees so her feet were resting on the edge of the seat. They sat like that in companionable silence, as they had done so many times, in front of the TV, or in each other's rooms. They fought, the two of them, of course they did, but underneath it all they were still close. Throughout all the turmoil of their parents' break-up they had clung to each other.

Jamie didn't know where it had all gone wrong with Mum and Dad. Of course, they were both control freaks. Dad had strong ideas about how he wanted things to be, and he made sure they were, quietly. And Mum – if things didn't go *her* way, she completely lost it. They were two strong personalities who constantly went head to head, even over the most trivial thing.

Maybe after a while that became too tiring to maintain? Maybe you reached a point in your life where the person you married was no longer the person you needed, and you went for the opposite? The guy Mum had run off with, Keith, was so laid back he was almost horizontal. Maybe she found that a relief after Dad, who was always on it, always on the case.

And Stephanie was as unlike Mum as you could get. She was quiet, calm, organised, sensible, low-maintenance . . . But quite a laugh, thought Jamie, in a way. She certainly wasn't boring. He'd thought at first she was a bit mousy, but once she'd got to know them, she had strong opinions. Different opinions entirely from Mum's. She'd certainly made Beth stop and think a few times, about how she presented herself, about what she aspired to. When you compared the two of them, all Mum was any good at was spending Dad's money, while Stephanie had built that café up from nothing. You had to admire her for it.

Beth was chewing her thumbnail as if it held the only

nourishment she was likely to get for the next few days. Jamie patted her shoulder. Beth and Mum were close, even though they rowed all the time.

'It's going to be OK,' he told her. 'Stephanie's sound. She's not wicked-stepmother material.'

'I know. She's cool. Mostly,' said Beth. 'But it is weird. It's like, now Stephanie's moved in, and we're all going on holiday together, that's it. Mum won't ever come back.'

'She won't come back anyway.' Jamie was sure of that. 'And look on the bright side – at least Stephanie can cook.'

They both laughed. Their mother's ineptitude in the kitchen was legendary. She simply had no interest in food and its journey from the kitchen to the table. Stephanie, however, could make even beans on toast a gastronomic adventure. She served them on sourdough bread rubbed with garlic, with oven-roasted tomatoes on the side, and melted Taleggio cheese over the top.

Mind you, their mum knew she was useless.

'I'm a terrible role model for you, darling,' she used to tell Beth, though she never looked sorry. 'All those other mums at school, with their online jewellery businesses and their organic-baby-clothing emporiums – I must be such a disappointment to you.'

The problem was, Mum was lazy and had the attention span of a gnat. She was good fun, though, far more fun than most people's mothers, and Dad's work ethic more than made up for her lack in that department.

Which brought Jamie back to the hoop he still had to jump through. He'd put it off long enough – after all, he'd known about it for more than three days now. He was going to have to confront it tonight.

Thirteen

Riley felt as if he was coming home whenever he stepped back on board the Orient Express. It almost seemed to embrace him. The knowledge that he didn't have to lift a finger throughout the whole journey was a luxury that he still appreciated, even though he had been on the train more times than he could count. He knew every inch of it backwards, yet it delighted him anew every time.

Even at his age, life was still frenetic, and although his assistant tried to keep control of his diary and his commitments, he worked flat out. It was gratifying to be in demand, as he knew it was tough for all but the very best photographers. He brought some quality, some mystery, some magic to his pictures that editors still wanted, that the younger generation, despite their unarguable talent, hadn't been able to provide. Whether it was technical brilliance or simply an injection of raw genius no one could ever say, but a Riley picture stood out.

As he started to make himself at home, Riley knew he wouldn't be able to fully relax until Sylvie was on board. Their cabin felt cavernous without her presence, and he longed for her arrival. Ever since his accident he had been carrying with him a sense of foreboding. He knew it was fanciful, and he didn't know exactly what it was he feared, but he knew he wouldn't settle until he had her in his arms.

She would have flown over as soon as she heard about the accident – of course she would – but Riley hadn't told her about it. At the time, she'd been working on a film in Paris, a romantic comedy that oozed Gallic charm and wit and was bound to sweep the board at the Cannes Film Festival. Riley knew Sylvie found filming gruelling these days, although she would rather die than admit it, but he had seen the shadows under her eyes after a long day on set. Gone were the days where she flitted through a scene with little preparation. She didn't need anything else to worry about, so he had kept the accident a secret from her. Luckily the press hadn't cottoned on to it, so it had been easy to keep up the subterfuge.

As he settled into his seat, Robert arrived with a tray of afternoon tea. Riley didn't want to drink champagne yet. Those days were also gone, when he could drink from dawn until dusk without missing a beat. He got to his feet and shook Robert's hand; the lad had looked after him and Sylvie a number of times now. That was one of the great things about the train: the staff rarely changed. They felt almost like family.

'Robert,' Riley said. 'I need your help. Correction, I need your advice.'

'Anything I can do. You know that,' replied Robert as he laid out the tea things.

'We're going to have to engage in a little bit of subterfuge,' Riley told him, and brought out a tiny box from his pocket.

'Oh,' said Robert, and his eyes opened wider as Riley

snapped the box open. 'Wow. Is that real? I mean, I've seen some sparklers on here, but . . .'

Riley looked anxious. 'Do you think it's too much? Do you think it's vulgar?'

'If anyone can carry it off, it's Sylvie. And I've never heard a woman complain that a diamond is too big.' He looked up at Riley. 'Is this her birthday present?'

Robert knew they always came on board for Sylvie's birthday. It was Robert who organised the celebratory dessert, liaising with the chef for something special to be brought to the table.

'Well, I shall give it to her even if she turns me down.'

Robert grinned. 'You're going to ask her to marry you.'

It was the first time Riley had heard the suggestion spoken out loud. It suddenly made it seem real.

'Yes,' he said. 'I am.'

Fourteen

Archie and Emmie decided to have cocktails in the bar car before dinner. It seemed the only way to kick off the evening in style.

'It'll take me ages to get ready,' Emmie warned as they conferred in the corridor outside their adjoining cabins. 'It's one of my more annoying traits.'

'It'll take me five minutes, if that,' admitted Archie. 'But that's OK. You take your time.'

He got changed swiftly, examining himself in the mirror as he put the finishing touches to his bow-tie and adjusted his collar. He gave a nod of satisfaction. He didn't look too bad: his dinner jacket inky black, his dress-shirt pristine, his gold cufflinks just visible. Somehow, getting changed had lightened his mood and given him a sense of expectation that dispelled his ill-humour of earlier. He decided to take a wander up and down the train while he waited. Darkness had fallen outside, and the blinds had been drawn, giving an even greater sense of being locked away from the rest of the world.

It took a little while to get accustomed to the sway of the train as he walked along. Quite a few people had their cabin doors hooked open, and he found it fascinating glimpsing inside, seeing their belongings strewn about, how they chose to spend their time: reading, dozing, chatting, drinking. The interiors of each carriage were different, but all equally inviting.

There was a wonderful sense of people preparing for the evening ahead. He watched a man fumble with the catch of his wife's necklace, her skin glowing gold in the evening lamplight. She turned to her husband with a smile, warmth in her eyes, and they embraced. Music drifted out of another cabin – smoky, sultry jazz. A young girl shimmied past him, and he caught the drift of her scent: violets, he thought, or perhaps roses.

Eventually Archie ended up in the boutique, which was crammed with a plethora of mementos, from photo frames to a pair of crystal glasses emblazoned with the Orient Express crest, to a diamond brooch. He thought he should get Emmie something, to make up for being so curmudgeonly. She was probably dreading having to sit through dinner with him. And he felt sure this was the sort of gesture Jay would have made. He tried to get into his friend's mindset, to imagine what he would buy; Archie considered himself to have little imagination when it came to this sort of thing. Jay had been a present person.

'Can I help you?' the assistant asked him. He was Italian, in an immaculate suit, with chiselled cheekbones. He looked as if he had stepped from the pages of a magazine.

'I'm looking for a souvenir, for my . . .' For my what? What was Emmie to him? 'Companion,' Archie managed finally. Companion was just the word.

'Are you on a special trip?'

Best not to even try and explain.

'Just general sight-seeing,' he told him.

The assistant nodded sagely. The answer seemed to satisfy him.

'Well, we have a huge range of gifts, at all prices. Just let me know if you want to look at anything.'

Archie looked at scarves, and pens, and salt-and-pepper shakers. He was tempted by a Limoges porcelain box, then was rather taken by a silver guard's whistle on a string. Actually, he rather fancied that for himself.

And then he saw the perfect thing. A copy of Agatha Christie's *Murder on the Orient Express*. It was a special hardback edition, with an ornate cover embossed with gold. He remembered reading on her application that Emmie liked Agatha Christie. Archie was not a great reader, but even he could see the appeal of a book like this. As a souvenir, it was perfect. He bought it, and it was placed in a special Orient Express carrier bag, and he felt rather pleased with himself.

When Emmie finally emerged from her cabin half an hour later, his jaw dropped. She wore a silver beaded dress with a fringed hem, suede shoes with a Louis heel and long black velvet gloves, all topped off with a flapper-style cap that shimmered with sequins. Her face peeped out from underneath, transformed with silver eye-shadow and dark-red lipstick and the longest eyelashes Archie had ever seen.

'Bloody hell,' he said admiringly. 'Is that one of your creations?'

She touched the hat.

'It's part of my Gatsby collection. Is it too much?' she asked, laughing. 'I wanted to get into the spirit.'

'You look incredible,' he told her.

He thrust the gift bag at her.

'I bought you a present,' he said. 'A souvenir . . .'

She pulled out the book and gasped. 'It's beautiful – the most beautiful book I've ever seen.' She threw her arms around his neck and gave him a kiss. She smelled of sugar and cherries. 'Thank you.'

She held out her arm and he took it. A little jolt went through him.

Time for a drink, thought Archie. Very definitely time for a drink.

They made their way through three carriages before reaching the bar car. There was a long, curved counter from where drinks were served, with every bottle imaginable on the shelf behind. Two white-jacketed barmen were busy making cocktails, scooping ice into shakers, slicing fruit, pouring multi-coloured concoctions into chilled glasses.

In front of the bar was a grand piano; the pianist acknowledged them with a welcoming smile as they walked past to find a seat. Mirrors and brass lamps enhanced the art-nouveau style, and the atmospheric lighting added to the sense of sophisticated luxury. They sank into a pair of chocolate-brown armchairs facing each other across a little table.

The head barman, in a white jacket with gold braid, came to help them with the very difficult business of choosing what to drink.

'Oh!' said Emmie, looking down the extensive list. 'It has to be an Agatha Christie cocktail. We can't come on board the Orient Express and not raise a glass to her. What's in it?'

The barman's eyes twinkled with mischief.

'Well, it is a secret, but it contains an ingredient from each of the countries we travel through on our way to Venice. There is kirsch, for example, and anise, and champagne, but more than that I cannot say.'

'Well, I agree we should definitely try it,' agreed Archie. 'Could we have two?'

Minutes later, they each had a heavy crystal glass filled with a light green liquid.

'Well,' said Emmie. 'I guess we should propose a toast to Agatha, for the greatest train story ever written.' She grinned. 'I can't help thinking how much she would have loved our story – the reason for us being on here. I mean, nobody would guess, looking at us. Would they? We look like a normal couple.'

'Do we?' The thought made Archie feel a little warm under the collar.

Emmie took a sip of her drink, pronounced it delicious, then leaned forward to ask Archie about himself.

'So you live on a farm?'

'Yes. Well, I live on my parents' farm. I've got what was once one of the workers' cottages.'

'It sounds idyllic.' Emmie was enchanted.

Archie shook his head. 'Not really. It's full of cobwebs and spiders and mice and dust and the wind howls through it. And we can't have double glazing because it's Grade Two listed, which is a complete pain in the neck. And the insurance is astronomical because it's thatched . . .'

As Archie spoke he could see the cottage in his mind's eye. It was basically falling down around his ears, but there never seemed to be the time to do anything about it.

'It's got to be better than a one-bedroom flat on a grotty council estate in Hillingdon.'

'You don't look as if you live somewhere like that.'

'No,' said Emmie. 'I try to forget I do as much as I can. But thanks to Charlie, I'm going to be stuck there for a while.'

A cloud flittered across her face. It dawned on Archie that Charlie's betrayal had had long-term consequences for Emmie beyond the emotional.

'I'd swap for a centrally heated flat in a heartbeat. It's bloody freezing. Sometimes there's ice on the inside of the windows in winter. Actually, I need to get to grips with it. But I haven't had much time lately . . .'

He noticed he had already finished his cocktail. It had slipped down rather quickly.

'Another?' he asked Emmie.

'I haven't finished this one yet. I'm not much of a drinker, I'm afraid. But you go ahead.'

Archie signalled to the barman to bring him another. It would help ward off the sense of gloom that was threatening him again. Talking about home had reminded him of Jay and here, in the bustle of the bar, amidst the camaraderie, he felt a heightened sense that his friend was never going to come back. This was exactly the sort of occasion that Jay would have adored. He could imagine him lining up the cocktails, chatting to the other passengers, grilling the staff about what it was like to work on the train. He'd have been firm friends with everyone by the end of the evening.

Archie finished his second drink before Emmie had finished her first.

Fifteen

The Stones were dining in the Voiture Chinoise, glamorously intimate with its creamy yellow ceiling and black lacquer panels, inscribed with a menagerie of animals – elephants, monkeys, alpine sheep and a pair of whales. Stephanie felt a squiggle of pride in her stomach as she sat down at the table opposite Simon.

Jamie was on her left, next to the window, and Beth was opposite him. They looked, she decided, like the perfect family, the men in their suits, and she and Beth in their little black dresses. She supposed the more cynical observer would work out that she was unlikely to be the matriarch, unless she'd been a child bride or had an awful lot of plastic surgery, but she didn't care.

Simon was feeling very jovial. He'd spent most of the afternoon poring over the map in their cabin, trying to identify exactly where they were on their journey by the landscape outside, and getting excited when they passed another train.

'Did nobody tell you?' he laughed to Stephanie, 'about my trainspotting tendencies?"

Stephanie put a hand on her chest in mock panic.

'Oh my God – I'd never have come if I'd known I was going to be trapped on a train with a trainspotter.'

'He's not kidding,' said Jamie. 'He spots planes too. He's got a plane-spotting app on his phone.'

Simon groaned. 'Jamie. You promised not to give me away.' He held up his hands in helpless defence. 'We live near the flight-path. So I like to know what's flying over. What's wrong with that?'

'You're an anorak, Dad,' Beth told him. She pointed at him. 'Even worse, you *have* an anorak. That beige thing you wear.'

'It's a ski jacket.' Simon feigned indignation. 'And it's off-white.'

Beth shook her head.

'Beige anorak.'

'Beige anorak,' agreed Jamie. 'With an elasticated waist.'

'And a hood.' Beth indicated a hood with her hands.

The two kids fell about laughing.

Stephanie couldn't stop herself either. Simon crossed his arms.

'Well, if I'd known I was going out for dinner with the fashion police . . .'

Stephanie leaned over and stroked his arm.

'It's OK. I love you. Anorak, trainspotting manual and all.'

'Good!' Simon held the wine list at arm's length, then looked at Jamie and Beth with an arch expression. 'I'm guessing you both want lemonade to drink? As you're behaving like children?'

Stephanie was about to protest that they should be allowed to have wine when Simon grinned and ordered a bottle of Pouilly-Fumé. She sat back in her seat, wondering if she would ever acclimatise to family banter: the constant teasing, the verbal parrying and thrusting. She was still never quite sure when anyone was joking or if they really meant it. It was a learning curve, that was for certain.

Jamie waited judiciously until everyone was tucking into their main course: a Charolais roast fillet of beef with a tarragon mousseline sauce. Simon had chosen a bottle of Gevry-Chambertin to go with it, and Jamie made sure his dad had drunk half a glass before he broached the subject. It was important with adults to hit them with tricky propositions after they'd had something to drink, but not too much. You needed to get them when they were relaxed, but not reactionary. It was a skill.

'Dad . . . I've got something I need to talk to you about.'

Simon carried on cutting his beef. He smiled over at Jamie for reassurance.

'Go on.'

'Our new bass player. Connor? He's got some amazing contacts. And he got this manager guy to come and see us the last time we played. We got an email from him. He's offered us a tour. A European tour, supporting this really great band he represents.'

Stephanie reached over and touched his hand.

'Jamie, that's amazing. That's fantastic. Why didn't you say before?'

Simon didn't say anything.

Nor did Beth. She was looking from Jamie to Simon, a wary look in her eye. She sensed trouble.

Jamie looked awkward. 'Because – the tour starts in October.'

Simon put his knife and fork down and looked at his son.

'When you go up to Oxford.' His tone of voice was not congratulatory.

'Yeah. Basically, yeah.' Jamie grabbed his glass. 'The thing is, Dad, we'll never get a chance like this again. You don't get offered tours like that. And this guy knows his stuff. He manages some really great bands.'

'Like who?'

'Well, no one you'd have heard of.'

'Really?' Simon's tone was dry.

'That's more of a reflection on you than them.' Jamie's quick repartee demonstrated why he'd managed to get a place reading jurisprudence.

'And who are the band you're supporting? Have they got a recording deal?'

Simon was employing his barrister skills too. Closing in.

'Not yet. But they will have by the end of the tour. They've got a massive fan-base, and a huge following online, and they're supposed to be doing the soundtrack to this new TV show—'

'All of this is guaranteed, I presume?'

'No, Dad – it's not *guaranteed*. There's no such thing as a guarantee these days. You have to put in the graft first – get the live following. Then it all happens. And if we can grab a piece of that, then we might be in luck too. The tour's all set up. We just have to pack our toothbrushes and go.'

Simon nodded thoughtfully.

'Except for the minor detail of university starting at the same time.'

There was silence. Stephanie sipped her wine. Beth drew

183

circles on the table in the breadcrumbs that had fallen from her roll.

Jamie swallowed. 'I want to defer for a year.'

Simon was shaking his head.

'Out of the question.'

Jamie gave a heavy sigh. 'Why not? What's the problem?'

'The problem is you've already had a gap year. The problem is you need to get on and get qualified. The problem is the guy is stringing you along—'

Jamie slammed his glass down.

'You always have to know best, don't you? Why are you so obsessed with me following in your footsteps? Why can't I do what I want? It's my life.'

Stephanie noticed the people at the adjoining table were looking over at them. She put out a placatory hand. 'Jamie. It's OK. You don't have to get upset—'

He raised his eyebrows. 'Really? When Dad's refusing to take what I want to do remotely seriously. Of course I'm upset.'

Simon remained the picture of calm.

'I thought you wanted to do law? That's what you've been working towards for the past few years. And you've done very well – extremely well – to get into Oxford. And you want to throw it all away because some guy with a Svengali complex has set up a third-rate tour and thinks you lot are gullible enough to swallow everything he says—'

Stephanie felt she had to intervene. 'Simon – you don't know all of this. You're being unreasonable.'

Jamie turned to her.

'Yeah. Thanks, Stephanie. At least you've got some faith in me.'

Simon pointed at his own chest.

'I have total faith in you. Total faith in you and your ability to become a great lawyer. I have no faith whatsoever in some fly-by-night turning you lot into the next big thing. Because unless you haven't noticed, Jamie, the music industry is officially dead. There's no money in it.'

'Maybe I'm not in it for the money?'

'Oh, right, so you're in it for the grotty hotel rooms and endless journeys in the back of a transit van.'

'Jamie's allowed to have dreams, isn't he?' Stephanie ventured. 'Maybe he should try it. Oxford can wait.'

'That's just the point. It can't. I know how the business works. He needs to get on with it.'

'One more year won't make a difference,' said Jamie.

Simon took a deep breath, trying to keep a lid on his temper.

'Jamie, I know you think I'm a loser because I've got Adele on repeat on my iPod, and maybe I'm not *down* with the *happening* bands, but I know when someone's spinning you a line. There is no guarantee that you'll be paid, for a start. Worse, you might incur massive costs. There is no protection – this guy could throw you off the tour after three days if he felt like it—'

'You don't know any of this. You haven't spoken to him.'

Simon looked pained. 'Trust me, Jamie. I know.'

'Yeah, yeah, sure you do, because you're, like, Richard Branson all of a sudden?'

Simon leant back in his chair. His eyes went very cold. Stephanie shivered slightly. She'd never seen him like this.

Jamie ploughed valiantly on.

'Anyway, Keith's already promised to check this guy out.

He's got a friend who used to engineer for Pink Floyd. Or something.'

Keith was Tanya's boyfriend. He always had a handy friend who knew everything there was to know about everything.

Simon nodded. 'So Keith knows your plan, does he?'

Jamie realised he'd made a tactical error.

'Well, I was kind of telling Mum and he heard. And he offered to help.'

'Which was kind of him,' Stephanie interjected. 'Maybe he can put your mind at rest, Simon?'

Simon's expression said that he doubted it very much.

'In that case, maybe you should think about moving in with your mother, if they're so much more supportive.'

'You know what? You're just jealous,' Jamie told him. 'You hate it when someone does something you can't do. Doesn't he, Beth?'

Beth had been keeping very quiet through the whole debate. Which was unusual. She shrugged. 'Leave me out of this. I don't want to get involved.'

Simon tightened his lips.

'I'm not saying any more. You're eighteen. You're an adult. It's your call.'

'I was hoping you'd be pleased for me.'

The waiter was approaching the table to clear their plates, which had now been abandoned. He hesitated, seeing they were in heated debate, but Simon leant back and indicated with a wave of his hand that he should go ahead.

'Can we change the subject? I'd like to enjoy the rest of my dinner, if that's all right with you.'

Stephanie glanced over at Beth, who made a face, as if to

say she had witnessed this kind of scene a million times. Jamie put his elbows on the table and rested his head in his hands. Simon reached out for the wine bottle but the waiter beat him to it, refilling both his and Stephanie's glasses.

Stephanie looked down at the table. This wasn't banter anymore. This was proper arguing. She couldn't believe how dictatorial Simon was being. He didn't seem to want to hear Jamie's side of the story. She understood his misgivings, but she thought he was being unnecessarily harsh. She knew he expected high standards from his children but she'd never seen him this draconian. It unsettled her.

And she felt very awkward. People in the carriage were aware that there was a dispute going on. She could see them looking over. It wasn't fair to spoil other people's enjoyment of their meal.

What she needed to do right now was jolly things along. She wasn't going to let the issue drop; she would tackle Simon on it when they got back to the privacy of their own cabin. The dinner table wasn't the place for a family row, and she thought both Jamie and Beth look stressed enough.

She picked up the menu.

'Who's going to have dessert? I am definitely going for the chocolate fondant. With salted caramel sauce.'

She smiled round, hoping against hope that Simon would pick up on her cue.

'That sounds perfect,' he said. 'Bethy? You're a chocoholic.'

Beth shook her head. 'I don't want anything else.'

'Nor me,' said Jamie, chucking the menu back onto the table and sitting back in his seat, sulky.

Simon gave an exaggerated sigh. 'We could be arguing like this at home,' he said. 'For nothing.'

Stephanie cringed inwardly. The situation was incredibly awkward. Jamie caught her eye and she gave the tiniest of shrugs to indicate she had no idea what to do.

Jamie flushed and looked down at the table.

'Actually,' said Jamie, 'go on. I'll have the fondant thing. It sounds awesome.'

Stephanie watched for Simon's reaction carefully. To her relief, he smiled at his son, grateful for his cooperation.

'I will too,' he said. 'Bethy, you can have a taste of mine. The desserts on here are legendary. You really shouldn't miss out.'

Peace, it seemed, was for the moment restored.

Sixteen

Yet again, Imogen marvelled at Adele's ability to know just what would appeal to her. This was a far more civilised way to travel to Venice than battling with the Heathrow Express and the inevitable delays of air travel. She was utterly charmed by the compact perfection in her cabin. She was only going to be on the train for twenty-four hours, but she unpacked properly, hanging up her evening dress on one hook and her nightdress on another, putting out her evening shoes, placing her wash things in the little cupboard containing the sink, and finally squirting a spritz of Jo Malone room fragrance into the air – the scent of Pomegranate Noir always made her feel at home straight away wherever she was.

She was just settling down to write a list of what she would need to take to New York with her – Imogen was a great believer in lists – when there was a knock on her door. It was the steward, Robert.

'Would you like me to bring you an aperitif while you get ready for dinner?'

She hesitated. 'I'm fine, thank you. I think I'll just have some wine with my meal.'

'OK.' He handed her a slip of paper. 'This is your table.

You're in the Cote d'Azur car. It's my favourite. You'll love it.'

She took the slip from him. For a moment, she wondered about asking to have dinner brought to her cabin. She could please herself, not even dress properly, just have a couple of glasses of wine and then go to sleep. She wasn't being reclusive or anti-social: it was genuinely what she wanted to do.

But that would be shunning the spirit of the Orient Express. The essence of the trip was dressing for dinner and enjoying the ambience, even if she was on her own. She was being lazy. She should jolly well make the effort, she told herself. Adele would be horrified to think she'd holed up in her cabin with her slippers on.

As a consequence, she pulled the stops out getting ready. She teased her shoulder-length hair into glossy curls and rubbed shimmering lotion all over her body before putting on her dress – an emerald-green Grecian maxi dress with a plunging neckline that she knew she had the cleavage for. The dress skimmed her figure and settled over her curves, revealing just enough to be tantalising. At her ears she placed a pair of diamante chandeliers, and the crystals sparkled in the soft light thrown out by the cabin lamps. She added no other adornment; the dress and the earrings complemented each other perfectly.

As she bent to pick up her beaded evening bag, she heard a text arrive. She felt her stomach contract and turn over. Was it from Danny? She couldn't pretend to herself that she didn't care. The text had invaded her little bubble. She had felt safe in her cabin, as if the real world was a million miles away. She should have turned her phone off. But now the text was sitting there, waiting to be read. Taunting her.

How's life on board? Have you met a handsome stranger? xx
It was from Nicky.

Imogen tapped out a quick reply. *Gorgeous! No handsome strangers yet but there's time xx.* Then she turned the phone off and put it back in her day bag. Of course he hadn't texted her. Why on earth would he? Her letter had been final. It had left him no room for negotiation. She would never hear from him again for as long as she lived.

She had to take a few moments to gather herself before leaving the cabin. She felt a bit shaky. She had thought herself so in control and so invincible. She had felt so sure about her future and where she was going.

'You're going to live in New York,' she reminded herself. 'And you and Danny wouldn't have worked in a million years.'

It was fast becoming her mantra.

The Cote d'Azur dining car took Imogen's breath away. The seats were upholstered in smoky blue and the windows were hung with silver-grey curtains, setting off the Rene Lalique glass panels. The lamps inside the carriage bathed the passengers in a rosy glow as liveried waiters passed amongst them, seamlessly ensuring their every need was met, each one as charming and handsome as the next. Outside, the night wrapped itself around the train as it pushed on down through France towards Paris, occasionally flashing through a small town, a reminder that there was another world out there, a real world.

Around her, other guests were already seated at their tables. Most of the men were in black tie. The women were radiant in the flattering lighting, dressed in silk and satin and velvet. Diamonds flashed on fingers and rested on shimmering décolletés. Ruby lips and flashing eyes spoke of intimacy and secrets and promises. There was a gentle hum of conversation, the clink of glasses, the popping of a cork. An occasional laugh; fingers entwined across a table. There was a sense of celebration and romance and indulgence.

For a moment she quailed, feeling unusually self-conscious and alone. Then she slid into her seat, her head held high, and picked up the menu. Outside, the banlieues of Paris began to flash past the window. They were stark and depressing: not a great trailer to the romance of the city itself. Tower blocks and concrete and graffiti were lit up by the harsh streetlights. Imogen thought perhaps this bleak landscape suited the mood that had suddenly settled upon her far better than the Paris that was for lovers.

Seventeen

There was nothing more romantic than looking out for someone at a train station, thought Riley. Airports didn't cut it in nearly the same way, with their inevitable delays. There was something so much more immediate about a train. As the Orient Express started to slow down on the outskirts of Paris, his heart speeded up. He fiddled with the catch on his window, pulling it down so that he could lean out and get a glimpse of her as soon as he could.

At last, they slid into the Gare de l'Est with its magnificent domed glass roof. A huge clock, its face luminous and its numbers black, showed time ticking away. How many more seconds until he saw her? He thought he would explode with impatience.

And then suddenly there she was, on the platform. A tiny figure, dressed in an oversized mac, Capri pants and laced-up sneakers, her hair in a chignon, a trademark scarf around her neck. So French. So Sylvie.

As the train drew to a halt, Riley left his cabin and hurried down to the door, where Robert was already helping Sylvie on board, carrying the faded red carpet bag she had brought with her for as long as he could remember. No matter where she was going, or how long for, it was all she ever took, and it was always big enough, holding her extensive collection of clothes – a mixture of couture items given to her by doting designers, and other people's cast-offs that she gathered wherever she went. She had at least five of Riley's jumpers, several shirts and innumerable pairs of socks, as well as a pair of his striped pyjamas she habitually slept in.

'Sylvie. Darling.' He held her tightly in his arms, breathed in the scent of Havoc.

'Riley . . . !' She was laughing with happiness. The way she said his name still made him glow with pleasure. Her accent was ludicrously Parisian, even though she had spoken more English than French for most of her life.

She held him at arm's length and frowned, peering at him in the light of the corridor. 'But you are so pale. You don't look well. What's going on?'

'I had an accident. But I'm OK.'

'An accident? What kind of an accident? You didn't tell me.'

'No. Because I knew you would get straight on a plane. But I'm fine. I promise you.'

'*Complètement fou.*' She held her hands up in a gesture that supported her statement, and rolled her eyes at Robert. 'He's completely crazy, Robert; what can I do with him? He needs a chaperone. Are you tired with your job on here yet? You could be Riley's chaperone . . .'

Robert smiled. 'I never tire of my job on here. You know that. You ask me every time.'

This was true. It was a ritual. Sylvie was always trying to get Robert to leave and look after her apartment in Paris. Luckily for him, he had never succumbed. Sylvie had whims, and didn't always consider how they might affect other people or if they were in any way practical. It was, of course, part of her charm. Robert was wise enough to see through it, but he was fond of her nevertheless.

She dug in her handbag and handed him a box of Ladurée macarons with a smile.

'Pistachio and lime and salted caramel. All your favourites.'

'Thank you.'

It was another of Sylvie's traits. To make you feel as if you were never far from her mind.

Riley put his hands on her shoulders. 'Come on. You must get ready for dinner.'

He exchanged a fleeting look of complicity with Robert before whisking her off to their cabin.

It took Sylvie no time at all to get ready; as an actress, she was used to quick changes. From her bag she produced a black Balmain evening dress – silk with a slashed neck, long sleeves and a full skirt. The dress must have been as old as she was, but it still fitted like a glove. She pulled her hair out of its knot and shook it loose, dabbed scent behind her ears, and applied a deep red lipstick. She turned and held out her arms for Riley's inspection. She was silhouetted against the train window, Paris receding behind them, and he was taken back to that day on the Tube. He only had to narrow his eyes a tiny bit and she was sixteen, with her blonde fringe and dark eyebrows and that defiant pout, posing . . .

The day, he realised now, that he had fallen in love.

'Will I do?' she asked.

'Oh yes,' said Riley, and he felt in his pocket for the tiny box. 'Come on, our table's waiting.'

Eighteen

As the train drew out of Paris, Imogen wondered how many more passengers had come on board. She found being on her own was less of an ordeal than she had first feared, as the dining car was as entertaining as any soap opera. She amused herself guessing why the other passengers were on board, and what their relationships were with each other. She was particularly intrigued by the young couple two tables up. The girl was stunning, dressed like Daisy Buchanan. It was clear they didn't know each other well. They deferred to each other far too much, and there was a politeness between them which would have long since evaporated were they lovers. Yet Imogen could see they were enjoying each other's company. It was charming to watch his deference, and her blossoming under his attention. Imogen smiled as a waiter placed a mouth-watering plate of smoked salmon in front of her, and a perfectly chilled glass of Chablis.

She had just picked up her fork when a figure strode into the carriage. She looked up with interest, eager to scope out the new arrival.

Then she dropped her fork.

It was Danny. Danny in a dinner jacket, thrown on over

jeans and a white shirt he had barely buttoned up, his black hair falling over his eyes, his expression thunderous as he strode through the cabin, looking from left to right. Looking, presumably, for her. And as he caught sight of her, he didn't miss a beat. He came up to her table and stood over her, glowering, and she shrank back slightly in fear.

'Don't ever do that to me again,' he said.

She swallowed. 'What . . . what are you doing here?'

'I want a proper explanation,' he said. 'Not just a note shoved through the door.'

'I'm sorry,' she said. 'I didn't know what else to do.'

'Talk to me?' he said. 'I thought I was worth more than that.'

'You are. Of course you are.'

Imogen's cheeks were scalding. The other passengers were looking over at them. The admiration in the eyes of the other women was blatant. Danny had never looked so devastating.

The maître d' came over to them, concerned. 'Are you dining with us this evening, sir?'

'Yes,' said Imogen. 'Yes, he is. I wonder if you could set him a place?'

'Of course, madam.' The maître d' nodded and moved away.

Imogen indicated the seat opposite. 'Sit down,' she said to Danny. 'I'll get you a drink.' She gazed at him in disbelief and awe. 'How on earth did you get here?'

'I drove. On my bike.' Danny slumped into the seat and sat back, pushing his hair away from his face and throwing one arm over the back of the chair. His dinner jacket fell open; she could see his chest under his unbuttoned shirt.

How could she ever have imagined that life without him could work? She wanted to drag him back to her cabin now, this minute. My God, had he really driven all this way just to find her?

She smiled, unable to help herself.

'You're wearing a dinner jacket.'

'I'm not a total savage.'

Imogen flushed. 'I didn't mean that . . .'

He was still glowering. He was still angry at what she had done. But he was here. A waiter arrived.

'I think,' she said, 'we should order champagne?'

Danny just nodded.

'You must have broken the speed limit,' she ventured.

'I'd imagine so,' he replied.

He raked his eyes down her. She thanked God she had made the effort to dress up. She sat up a little taller. She wasn't going to show she was ruffled. She wasn't going to show that her heart was doing triple time, that her stomach was fizzing, that she had never felt so unbelievably turned on . . .

'So,' she said. 'If I'd known you wanted to go to Venice that much—'

'Happy belated birthday,' he said, pulling a package out of his pocket and chucking it on the table.

She unwrapped the tissue. Inside was a glass heart, emerald-green shot through with flecks of gold, on a very fine gold chain.

'You bought this for me?' she said.

'Yeah,' he said. 'When I thought we actually meant something.'

She held it in the palm of her hand. It was perfect. It

matched her eyes. It matched her dress. 'I made a mistake,' she said.

He raised a dark eyebrow. 'So what do we do now?'

Imogen didn't reply for a moment. Then she smiled.

'We have dinner,' she said. 'And then we go back to my cabin. Or your cabin – I guess you've got a cabin? – and have very, very hot make-up sex.'

He looked at her coolly. 'Whatever you decide,' he replied. There was more than a hint of sarcasm, but she didn't flinch. She looked him straight in the eye. His gaze slid away. She stretched her legs out and entwined them with his under the table, feeling the rough denim against her bare legs as she put the necklace on. He didn't move, just stared out of the window, but at the corner of his mouth she saw the faintest glimmer of a smile. She looked down at the table and tried not to laugh.

Danny McVeigh wasn't half as cool as he made out he was.

Nineteen

Riley played down the full details of his accident to Sylvie over dinner. He didn't intimate to her how close he felt he had come to death, or how it had affected his attitude to life. He didn't want to give her any clue that he had changed, or make her suspicious.

Instead, he listened avidly to her news from the movie she'd just finished, laughing at the scandal the papers would give their right arms to be party to. On set, everyone told Sylvie their secrets, and she kept every last one to herself. Telling Riley didn't count. He was even more discreet than she was. In their world, you learned that spreading gossip only ever backfired in the end.

Sylvie had never had a big appetite. She toyed with her food, pronouncing it delicious, but she never ate a great deal, which was why she could still fit into the clothes she'd had when they first met. She did, however, have a sweet tooth, and saved any appetite she had for dessert.

The dessert arrived. A beautiful little box made of chocolate. On the top was piped Happy Birthday, with a garland of flowers that matched the marquetry in their cabin.

'That's so pretty,' she said with a sigh. 'It seems a shame to spoil it.'

'You can't keep it. It'll only melt,' said Riley. 'Go on. See what's inside. A wild cherry ice-cream, I think . . .'

She picked up her spoon and began to lever off the lid. Inside, instead of ice-cream, was a ring, nestling on a bed of white satin. She looked at it in bewilderment.

'What?' she said. 'I don't understand.' She looked at Riley, puzzled. 'You always give me a scarf for my birthday. Always . . .'

'This year's different, Sylvie.' He still had the scarf, the one he had bought just before the accident. He would give it to her later. Riley was superstitious – he didn't want to break the ritual. But he had a more important matter to attend to first. He leaned forward. 'This is my way of saying . . . of asking . . . will you marry me?'

'Oh Riley,' she sighed, and his heart sank as he saw tears glistening in her eyes.

She was going to turn him down. He supposed he was prepared for it. It had been a gamble. She was a fairy, a firefly; like Tinker Bell – the sort of woman who didn't want to be someone else's, who didn't want to be tied down. He braced himself for her rejection. It was going to break his heart. But he supposed he'd still have her in his life, even if he couldn't make her his wife.

She put her hands on his. He didn't really want to hear the words. He wished she would get it over with. She could keep the ring, regardless. He wasn't going to humiliate himself by taking it back to the jeweller. He willed her to hurry up.

'What took you so long?' she asked finally.

He blinked. 'What?'

'I've been waiting for you to ask me that since the day we met.'

Riley tried to make sense of what she was saying. 'What do you mean?'

She threw back her head and laughed. 'Of course I'll marry you, Riley. Come on.' She held out her left hand. 'You must do the job properly.'

Riley picked the ring out of the chocolate box and slid it onto her finger. It was a perfect fit. Around them, the passengers were smiling with delight. Someone began to clap, and soon the whole carriage was joining in.

Sylvie, a performer to the end, leapt up and paraded down the train, holding out her hand for all to see. As the women admired and cooed, the men nodded their congratulations, wryly accepting that the bar had been set for romantic gestures for the rest of their lives. Nothing else but diamond rings hidden in handmade chocolate boxes would do from now on.

And when she got back to her seat, she threw her arms around Riley and kissed him, to another round of applause.

'This will be all over the papers tomorrow,' he said, but he couldn't stop smiling.

'Good,' said Sylvie. 'I want the whole world to know. I love you, Riley. But you took your goddamn time.'

Twenty

Once they returned to their cabin, Stephanie wasn't sure how to talk to Simon about what had happened at dinner. It had disturbed her. She busied herself taking off her make-up and brushing her hair while she decided how to broach it.

Simon took off his jacket and hung it up, then came and stood behind her. He looked at her in the mirror. She stared back at him, not sure what to say.

'I'm so sorry,' he said eventually. 'This is a long way away from how I wanted this trip to be.'

She put down her brush. She had to say what she thought. Stephanie was never one to pretend.

'I thought you were a bit hard on Jamie.'

He frowned.

'Hard?'

'Isn't it every kid's dream to be a rock star?'

'*Kid's* being the operative word.'

'But this could be his big chance,' Stephanie persisted. 'Not everyone gets offered a tour, whatever you might say.'

Simon ran a hand over his head. He was obviously thinking carefully about what to say next.

'Jamie is a very clever boy with a brilliant future ahead of him,' he said eventually. 'It's much harder to be offered a place at Oxford than to get the chance to tag along with some second-rate band.'

Stephanie crossed her arms. 'Maybe you're projecting your own ambitions onto him?'

'What?'

Stephanie wasn't going to let herself be intimidated.

'I think you're being unfair. I think you're being narrow-minded. The whole world could open up for him and you're not giving him the chance to find out for himself.'

Simon looked up to heaven with a heavy sigh. He turned away from her. He walked over to the window and pulled up the blind, staring out into the black night. He looked angry.

'It's just another point of view, Simon.' Stephanie kept her voice as even as she could, but she wasn't going to head any further into this relationship thinking she couldn't have an opinion. Even if they weren't her children.

He didn't answer. She could see his tension by the way his shoulders were hunched. Part of her wanted to massage the stress out of him, but the air between them needed to be cleared first.

'I can't believe she's still doing this to me.' Simon's voice was tight. 'Even though I've been officially divorced for two years and I've paid her off, she's still controlling my life.'

'What do you mean?'

Simon turned round. He looked tired.

'I know it's Tanya behind this. I guarantee it. It's absolutely her style. Her way of making sure she spoils our trip.'

'That's crazy.'

'*She's* crazy.' He came towards her. 'This is how it works, Steph. Jamie will have run the whole thing past Tanya first. He'll have asked her what she thinks I'd think of the deal. And she will have egged him on, given him all the ammunition to present me with a virtual fait accompli that I can't argue with, including getting Keith involved. And she'll have made sure Jamie dropped the bombshell at the worst possible moment. Right in the middle of our trip. *Wait till your dad's on the train. Wait till he's all relaxed and he's had a few drinks. He won't be able to say no.*' His imitation sounded just like the voice Stephanie had heard on the phone. 'Tanya plays these games all the time. She manipulates those kids and they have no idea. It was why our marriage ended. And she still can't resist it. Honestly, I have been here before so many times.'

Stephanie frowned. 'How could anyone behave like that? Why would they want to?'

Simon put his arms round her and pulled her to him. 'Stephanie – that's one of the reasons I love you. Because you don't get it and you never will. Long may you stay like that.'

She looked up at him.

'Am I being patronised?'

'No. You're being adored.' He dropped a kiss on her shoulder. 'Jamie knows I'm right. He's just putting up a fight for the sake of it. Deep down, he wants me to put my foot down. And I don't want to talk about it anymore. This is our trip, remember?'

Stephanie opened her mouth, and shut it again. She wasn't sure what to think. Now she saw it from Simon's perspective, she could see he had a point. But then, she reminded herself, he was very persuasive. It was, after all, what he did for a living.

He was stroking her face, her hair. He was murmuring in her ear. 'I love you. I want us to be as close to a family as we can be. And I really value your opinion. On everything. But I'm not going to let Tanya come between us. Or let her screw up Jamie's future. You can see that, can't you?'

Stephanie put her arms around his waist. He was so warm, so solid. She wasn't going to pick up the baton from his ex-wife and make his life difficult. She wasn't just rolling over, but sometimes, she knew, it was time for a tactical withdrawal.

'She's not going to come between us,' she whispered. 'Nothing's going to come between us.' She began to un-button her black lace shirt-dress, gradually revealing her ivory skin. 'Nothing.'

Next door, Jamie lay on his bunk. His head felt a bit swimmy from all the heavy red wine he'd drunk at dinner – he usually drank vodka shots or St Miguel. He twirled round on his iPod until he found the latest demo he and the band had recorded in the garage. It was good, he thought. In fact, better than good. They were definitely going to go places. He thought about the tour they'd been offered. Dad's reaction had been about as predictable as it got, he thought. How had he ever imagined for a minute that he'd get his dad's blessing?

Well, he didn't need his blessing.

Dad thought he knew everything about the world and how it worked, but he didn't. Mum and Keith had been amazing. They'd promised him their support. Mum had even said they'd come and see the band when they hit Europe, though Jamie thought maybe that was taking things too far. His friends all thought his mum was hot but did he really want her jumping up and down at one of his gigs? Maybe not, but at least she had been supportive.

Not like Dad, who had made it pretty clear to him what the deal was. His dad didn't care about him at all. His mum was right. All his dad cared about was himself.

Twenty-one

After dinner, Archie and Emmie went back to the bar for a nightcap. Well, several. Archie spotted a bottle of his favourite malt, and once he got started on Laphroaig it was difficult to stop. He had a horrible feeling he was sliding into drunkenness, but Emmie didn't seem to mind. And drunkenness was better than remembering.

Besides, Archie was a very jolly drunk. He never got maudlin, or aggressive, just more benignly amiable. So he sipped his malt while Emmie toyed with an Irish coffee. For a while they sat in companionable silence. It was cosy in the bar – the blinds had been drawn and the lights dimmed. Some of the guests had already made their way back to their cabins to bed; the hard core remained. The pianist was playing 'My Funny Valentine', slowly, dreamily. Emmie swayed in time to the music, a smile on her face.

'I'm having such a lovely time,' she told him. 'It's been great, getting to know you, and knowing there's no pressure. I was terrified that whoever won the prize was going to try it on. That they might think winning the prize gave them the right to . . . you know . . .'

Archie clutched his glass more tightly, went to drain it, then realised it was empty already.

'I'm . . . just going to get a refill,' he told her.

He got up to go to the bar to have his glass replenished, even though he knew the waiter would get him one if he so much as raised a finger. He staggered slightly on the way, and tried to estimate how much he had drunk. There'd been the champagne at lunch, then a couple of cocktails, and he'd certainly had the lion's share of the bottle of white followed by the bottle of red they'd had with dinner. Then he'd had port with his cheese . . .

He'd slow down after this one, he thought.

On the way back to his seat, he stopped by the piano.

'Hey, mate – do you know Van the Man? Van Morrison? Can you play . . . "The Right . . . Bright Side of the Road?" ' He corrected himself, trying not to slur.

The pianist nodded. 'Sure.' With the ease of the consummate professional, he started up the opening bars.

Archie stood in front of the piano and raised his glass.

'Ladies and gentlemen,' he began. He was used to commanding attention. He was the expert toast-giver, best man, speech-maker.

He saw Emmie look up at him with a slightly alarmed expression on her face. Maybe he should go and sit down? He didn't want to embarrass her. But no: he wanted to toast his friend, his friend who should have been here. Surely no one would mind?

'This song is for my mate Jay,' he told the remaining guests in the bar. 'We've been friends since we were so high.' He held his hand down low. 'We grew up together. Did all the usual stuff: the rites of passage. We looked after each other. But sadly he died a couple of weeks ago. Anyway, this was his happy song. When we went on road trips, it was the first thing he put on in the car.'

There was a moment of suspended horror as the rest of the guests in the carriage took in what he was saying. Emmie froze. But then someone at the end of the carriage raised his glass.

'To your friend,' he said boldly. And moments later, everyone else followed suit, until the entire carriage combined in a toast, as the pianist started to play.

Archie held up his glass and smiled. He sang along, surprisingly tunefully.

Emmie stood up, not sure what to do, whether to get one of the bar staff to take him out, tactfully. Then she realised that no one seemed to mind his impromptu eulogy, that they were caught up in the spirit of it. So she came and stood by him, took his glass and put it on the bar, then held out her hands to dance. Gradually, they were joined by other guests and the bemused waiters hung back while the bar was filled with dancers.

Archie entwined his fingers in Emmie's and spun her round. She looked beautiful, he thought, and realised she had kicked off her shoes. She barely came up to his shoulder without them.

The pianist was smiling from ear to ear as he played the last chord. There was applause, then everyone went back to their seats. It was almost as if the spontaneous dance had never happened. Archie swayed slightly, blinking.

Emmie took him by the arm. 'Come on,' she said. 'You need some sleep.'

She steered him back to his cabin, holding her shoes in one hand.

Archie stumbled in, loosening his tie and shrugging off his jacket.

'I'm sorry,' he told her. 'I think I've had one too many.'

'Hey. Don't be sorry. It's understandable.'

'I'm pretty sure you're not supposed to end up doing karaoke in the bar on the Orient Express . . .'

'It was wonderful. Everyone loved it.'

'I'm surprised we didn't get asked to leave.'

'They couldn't just throw us out in the middle of no-where.'

Archie crashed onto the bottom bunk. He groaned, dropped his head back onto the pillow and went out like a light.

Emmie covered him up gently with the blankets. She reached out a hand to stroke his head, then stopped. She'd had a sudden urge to comfort him, but he might think that was a bit weird. She hovered, not sure what to do. She felt uncomfortable leaving him alone in that state. He was obviously taking his friend's death harder than he cared to admit.

She left his lock on the latch and went back to her own cabin, changed into her night things and dressing gown and picked up the book Archie had bought her. Then she crept back into his cabin and sat on the stool opposite his bed, wrapping herself in a spare blanket. She would stay there for a couple of hours and read her book, just in case he woke and wanted someone to talk to. She didn't want him to feel as if he was on his own.

The train pressed on through the ink-blank night, undeterred by the lack of moon and stars to guide it, for the cloud had seen fit to cover them over just after midnight. On board, the air was thick with somnolence as the passengers succumbed to sleep one by one, their blood running slow with rich food and wine. The train's swaying motion as it curved along the track acted like a cradle, soothing even the biggest insomniac. Robert walked along the corridor, satisfied that his charges were all tucked up safely for the night, before settling into his bunk for a cat-nap. If anyone needed anything in the night, they only had to ring for him. He would be up again as soon as dawn broke, only a few hours away.

In her cabin, Imogen lay with Danny in her arms. He was nestled into her, fast asleep. She relished the warmth of his body, the rise and fall of his chest in time with hers, but her mind was racing. She wasn't sure what the future held. She had a lot to think about. A lot of decisions to make. But in the meantime, she was going to make the most of the deliciousness of having him with her.

As she drifted off to sleep, she thought perhaps this wasn't what her grandmother had had in mind when she had booked her ticket . . .

Twenty-two

*A*nd so began Adele's affair with Jack Molloy.
    She wasn't proud of it. And she couldn't defend it to herself, except to say that the affair swept her up and carried her away and she barely had any say in the matter. It sounded ludicrous, but she felt it was meant to be, that Jack had been sent to change her life and her outlook, and she was utterly powerless to walk away.

The terms were clear. She was, she knew, one of many women with whom he had been unfaithful. He wore his infidelity like a badge of honour, yet he was so disarmingly open and honest about it that she couldn't judge him.

Open and honest with everyone except his wife, of course, whom he kept on a pedestal. He would never in a million years compromise his marriage or entertain leaving Rosamund. Jack was only ever on loan to anyone. He never promised his paramours anything. He was also, Adele sensed, something of a coward. He liked his security, his home, Rosamund's social position and, of course, the family money. His philandering could never get in the way of that.

Fool that Adele was, she accepted the deal. After all, she had no intention of leaving William either. She, too, liked the security of being the doctor's wife – but not, apparently, she scolded herself, the tedium. Wasn't that why she was opening the gallery? Wasn't that enough excitement?

In moments of rationality, in the calm of the kitchen when she was drinking cocoa with Mrs Morris, the voice of reason inside her told her to walk away, before she got hurt – or, indeed, before she got caught. Both were equally likely, but the latter would have spelt disaster. Hurting herself she could cope with, but the thought of hurting William was anathema to her.

Despite all this madness, she loved her husband deeply. It was just that recently he had made her feel so very meaningless. She felt as if William could have managed life perfectly well with his secretary at the new surgery and Mrs Morris to run round after him at home. Adele really wasn't sure where she fitted in, or what purpose she served. Sometimes, at the breakfast table, when he was preoccupied, William looked right through her and didn't hear a word she was saying. Once, what she was saying might, she agreed, have been unutterably dull, but things were now moving apace as she got the gallery together and she did think he might have shown the tiniest bit of interest. Instead, he seemed to think that giving her a blank cheque to cover the expense was adequate. She didn't want his money. She wanted his admiration.

Something Jack was only too happy to give her. Jack was always capable of firing her up to achieve greater things. He guided her, moulded her, challenged her. He taught her how to differentiate between a good painting and a great one, how to spot a copy or a fake, how to assess damage, how to check provenance – it was a complex world she was entering, and it wasn't enough to have a good eye. It needed to be backed up with knowledge and experience. And it thrilled him to have an eager pupil. He accompanied her to sales and auctions all over the country, and artists' studios and openings and private views.

If she could have left it there, the relationship would have been entirely defensible. He was her advisor and nothing more. But it never stayed in the auction house or the sale-room. It inevitably strayed further, and that was the part that Adele found so intoxicating. Both her mind and her body were being stimulated in ways she hadn't thought possible. She felt as if she could take on the world. But at the same time the guilt never really left her; she knew she couldn't maintain this double life indefinitely.

She never told anyone of her affair, no matter how much she longed to share the burden, because she knew she would garner no sympathy from anyone with a modicum of backbone. Her friends would be horrified; affairs simply weren't acceptable behaviour in their social circle, even though Jack tried to convince her that people had them all the time. And whenever she tried to rationalise it, she failed. You can't rationalise chemistry, what the French call a coup de foudre, *a thunderbolt. She even made lists of Jack's flaws and his qualities: the first was always much, much longer than the second, but even seeing the evidence in black and white didn't give her the impetus to stop.*

She couldn't live without him and the way he made her feel.

The strain of it all started to take its toll. She would start awake in the night, panicking, not sure whom she was with. She had nightmares about giving herself away to William, nightmares so real she woke sobbing with fear.

These weren't as terrible as the nights she dreamt she lost Jack. It was never clear how, but the grief tore at her, and the horror of it would cling on to her all through the next day, leaving her hollow-eyed with exhaustion.

The emotion of it all was draining. She became very thin. She told William it was because the boys were away, and so she wasn't eating so many cakes and biscuits. She could see he was concerned.

'I wonder if this gallery lark is becoming too much for you,' he commented. 'I mean, it's not even open yet and you look wrung out. I think you should think about taking someone else on. Or ask yourself if it's such a good idea after all.'

'I can manage,' Adele insisted. 'It's all new to me, that's all. And there's a lot of running about. Keeping an eye on the workmen, and going to sales, and managing the house on top of all of that . . .'

Managing the house? She barely did a thing there anymore. Not that William would know, or notice. She had increased Mrs Morris's hours, had everything delivered and she never made cakes or puddings anymore. All of this brought her guilt into focus. Time and again she determined to stop the affair. She was a strong-minded woman – surely she could find the strength to walk away? She tried, on more than one occasion.

'I can't do this anymore,' she would sob to Jack.

'Then don't,' he would reply mildly. Everything was so black and white to him. Everything was so simple. He had no conscience. He could never understand her dilemma, not really. But he was very patient with her and her outbursts. He would look at her, bemused.

'Tell me it's all going to be all right,' she would beg.

'Of course it is. Why wouldn't it be?'

For a million reasons. Because she might break down. Because she might betray herself. Because it was driving her mad, the fact that she couldn't control it, that she was obsessed, that she couldn't stop it when she knew she should. The fact that her love for Jack was twisted and wrong and hollow and based on deceit.

'I wish I'd never met you,' she gasped one night, as the ecstasy threatened to engulf her.

'Really?' he smiled down at her, knowing full well she would have made the same choice over and over again until the end of time.

It was a kind of madness. That was her only defence.

One afternoon at Simone's, Jack introduced Adele to a young man called Rube. He was painfully thin and charmless, with claw-like hands that fluttered as he talked and eyes that bulged white as hard-boiled eggs. Jack seemed enthralled by him.

'Trust me, he is going to be famous. Properly famous. His work is astonishing. In fact—' he looked at her, and she could see he'd had an idea. 'I'm going to commission a painting from him while I can still afford it.'

He marched over to Rube and Adele could see them both looking over at her while they talked. She felt a strong sense of misgiving, which was confirmed when Jack told her Rube had agreed to paint her.

She didn't want to be painted. The idea filled her with dread. It was stepping over a line.

'But I want something to remind me of you,' Jack persisted, and of course her vanity won out. Jack could always use flattery to get what he wanted. He rarely made sentimental gestures, so she clung to this as a sign that she meant something to him.

Rube's studio was a disgrace. It was vast and cold and the most unhygienic place she had ever set foot in. There was damp and dust and dirt. Discarded plates bore the remnants of food that had grown furry with mould. There was no proper loo, just a bucket which she suspected he rarely emptied. She quickly made an arrangement with the café next door to use their facilities.

He indicated a green velvet chaise longue for her to lie on. She began by sitting on it awkwardly, not sure who might have sat on it before or what they might have engaged in.

He stared at her.

'Naked,' he said. 'I need you naked.'

'Absolutely not,' she told him. She wasn't taking her clothes off to be painted.

He threw his coffee cup across the room. It hit the wall. The coffee trickled down.

'You're wasting my time,' he said accusingly. 'I've set aside two weeks for this. I need the bloody money. I don't paint clothed women. There's no point.'

Adele didn't know what to say. She could tell he was furious. She could also tell she'd been set up, that Jack had omitted to tell her this part of the deal because he knew she'd refuse.

'Either you take your clothes off, or you reimburse me for the time wasted. I'm not bothered which.'

Rube had an arm up inside his jumper and was scratching furiously. Adele felt sure he had fleas. She wanted to get out of that studio as quickly as she could.

Then behind him she caught sight of a canvas, presumably his most recent work. It was of a young girl drying her feet with a towel. It was glorious. Her skin was luminescent; her beauty sang out from the canvas. It was fluid and sensuous yet respectful – everything a good nude should be.

She gasped, and walked over to the painting to examine it more closely.

'It's exquisite,' she told Rube, who glowered.

'Have you made up your mind yet?' he demanded.

Adele hesitated. She turned back to the painting. She saw now what Jack had recognised in Rube. He was exceptionally talented. His work went above and beyond mere talent. In her gut, she knew that if she didn't sit for him she would regret it for the rest of her life. This was history in the making.

She walked back over to the chaise. 'I'll do it,' she told him.

She put her hands up and started to unbutton her dress.

Rube glared at her. 'Right decision,' was all he said.

As Rube relaxed into the job he became more amenable. And Adele got used to disrobing and sprawling on the chaise longue for him, like some insatiable courtesan. What she did find disconcerting was the way Rube watched her whenever they were all in Simone's. She didn't like to think about what was going through his mind. In the studio, he studied her as an object, not a human being and kept himself very detached, so she was never afraid. But in Simone's, he watched her like a hawk.

It was when the painting was nearly finished that she discovered the reason for his fascination.

'Jack loves you, you know,' he told her out of the blue. 'When you're not looking, he can't take his eyes off you. I know you think he doesn't care. But I think you'd be surprised.'

Adele opened her mouth to protest that none of this was any of his business, but he waved a hand to shut her up.

'You're very important to him. Never forget that. You are more important to him than he is to you.'

She closed her mouth, rather nonplussed. She wondered if what Rube said was true, if he had some insight into Jack that *she was never able to penetrate. She knew Jack was fond of her, of course she did, but she had never felt as if she ranked higher than any of his other conquests. She still hated herself for pursuing the affair, for letting him exploit her weakness. But she was addicted: to him, and his world, and the person he made her.*

She saw exactly who she was and what she had become when she finally saw the painting.

It was her thirty-third birthday. William had given her a card, and a blank cheque. 'Buy yourself something nice,' he said. She wanted to rip the cheque up and throw it at him.

'Don't you understand what you are doing to me, with your patronising disinterest?' she wanted to scream.

How cunning of her, she thought afterwards, to shift the blame onto William. She had what so many women of her generation craved – independence and a long rein. Had it left such a big hole in her life that she had to behave how she did?

Her disgust with herself only lasted as long as it took for Jack to give her Rube's painting. He had it waiting for her in his flat, resting on an easel. It was in a heavily carved pale wooden frame, a red organza ribbon wrapped around it. On a bronze plate on the bottom of the frame was inscribed 'The Inamorata by Reuben Zeale'.

It was Adele, undeniably, but an Adele she never saw when she looked in the mirror. An Adele she knew William never saw either. She had always posed for Rube stretched out on her side, one arm behind her head and the other across her body in an attempt at modesty. Yet somehow he had captured something post-coital in her, a woman who was still in the afterglow that only lovemaking with the love of your life gave. It was primal. And breathtaking. And utterly incriminating.

As she surveyed it, half with pride and half horror, she realised this was why Rube had surveyed her so fiercely in Simone's. He didn't want to paint the woman she presented to him when she posed on the chaise. He wanted the other her, the Adele who lived dangerously, the one who lit up from inside when she was with her lover. And he had captured her, in spades.

'No one must see this,' she gasped. And they mustn't. If anyone needed evidence of her infidelity, this was cast-iron proof.

She felt very uncomfortable about the painting, as if it was an omen. As long as it existed, her reputation and her marriage were in peril.

'I shall keep it for you here,' Jack promised. 'No one shall see it but me.'

'And anyone else you bring back here.'

He gave her a warning look, the one that meant she had stepped over the mark. 'I'll turn it to the wall.'

If this was meant to reassure her, it didn't. She pointed out to him that there wasn't a woman on the planet who wouldn't turn such a painting back again to see what it was hiding.

He started to get cross then. 'We'll just have to take that risk. Anyway, it's yours, to do with what you will. And if you ever want it for yourself, you only have to ask.'

She knew he meant that. For all his ways, Jack had a certain code of honour that he wouldn't break. He would keep it for her, until the end of time, or until she asked for it back, whichever came sooner.

Not long after the painting was finished, things started to go badly wrong between Jack and Adele. She knew that the honeymoon was over, that she wouldn't be able to sustain the *intensity and the physical stress of it all. It was high-octane, and she was extremely emotional, in marked contrast to what she considered to be Jack's bloodlessness. She knew he probably had other women, but he insisted that even if he did, it made no difference to how he felt about her, that she was special.*

'Not special enough to be enough!' she retorted.

'You can't expect fidelity in a relationship based on infidelity,' he shot back, and how could she argue? She knew if she protested too much, he would shut her out. He hated scenes and accusations and fuss. And so she tried to put up with it, because she couldn't bear the thought of losing him.

Although sometimes, in her more rational moments, she wanted him to push her too far so she could walk away. If his behaviour became untenable, then perhaps she could find it within herself.

It was only a matter of time.

One afternoon they came back to the flat after a late lunch. Adele was due to go home on the train, but there was time for them to spend an hour or so in bed before she went. Jack unlocked the door and she went to the kitchen to make a cup of tea – they had terribly domesticated moments. She even kept a supply of her favourite ginger nuts in the kitchen.

She heard a gutteral cry from the bedroom and rushed in.

There was a girl on the bed. There was blood everywhere. On the floor, on the sheets, on her clothes. She stepped closer and recognised her. It was Miranda. The girl who had been lying in the doorway the first time she had been to Simone's. She was a spoilt young debutante with more money than direction, who was drawn to the decadent atmosphere in the club. She spent her time drinking in Simone's, smoking cigarettes and seducing anyone who would have her.

Including, no doubt, Jack.

'What do we do?' said Jack, white-faced. He was rooted to the spot.

Adele was a doctor's wife. Of course she knew what to do. She pushed him to one side.

'Call an ambulance,' she barked at him 'then get her some bandages.'

'Bandages?'

'Anything I can use.' He looked blank. She could see he wasn't going to be any help. 'Don't bother.'

She grabbed a pillow, tipped it out of its case then started tearing the fabric up. Miranda was still alive – her eyelids were fluttering – but there was no way of telling how long she had been here or how much blood she had actually lost. It seemed like rivers.

Adele did what she could, tying the strips of sheeting round her arm tightly to stem the flow.

'Please don't die,' she begged. The girl was so young. What had happened to make her want to do this? Adele didn't want to think about it.

She heard the sound of the ambulance men on the stairs. They burst into the room, with an anxious Jack behind them.

'Good work,' one of them told Adele. 'You've probably saved her life.'

'Maybe,' said the other, looking doubtful. 'She's lost a lot of blood. Are you coming with her to the hospital?'

Adele hesitated. It wasn't her place. She was nothing to the girl. Miranda was in safe hands now. But she couldn't bear the thought of her going to hospital on her own. And, possibly, dying on her own. She shivered.

'Of course.'

The ambulance ride was terrifying. It racketed through the streets, swaying precariously from side to side, the siren blaring. Adele sat by Miranda. She wanted to hold her in her arms, but the ambulance men wouldn't let her. She felt as protective of the girl as she would her own boys. She kept wanting to check her pulse, but didn't want to interfere.

The hospital they arrived at was small and dirty and crowded. She had no idea which part of London they were in, and there was no time to ask. Miranda's stretcher was rushed down dingy corridors and through a set of double doors. A small team rushed forward, and Miranda's tiny, inert body was stretchered away.

A nurse stopped Adele from following. Her eyes were cold and judgemental above her mask.

'What blood group is she?' she asked.

'I'm sorry, I've no idea,' replied Adele, realising they thought she was Miranda's mother.

The nurse shot her a look of disapproval. Adele wanted to explain who she was, that she was a doctor's wife, but she was no one in this mausoleum of sickness and chaos. She was left in a waiting room with dirty green walls. Time ticked on and she realised with panic that she wouldn't be able to get home. She asked to use the telephone.

'The telephone is for the doctors,' the nurse told her, curt, so she made her way out into the street and found a phone box.

'I've been delayed today, rather, and Brenda has asked me to supper and to stay over,' she told William, thanking God both for her alibi and her husband's enduring lack of interest in her whereabouts.

Over and over again she read how to identify the signs of polio, and flicked through the old copies of Picturegoer

224

magazine, taking nothing in. It was close to midnight before someone came to tell her that Miranda was stable.

She crept to her bedside.

'I gather it was your quick work that saved her,' another less disapproving nurse told her.

Miranda looked tiny and pale and helpless, a million miles from the rapacious minx that propped up the bar in Simone's.

'I love him,' she told Adele when she gained consciousness, and then her eyes rolled to the side, as if the string holding them in their sockets had been snipped.

She couldn't have been much more than eighteen. Who did Jack think he was, breaking the hearts of mere children? thought Adele furiously. Her heart was fair game. He had warned her from the start. She had entered into the contract knowing the small print. But a girl who had no idea of the ways of the world?

Jack was unrepentant when she finally got back to the flat, although she could tell by his pallor that the incident had shaken him.

'Listen,' he said. 'I'm one of many where Miranda's concerned. If she's fallen for me it's because I don't exploit her, not like some of the other bastards who are only after her money. And she's twenty-three. She's hardly a child.'

'Oh, that's OK then. If she's twenty-three,' retorted Adele. 'The perfect age to cut your wrists in someone's bedroom.'

'She's unstable.'

'Then you shouldn't have got involved with her!' she shouted.

'I'm not involved with her!' he shouted back. 'I dragged her out of Simone's one night when she was in a bad way. I brought her back here and looked after her. I didn't lay a finger on her.'

Adele could imagine him soothing her, spoiling her.

'Really?'

He looked her in the eye. 'I'm not a total monster. I know your opinion of me is low . . .'

'Because you do nothing to reassure me otherwise.'

She sighed with exasperation. Jack was defensive.

'I'm honest with you about the fact that I'm easily tempted. But for your information, there's been no one but you for some time now.'

'So why do you let me think otherwise?'

'Because I can't take the pressure? Because I don't trust myself? Because once I've said it, then I can only spoil it?'

'That's ridiculous. Don't you have any self-control?'

'No! No, I don't. Don't inflict your view of how people should behave on me, Adele. We're not in Shallowford now. I'm not a doctor. And I'm sorry you think so little of me. Sometimes I don't know why you bother with me at all.'

Adele looked at him. 'Neither do I.'

And in that moment, she realised the whole relationship brought her far more unrest and distress than contentment.

She put her head in her hands.

'I can't deal with this anymore, Jack. The whole thing. It's too much.'

He looked at her. 'No one ever asked you to,' he said.

He was right, of course. And she had known from the start that he would break her heart. Yet it was pointless wishing she had never gone for that first lunch. It was her own fault for being unable to resist temptation. For being vain and shallow and needing attention when she was the luckiest woman she knew. What was so twisted inside her that she felt the need to jeopardise a perfectly happy marriage?

She went to embrace him but he put his hands up to stop her. Jack, when aggrieved, could play hard-done-by ad infinitum.

It was certainly easier to leave him without physical contact. Touching him always melted her resolve. She looked around the flat, as if she was trying to memorise it, although she already knew every corner, every surface.

The pile of sheets covered in Miranda's blood lay in a crumpled heap.

'What are you going to do with them?' she asked, practical to the end.

'The laundry will deal with it,' he told her. 'They never ask questions. Or judge.'

She flinched. It was true. She did judge him. She judged him by the standards of her other self, the doctor's wife, not the adulteress, and she knew that was a fault. She knew it was the kiss of death for their relationship.

'I'm sorry.' Her voice started to break as she said it. She didn't even know what she was apologising for. Adele walked to the door before she broke down. If she cried, she would throw herself at him and beg forgiveness. She owed herself a modicum of dignity.

A little bit of her hoped that Jack would learn something from today. That if he carried on playing fast and loose with people's hearts and not being open and honest that he would end up with nothing.

Adele was more shaken than she thought by Miranda's suicide attempt. Several times she started to cry when the image of the girl's inert body on that bed hit her in the middle of the day when she least expected it. She wondered how she was, and if *there was any way she could find out. She decided it was best not to delve. She'd turned her back on that world, and anyway there was nothing she could do or say to help the girl.*

If William noticed that she was remarkably sensitive, he didn't say anything. She did tell him she was under the weather, and missing the boys, which she was. She longed for their boisterous presence to plaster over the hole in her life. When they were around, the day had momentum and energy and she could feel carefree.

Instead, she focused on the gallery. She made plans for a grand opening. The word was out in the town, and people seemed excited by the prospect, which gave her a little cheer. She prepared business cards, sent out press releases, wrote up the history and provenance of every painting she had bought. She had each one re-framed, making sure that whatever she chose showed the picture in its best light.

At last she was ready. She spent an entire weekend hanging all the pictures. It was exhausting – people thought it was just a question of banging a few nails in the wall, but there was an art to an effective display. She swapped and changed and re-hung and bashed her thumb with a hammer and dropped a picture on the floor, damaging the frame, until finally she was satisfied.

One Sunday afternoon, she gave William the grand tour.

'I am so proud of you,' he said, and gave her a spontaneous hug. His sudden warmth took her breath away. 'Come on – let's go out for dinner and celebrate.'

'But I look a mess,' she protested.

'You look beautiful,' he teased. 'Your hair's all over the place and you've got dust on your cheeks, but there's a light in your eyes you haven't had for a while. You've never looked better.'

At dinner, he apologised for his lack of attention. 'I've been totally preoccupied with the new surgery. It was a difficult change for me, and I know I was pretty bloody. I'm sorry. Can you forgive me?'

'Of course.' Adele felt a sense of peace. Her marriage was back on track. Everything was going to be all right.

Adele planned her grand opening party for the first week in December. That way, she could take advantage of the festive season to decorate the gallery, and leave enough time for people to make purchases for Christmas if they so wished. She hoped and prayed that they did. She had made a huge investment in terms of time, money and emotion.

It was when she came to send out the invitations that she made her fatal mistake. She had been so busy, the memory of Jack had faded to just an occasional twinge. She didn't indulge herself in reminiscence or longing anymore, or relive the passion as she lay in bed at night. Her relationship with William had revived itself now she felt on more of an equal footing. Not passionate in the same way, but deep and strong.

For some reason, this made her think she was resilient enough to invite Jack to the opening. She wanted to prove that she was over him, mostly, but also to show him first-hand what a success she had made of the gallery. After all, she reminded herself, Jack had given her a huge amount of help and advice. It was churlish not to invite him. Of course she would be able to cope with seeing him. William would be at her side. It would be very civilised. And grown up.

She tucked the invitation into an envelope, wrote Jack's name and address on the front and added it to the pile, ready to take to the post office. By the next morning, it would be on the doormat in the entrance hall of his flat. Someone would pick up the post and put it all on the hall table. He would pick it up. Would he come?

The night of the opening party was bright, cold and crisp. Adele estimated that over a hundred people would be coming. It didn't unsettle her. She was a great hostess, and very organised. What could go wrong?

She and Mrs Morris spent the week preparing. The kitchen was a fug of baking smells. They made sausage rolls and vol au vents and cheese straws and mince pies. Adele concocted a brandy-based fruit punch. William tried it and pronounced it like rocket fuel.

'If I get the guests drunk,' she smiled, 'they might empty their pockets.'

She polished their two silver punch bowls and borrowed extra glasses from the local hotel. And then she set about decorating the gallery. She wanted to create something memorable that people would come back to. She spent an afternoon in the woods with the boys, gathering holly and greenery.

The afternoon of the party, she made a final inspection.

The banisters, the fireplaces and the larger paintings were all swathed in holly wreaths tied with festive red ribbon. Everything was lit by candles. Silver trays laden with glasses were waiting to be being passed around by the two waitresses she had hired. She had bought a Christmas tree to put by the fireplace, crammed with sparkling baubles that reflected the light, and underneath were piles and piles of presents. Not real presents, but books from the house that she had wrapped in gaily coloured paper. She had bought an LP by Johnny Mathis to put on the record player – Christmas songs that she would play just loud enough to be atmospheric but not intrusive.

Everything was perfect. She had bought a fitted off-the-shoulder black dress with diamante buttons. Her hair had been set the day before – it had grown a little, and the hairdresser had cut her a fringe and backcombed the rest into a bouffant style that made her look a little like Jackie Onassis.

William came behind her to fix the rope of pearls she had chosen to wear at her neck. When it was done up, she looked in the mirror. She felt pleased with how she looked. William dropped a kiss on her neck.

'I'm very proud of you,' he told her again.

The party was a roaring success. Even more people than she had invited seemed to have come. Luckily Mrs Morris had insisted on cooking double the quantities Adele had estimated she would need. Mrs Morris lived in horror of food running out. Several people bought pictures. Adele felt a rush of pleasure and excitement. She was going to be a success. The gallery was going to be a success.

And then she saw Jack on the other side of the room. She felt her heart quicken just slightly, but it wasn't the powerful reaction she used to have on seeing him. She felt quite calm, and ready to speak to him. She would be gracious and serene.

Then she saw that he had someone with him. It was Rosamund. It had to be. She was ravishing, of course. Dark hair cut quite short, and creamy skin, and navy-blue eyes – an unusual colour combination that made her stand out from the crowd. She wore a red dress that suited her perfectly, and in her ears were a pair of sapphires.

The calmness Adele had felt dissolved into panic. The

roaring fire made the room too hot and she'd had two glasses of punch. Jack was leading Rosamund over to her. She had no idea what to say or what to do.

Jack, of course, was as suave as ever.

'My dear, merry Christmas. And congratulations. This is a triumph.'

Adele managed to murmur a thank you, just as Jack drew his wife forward.

'Darling,' said Jack. 'This is Adele Russell. Adele, this is my wife, Rosamund.'

Rosamund was poised, perfect, polished. She took Adele's hand and held it for a fraction longer than was necessary whilst meeting her eyes, just to assert her superiority over her. Adele felt like an ogress next to her. The black cocktail frock that had seemed so right earlier made her feel matronly and outmoded.

William came forward and Adele found herself having to make hasty introductions.

'What a clever wife you have,' said Jack. 'I've no doubt this gallery is going to be a huge success. She has a great eye.'

'Well, she's worked her socks off,' said William in reply. 'She deserves any success she does get.'

Adele was furious. They were talking about her as if she wasn't there. Rosamund gave her a smile. She had no idea if it was a gesture of solidarity or a smirk of superiority. Rosamund was a blank page. A beautiful blank page.

'Excuse me,' she managed with a modicum of grace. 'I must go and circulate.'

Adele hid herself away in the cloakroom for five minutes while she gathered herself. How on earth had she imagined that she could cope with having her erstwhile lover in the same room as her husband? Hearing them chuckling about her accomplishments had been excruciating. And she had never in a million years thought Jack would bring Rosamund. But of course he had. It was Christmas. Party time. Why wouldn't he? Her palms were wet with anxiety. How idiotic she was. She'd brought it on herself by sending the invitation, foolishly and recklessly.

She came out of the cloakroom and took a deep breath, ready to go and mingle with her guests once more. People were showing no signs of leaving. The noise level had gone up a few decibels. The heat had risen.

When she felt a finger on the back of her neck, she thought she was going to faint.

'I've missed you.'

She could smell Zizonia. His finger moved in a small circle, massaging her gently. With each turn, she became weaker and weaker.

'Stop,' she told him. She didn't want him to, of course.

He was right behind her. She could feel the heat of his body as he spoke into her ear.

'I made a terrible mistake,' he said. 'I didn't realise how much you meant. I need you, Adele.'

Oh God. The very words she had longed to hear all the time they had been together. When he had insisted on tormenting her.

'I don't want anyone else,' he went on. 'I want you. You mean the world to me.'

She'd dreamt of him saying this so many times.

'It's too late, Jack,' she said. 'It's over. I can't go back. I'm happy now.'

'You're not,' he said. And he was right. She could fool herself she was content, but nothing William said could match the thrill of the words Jack was whispering in her ear. Or the feelings that his hands on her waist awoke.

'Please don't,' she pleaded, but she did nothing to remove herself from his grip.

'Come to Venice with me,' he said. 'In the spring. I'm going to visit some clients, see some artists. We can be together. Just you and me.'

She shut her eyes. This was sheer torture. How could she have imagined that Jack wouldn't put temptation in her way? His ego was too big not to try and lure her back, just to prove he could.

'Absolutely not,' she managed.

'I'm going from Paris. At the beginning of April. That gives you plenty of time to tussle with your conscience and find an excuse.'

He ran his finger down her spine, stopping where her dress began. Then he walked away, back into the throng of the party, leaving her barely able to stand.

Ten minutes later, he and Rosamund emerged from the throng and said their goodbyes.

'Happy Christmas,' said Rosamund, kissing Adele coolly on one cheek.

'Let it snow, let it snow, let it snow,' sang Johnny Mathis.

The final guests left just after midnight. Adele and William left the gallery and locked it. She had arranged for Mrs Morris to come in and tidy up the next day. She would be glad of the extra money to buy her grandchildren's Christmas presents.

In their bedroom, William chattered about what a success the evening had been, making comments on the guests and the *décor, but eventually he too fell silent, sensing she didn't want conversation.*

'Darling, I'm so sorry,' she told him. 'I'm absolutely exhausted and that punch was far too strong. Let's talk about it in the morning. I am desperate to go to bed.'

In the bathroom she finally let the tears stream down her face, just for a few moments, because otherwise she felt she would die with the effort of keeping them in. She splashed her face with cold water and hoped William wouldn't notice anything untoward.

Jack had told her he missed her. Jack had told her he needed her. Jack had told her she meant more to him than anyone. Once, those words would have been a dream come true. Now she just wanted to forget them. She couldn't go back to the turmoil, the torture, the madness.

She curled up in bed, feeling hopeless. She gave herself a strict talking to. It was Christmas. Christmas was for family, and for the boys. She wasn't to spoil it because she'd been a fool. She was to put her mistake behind her and look ahead to the New Year. There was no need for her to decide what her resolution was to be. It was obvious. Forget about Jack Molloy once and for all and never, ever be tempted to contact him again.

Twenty-three

It was five o'clock and dawn was thinking about breaking. The sky was gradually turning from deep navy to smoky grey as the Orient Express glided past Lake Zurich, an expanse of tranquillity the colour of the moon. The inhabitants of the houses on its shores were, if they had any sense, still tucked up in bed, as were most of the passengers on the train. Except a very few, who were bad sleepers. Or early risers. Or who had something on their mind.

Beth opened the door of her cabin and crept out into the corridor. No matter how hard she tried, she couldn't sleep. Her bunk was perfectly comfortable, but her mind wouldn't switch off. Over and over and over it all it went. One minute she could convince herself everything was going to be fine, that she had nothing to worry about. And the next she was breaking out in a cold sweat of panic. In the end, she decided to get up.

She sat at the little table at the end of the corridor that was there for passengers to look out at the scenery from. The blinds were down, but Beth lifted the end one carefully. By now, the sky was heading for palest pearl. She put her head in one hand and gazed out, wondering if there was anyone else awake out there. Anyone like her, who was worried sick about something.

It would be five weeks on Saturday since it happened, she estimated. She replayed it over in her head constantly, wishing she could stop at the point of no return and go back again. Where would she stop, she wondered? The point at which she had decided to go out? The point at which she had decided to go back to Connor's flat? The point at which . . .

What on earth had got into her? She had no time for girls who made idiots of themselves with boys and then got hysterical. Beth always liked to think of herself as sorted. She didn't get wild crushes. She always kept her head and knew what she was doing, even after a skin-full. She could, after all, drink for England. She and Jamie had put in enough training together. The one thing about divorcing parents was that they didn't notice when the drinks cabinet was suspiciously empty.

Beth's friends had persuaded her to go and see Jamie's band at a pub called the Greyhound. Because it was her own brother, Beth was far from enthusiastic – she could watch them play in the garage at home for nothing if she wanted to. But her friend Zanna was totally obsessed with the lead singer.

'They're not even that good,' Beth told Zanna. 'They're like a wannabe Nirvana. But they keep forgetting they're in Shepherds Bush, not Seattle.'

Like many nights that you don't look forward to, though, it had turned out to be amazing. Someone had decided that jugs of margaritas were the way forward. At the end, Beth had got chatting to the band's new bass player.

She hadn't met Connor before, and she was entranced by his grey eyes with the dark rings round the irises, and his shaggy long fringe which he continually brushed out of the way, and the shy, sexy smile that made her feel unsettled.

And when she realised that everyone else was going on to an after-party somewhere, including Zanna, and including Jamie, it seemed the most natural thing in the world to hang back and go home with him.

'I'm not an after-party person,' he told her.

'Nor me,' she agreed. Even though she so was. But it looked as if they were going to have their own party, for two, so that was OK.

At his flat, he put on a Nick Drake album and tossed her a can of beer. She curled up on the sofa, which looked pretty grubby, but in the candlelight it didn't matter so much. Especially when he came to sit next to her. Then started to kiss her.

He stroked her and it made her purr like a cat and she stretched out next to him, eager for more. When he slid his hand inside her jeans, she didn't protest. It was too wonderful. Even now, her skin tingled at the memory. It had seemed so natural at the time.

Afterwards, she had fallen asleep in his arms.

And woken with a sense of dread three hours later. He was out cold on the sofa next to her. The grungy hair she'd found so attractive the night before now just looked slightly matted. She shivered with dawn cold, crawling about in the semi-darkness trying to find her clothes, sick with the realisation of what she had done. She wasn't usually the sort of girl not to have safe sex. But she'd been so drunk. And she'd been so turned on. She could remember telling him it didn't matter. How the hell could she have been so stupid?

She sat by him on the bed for five minutes, trying to pluck up the courage to wake him. But he suddenly looked unapproachable. All her bravado and confidence had gone. Her mouth was dry with fear and the salt from the margaritas.

She went into the bathroom. She must have been in there last night, but she couldn't remember, because if she had seen what was in there she would have been out of his flat like a shot. A turquoise kimono on the back of the door. Bottles of Prada perfume, and lipsticks, and Dirty Girl body scrub and a pink toothbrush.

She stormed back out and thumped him in the back.

'Ow!' He looked up at her, indignant.

'You've got a girlfriend.'

'Chill. She's away till Tuesday. Some training course.'

'That's not the point. If I'd known you had a girlfriend I would never—'

He looked up at her from under his fringe. The grin she had found so alluring last night was now evident as a leer. 'Yes, you would. You were gagging for it.'

Beth, never knowingly lost for words, didn't know what to say. Sourness seeped up into her mouth from her stomach, terror mixed with tequila. She burst into tears.

'Oh Christ,' said Connor.

'Get me a taxi!' she wailed.

'Get one yourself,' he told her, and pulled a cushion over his head.

For a moment she stood there, open-mouthed in indignation. No one treated her like that. No one. But he

239

showed no sign of showing her any attention, so she found her bag, and her coat.

She kicked him.

'Where's the nearest Tube?'

He looked up. 'Ravenscourt Park,' he mumbled, and fell back to sleep.

For days afterwards she waited for Connor to contact her. Nothing nothing nothing. No text, no Facebook message. She didn't say anything to Jamie. She felt ashamed, and foolish, and she knew Jamie would be furious with her. He usually watched her like a hawk – what she was doing and who she was with – though he hadn't been so observant that night, she thought ruefully. Her fault – she'd told him she was going back to a mate's and he'd believed her. If he knew what Connor had done, he'd lamp him. They might fight like cats and dogs at home, but outside Jamie was fiercely protective of his sister.

Every time Jamie went off to a gig, she wondered if Connor was going through the same ritual. Picking up some unsuspecting girl, making her feel like one in a million – then dropping her. Or was he happily back with whoever's stuff had been in the bathroom? Had Beth just been a one-off, one-night stand? She felt humiliated, and used, and ashamed. She couldn't talk to any of her friends about it: they'd think she was a skank. Some of her mates were sleeping with their boyfriends, but they didn't sleep with people they'd only just met . . .

In the meantime, the other nagging worry wouldn't go away. Beth looked out at the lake. It was immense. She thought about walking into it, walking and walking till the

240

water went over her head. She could sleep forever then, and all her worries would vanish.

The door next to her cabin opened, and out came Stephanie, wrapped in her dressing gown.

'Hi.' Stephanie smiled at her. She was whispering. 'Are you OK? How long have you been out here? You must be freezing.'

She rubbed Beth's shoulders. It was a gesture of affection. It made Beth want to cry. She looked up at her.

'I think I'm pregnant,' she said.

Oh my God. Why had she said that?

Stephanie tucked her hair behind her ears and knelt down beside Beth, who was now weeping into her hands, her elbows on the little table.

'What do you mean? How do you know?'

'I'm two weeks late. I'm never late. Never.'

Stephanie took in the information. 'Ok. So . . . who . . . how . . . when?'

Beth wasn't about to divulge the more intimate details.

'You so don't need to know all that,' she told her.

She tried to wipe her tears away but they wouldn't stop.

'Oh you poor thing. Come here.' Stephanie reached over and gave her a big squeeze. 'So are you sure? Have you done a test?'

Beth shook her head. 'I haven't dared.'

'It's really early days, right? You need to find out for sure, if you are or you aren't. And then . . .'

Beth put a hand on her non-existent tummy. 'Don't even go there with the termination thing. I couldn't do it.'

Stephanie's face was a mixture of sympathetic and pained.

'No one's going to make you do anything you don't want to.'

'You want to bet?' Beth looked defiant.

'Of course they won't. They'll just help you make the best decision that's right for you.'

Beth shook her head. 'You don't understand.'

She was starting to panic. Her voice was getting louder. The last thing they needed was people starting to pop their heads out of their cabins to see what the kerfuffle was. It was still only just past five o'clock.

'Let's go to the bar,' said Stephanie. 'We can talk in there. We're going to wake everyone up otherwise.'

Beth acquiesced, somewhat wearily, and the two of them made their way up the train, padding along in their slippers. The bar was, not surprisingly, empty and the grand piano stood silent – it was strange seeing it so quiet, after such merriment the night before. A steward appeared, not remotely flustered that they needed attention at this hour of the morning, and offered to bring them hot chocolate.

'Perfect.' Stephanie smiled her thanks and turned back to Beth, who was huddled in her seat, miserable. How well she remembered the misery of teenagedom. How every problem appeared monumental and insurmountable, and everyone seemed to be against you. Not that she'd ever had Beth's particular problem. She'd had friends who had, though. Everything had always turned out all right in the end.

'Hey,' she said softly. 'It'll be OK.'

Two tears squeezed themselves out. Beth wiped them away with her sleeve.

'I just don't know what to do,' she said.

'First, we need to find out if you really are pregnant.' Stephanie knew the staff on board were obliging, but it was unlikely they could rustle up a pregnancy-testing kit at this hour of the morning. 'We'll have to wait until we get to Venice.'

'But I must be,' moaned Beth. 'I'm never late. And I did have . . .'

She shut her eyes tight at the memory.

'Unprotected sex?' Stephanie prompted.

'Yeah,' Beth managed. 'With Jamie's bass player. After a gig. He doesn't want anything to do with me now . . .'

'Jamie's bass player? Where was Jamie when this happened?'

'He didn't know anything about it. Honestly. It's not his fault. Don't tell him. He'll go mad. He'll kill Connor.'

'Connor?' Stephanie's tone was grim as she said his name. 'That's the one who's got them the deal, right?'

'Please. Don't tell anyone. Anything.'

Stephanie felt responsibility settle itself onto her shoulders, stifling and claustrophobic, like a too-tight sweater. Whatever she said and did now would have an effect on everything: her relationship with Beth, her relationship with Simon, Simon's relationship with Beth . . . Family life, she was starting to realise, was an intricate and complicated affair. You had to be answerable to every action, everything you said. And what of Jamie in all of this? Surely if he knew about this revelation it would affect his decision?

Stephanie's life up to this point had been uncomplicated. She had really only ever been responsible for herself, emotionally. Even in her previous relationships, she had always felt able to make decisions without considering anyone else, because of the way she had organised her life. She had been an island. The island of Stephanie. Was she intrinsically selfish? she wondered. Was the burden of negotiating her way through this minefield going to prove too much?

She tried to put herself in Beth's place. What would she have wanted at that age, had she been in the same predicament? A big hug, she decided, and unconditional reassurance that everything was going to be all right, whatever happened. Comfort, that's what she would want. And a sense that she wasn't in this on her own.

Did she have the right to give Beth that reassurance? She wasn't her mother. She wasn't sure what her role was at all. But she was an adult, and one whom Beth had trusted enough to tell. She tried to quell the panic inside and slid her arms around the girl's shoulders, pulling her in.

'Whatever happens, I'm on your side,' she told her. 'You can trust me.'

Beth's voice, buried against her, was muffled.

'You must promise me not to tell Dad.'

Stephanie felt uncomfortable. 'I don't know if I can promise that,' she replied. 'We don't keep secrets from each other, your dad and I. We agreed that right from the start.'

Beth pulled away. Her expression was stricken. 'You mustn't!' Her voice was a keening mew that echoed around the bar. Stephanie's eyes flickered towards the steward, but he didn't look up. He was trained to turn a deaf ear, no doubt.

'He'll make me get rid of it. I know he will. And I don't know if I want that. I couldn't kill my own baby.'

'I'm sure he won't force you into anything you don't

244

want to do.' Stephanie was confident this was true. Of course, Simon would be devastated by Beth's predicament, like any dad, but he would respect her and support her. 'And there's no point in doing anything or making any decisions until we know for certain if you are pregnant.'

'I am.' Beth gazed at her. 'I can feel it. I feel sort of . . .' she waved her hands over her body and shrugged. 'Full. A bit like I'm going to explode.'

Beth rubbed her face. Her hair was sticking out everywhere. She looked so young.

'Look,' Stephanie said. 'Why don't you go and snuggle back into bed and have a sleep? You look exhausted. You've obviously been awake all night worrying. It's not even six yet. You can get another couple of hours' sleep before breakfast. You might feel better.'

She walked her back to her cabin, then stood while Beth clambered back into her bunk and drew the sheets and blankets up round her. She made sure the blind was shut tight then turned out the light.

Beth sat up.

'Don't leave me,' she said.

Stephanie sat on the edge of her bed. Simon would be wondering where she was, if he was awake. But she didn't care. She sat by the bed stroking Beth's hair as she drifted off. When she was certain she was fast asleep, she crept back to her cabin.

Simon was still out for the count. She looked at him for a moment, wondering about what Beth had told her. Should she tell him? No – it was too early yet. It might be a false alarm.

She wondered how he would react either way. She still

felt uncomfortable about the way he had responded to Jamie's news, which wasn't nearly as controversial as Beth announcing she was pregnant. She watched him while he slept. He was still handsome, his salt-and-pepper hair cut close, his brow strong, his nose straight, his skin smooth. There were still those smile lines either side of his mouth, even in repose.

She wondered what was going on inside his head. She wondered what he was dreaming, what occupied his subconscious, what secrets lay just beneath. She wished she could reach inside his mind and scoop out his thoughts, then sift through him to discover who he really was.

She pulled her dressing gown around her. It wasn't cold in the cabin, but she felt a slight chill on her skin. She decided she would get back into bed and try and get some sleep. It was far too early to wake, and she was going to need a clear head.

She was just climbing the bottom rung of the ladder when she felt a hand caress her ankle.

'Hey,' whispered Simon. 'Where've you been?'

'It's still really early. I just went to the loo. Go back to sleep.'

'Come and keep me company.'

It was the last thing she wanted to do. She wanted to be alone to gather her thoughts. But she couldn't refuse without arousing suspicion. She slid into the bunk beside him. He pulled the covers over them both and scooped her into him, cuddling her from behind as he drifted back to sleep.

She lay there wondering, about the man in whose arms she lay, what to do about Jamie, what to do about Beth, wondering just how on earth she fitted in to all of this.

Twenty-four

Emmie started awake. Her neck was stiff and she was cold. The blanket she had covered herself with had fallen to the floor, together with her book. She realised that she had fallen asleep and was still in Archie's cabin. He was slumbering contentedly, out for the count.

She lifted up the blind and gasped. She couldn't believe the scenery outside the window. Emerald-green mountains topped with wispy cloud stood out against a pale-blue early-morning sky. Chalets with pointed roofs hooked onto the hillsides in little clusters. Longhorn cattle grazed the slopes. She almost expected to see Heidi running down the mountainside, hair streaming behind her, milk pail in hand. It was beyond anything she could have imagined, and Emmie had a pretty vivid imagination.

She rewrapped her dressing gown around her and slipped out into the corridor, making her way up to the steward's cabin at the end of the carriage where Robert was preparing breakfast trays for the earlier risers. The enticing scent of fresh coffee hit her and she realised that, despite last night's dinner, she was hungry already.

'I wondered,' she asked, 'if you had anything to ward off

a hangover? I think my companion might be waking up with a bit of a headache.'

Robert grinned. 'You're not the first person ever to ask.'

Moments later, he produced a glass of water into which he dropped two Berocca, accompanied by a brace of pain-killers.

'Then I recommend breakfast as soon as possible. I'll bring it to your cabin when I've delivered these. A couple of croissants and a decent coffee and he'll be as right as rain.'

Emmie carried the cure carefully back to Archie's cabin. She sat on the bed next to him and tickled his cheek. He started to wake, flapping his hand at her to stop.

'What?' he said, sitting bolt upright.

She laughed at his confusion when he saw her.

'Hangover?' she asked.

'No,' he told her cheerfully. 'Never have 'em.'

She thought by the paleness of his face that he was protesting too much. She handed him the Berocca and two tablets regardless.

'Take these,' she said. 'Breakfast is on its way. I didn't want you to waste another moment of the journey.'

'Quite right,' agreed Archie. 'But . . . what are you doing in here?'

'I fell asleep in the chair,' she told him. 'I didn't want to leave you on your own.'

'You're kidding?' He ruffled his hair and it stuck up at all angles. 'I'm so sorry. I was a total idiot, getting drunk like that. You really drew the short straw, getting me as your blind date. I'll make it up to you somehow.'

'It's not a problem,' said Emmie. 'I had a great evening. It was only at the very end . . .'

Archie rummaged in his mind for what might have happened. He shook his head. There was no memory there.

'When you sang Van Morrison to the whole of the bar,' prompted Emmie.

'Oh no . . .'

He shut his eyes, remembering.

'I'll go back to my cabin and get dressed,' Emmie told him. 'I won't be long. Then we can have breakfast.'

A second later, she was gone. Archie slumped back onto his pillow.

'Nice one, Archie,' he told himself. 'What a gent.'

Twenty-five

Jamie was hovering by the steward's door, wondering quite how he was going to broach the subject. He wished Robert would hurry up and come back. The longer he loitered here, the more likely it would be that one of his family would see him. He couldn't carry out his plan unless he got his passport back, and they'd all handed over their passports when they got on the train. They were kept safely together, ready for inspection at any of the borders if necessary.

Thank God. Robert was coming back down the corridor. He saw Jamie and smiled.

'Can I help?'

Jamie decided to go for it. Not make a big deal.

'Uh, yeah. I need to get my passport back.'

Robert frowned. 'They're all with the train manager, I'm afraid. You'll get them back just before we arrive in Venice.'

'That'll be too late.' He was going to have to explain. 'I'm getting off at Innsbruck. I've got to get back home. There's been a bit of a crisis.'

'Oh. Well, I'll have to let the train manager know. We have to keep very strict lists of who's on board.'

'OK. But if you can get it back to me, that would be

great.' He paused. 'But, um – if you could . . . not tell anyone else. None of my family.'

Robert looked at him. 'Right.'

Jamie smiled, awkward. 'It's my mum. Back home. It's all kicked off. She's a bit . . .' He waved his hands to indicate neurotic. 'But I don't want to tell my dad and spoil his trip. I'm just going to slip away. Go and sort her out.'

'I see.' Robert could see the lad was stressed. He was doing that classic thing of trying to be all cool and casual when underneath he was petrified. He could remember that feeling only too well. It was part and parcel of being that age. 'Anything you want to talk about?'

Jamie put up his hands. 'No thanks. It's all cool. I just need my ID.'

'OK. Give me half an hour and come back and get it.'

'Cheers.'

Jamie walked off down the corridor. Robert watched him. He felt uncomfortable about the conversation. Something wasn't quite right there.

Archie and Emmie were tucking into their breakfast. There was fresh fruit salad, and baskets of pastries, and creamy yogurt, and pots of tea and coffee, all served on white china at the table. The blinds were drawn up and outside, the mountain scenery grew ever more spectacular as the train pressed on through Switzerland, distant churches and castles peeping through the tree-laden slopes.

'I'm more of a bacon-and-egg man myself,' said Archie, eyeing up a tiny pain au raisin suspiciously.

'This is just heaven for me,' Emmie told him. 'I'm lucky if I can find milk in the fridge.'

'You're not a homemaker, then?' Archie slathered a roll in butter.

'I don't have time. I'm in my workshop from eight till eight most days. Then I have market stalls at the weekends – I have to get up at dawn to get there and set up. So I hardly ever cook.'

'Me neither. I get force fed by my mother. She's not happy unless she's pushing food down people's throats.'

'You're lucky.'

'I should be the size of a house. But the farm keeps me fit. And the dogs.'

'Oh yes – border terriers? Isn't that what it said on your application?'

'I don't know. I have no idea what Jay wrote.'

Emmie smiled. 'He made you sound wonderful.'

'Oh dear.' Archie spooned two sugars into his coffee. 'You must be very disappointed.'

Emmie didn't answer for a moment.

'No, I'm not,' she said eventually, and turned to look out of the window. 'Look! We're passing St Moritz. I've always wanted to go there. It sounds so glamorous. All film stars and fur coats and sleigh rides . . . I don't suppose I ever will.'

She was babbling. She knew she was. So she took a bite out of an apricot croissant. At least if her mouth was full she couldn't talk any more nonsense.

Sylvie was sitting cross-legged on the bottom bunk in Riley's old pyjamas, sipping black coffee.

'St Moritz,' she said dreamily. 'Do you remember that Christmas?'

252

Riley looked out of the window. There was still snow at this high altitude, though it was gradually melting, giving way to lush green grass which would soon be peppered with spring flowers. Of course he remembered. Riley wasn't a big fan of Christmas, but that had been one of his favourites, when he and Sylvie had rented a chalet in the mountains. They didn't always spend Christmas together, but he always loved it when they did. They'd been with a big group of friends. Riley wasn't a keen skier – he was too scared about breaking a wrist and messing up his work to relax enough to be good – but Sylvie was fearless. She'd skied since she was three.

She wasn't a show-off, though. Not like one of the other members of their party, Roger Bardem, a man who was an expert on everything and liked everyone to know it. All evening he had droned on about his skiing prowess. No one quite knew who had invited him, and he had a complete lack of self-awareness which meant he had no idea the entire chalet wished him smothered by an avalanche.

Sylvie couldn't take it any longer.

'We'll have a race tomorrow, Roger, you and me. Yes?' Sylvie had looked at him across the table. 'The loser buys everyone lunch.'

Roger had raised his glass to her, smugly confident. 'Done.'

Riley had been petrified on Sylvie's behalf, but there was no stopping her now the challenge had been set. There was no point in trying to talk her out of it. In a white snowsuit, with black Courrèges sunglasses and a white fur hat, she had been defiantly certain that she would beat her competitor. And she had trounced him, swooping down the mountainside through the fresh powder with as much style and grace as speed. His fearless Sylvie. Riley had known she would win, but tortured himself nevertheless, imagining her coming to a terrible end, carted off by the blood wagons, just because of a dinner-table bet.

At lunch, Sylvie had made sure everyone ordered the most expensive wines. She relished watching Roger shrivel inside, pride stopping him from protesting as he totted up what this was costing. Just before the meal ended, Sylvie had slipped away and paid the bill. Her pleasure had come in making him squirm, not making him pay.

Riley had adored her more than ever for it. She was laughing now, remembering it.

'Roger Bardem. You remember? His face when we ordered the Chassagne-Montrachet?'

'You were evil,' he told her.

'He was a boor,' she said. 'A boor and a bore. He deserved everything he got.'

Riley looked at her. 'Don't ever change,' he said.

She gave him a quizzical look, a croissant in one hand. 'Why would I change?' she said. 'You know exactly what you've let yourself in for.'

'I do,' he said. 'I do indeed.'

Robert tussled with his conscience for half an hour before deciding that actually, intervention was the right thing. He imagined he would get into more trouble for keeping Jamie's plan quiet than he would for revealing it.

He went to find Jamie's father. He and his girlfriend were in the bar, where they were drinking coffee and taking photos of the scenery outside the window. They were passing the ancient fortified town of Bludenz, and the gradients were getting steeper and steeper.

'I'm terribly sorry to interrupt you,' Robert said, 'and I'm not sure it's my place to tell you this, but your son's planning to get off at Innsbruck. He asked me to give him his passport back.'

Stephanie looked shocked. 'Jamie, you mean?'

'Yeah. He asked me not to tell you.'

Stephanie's face filled with consternation. Simon merely frowned. 'Have you given it to him?'

'I couldn't really refuse.'

'Well, thank you for letting us know.' Simon looked back down at his camera, adjusting the settings.

Robert walked away, not sure if he had done the right thing or not.

Stephanie looked at Simon. 'What are we going to do?'

Simon shrugged. 'Nothing we can do.'

'Aren't you going to stop him?'

'I can't stop him. He's eighteen. He can do what he likes.' He fiddled with his settings. 'If I set this at 1/250 . . .'

'You can't just let him go! Aren't you bothered?'

Simon sighed.

'Of course I'm bothered. I'm deeply upset that it's come to this. But my intervention isn't going to change anything. In fact, it'll probably make it worse. I don't want a *scene* on board the Orient Express, thank you very much.'

'But it's your intervention that's brought this about. You telling him he couldn't—'

'Give up university to go messing about with his mates?' Simon interrupted her. 'None of whom, I might point out, are giving up the same kind of opportunity.'

'So that's it? You're not even going to say goodbye?'

Simon sighed again. 'It's lose-lose as far as I'm concerned. Whatever I do will be wrong. I can't stop Jamie going. He wants to prove a point. And I am not going to be manipulated into backing down. End of.'

Stephanie was absolutely floored. How could Simon be so hard-hearted? Poor Jamie – of course he was being a bit silly, but all he probably wanted was his dad to intervene and put his foot down. What could she do?

She sat back in her chair, drained.

Outside the window, the track ahead was tortuous, winding dramatically so the front of the train could be seen snaking ahead.

'Spectacular,' said Simon, pressing his lens to the glass and snapping several photographs in quick succession.

Stephanie's mouth was dry. How could he just sit there and do nothing? Couldn't he see he was playing right into Tanya's hands?

It had taken a woman to create this toxic situation. Maybe it would take a woman to get them out of it. What was more, Simon was blissfully unaware that Jamie was the least of his problems. He'd need his family round him, not fractured.

She stood up.

'If you won't go and talk to him, then I will.'

Twenty-six

Jamie was in Beth's cabin. He'd packed his bag and he had his passport. He'd checked his bank account on his phone and there was plenty of money in there. He'd been good about saving half of what he'd earned as a barman during his gap year, and now thanked God he hadn't blown it all on stuff for the band.

Beth was lying on her bunk looking sulky, but what was new?

'I'm going home,' he told her. 'I'm getting off at Innsbruck.'

'Don't be an idiot,' she replied.

'I'm not being an idiot! If Dad can't respect my decision-making, then I don't see why I should hang around.'

Beth sat up. 'So you're going to spoil the whole trip? What about Stephanie?'

'Like she cares?'

'Yes. I think she probably does.'

Jamie scowled. He'd expected Beth's support. In fact, he'd been going to suggest that she should come with him. Let the grown-ups enjoy their holiday in peace.

'He's a control freak.'

'Jamie – all dads are control freaks. It's part of the job description.'

'No one else's dad has told them it's a bad idea. Everyone else has got their family's support.'

Beth rolled onto her side and rested her head in her hand.

'That's because they're all losers. Half of them were only going to go and do music technology at the local college. Not exactly a big sacrifice.'

Jamie stared at her.

'You've been brainwashed.'

'Jamie. I'll be honest. The band isn't even that good.'

His mouth dropped open in outrage.

'You said they were great. You said you *loved* them.'

'I was being *supportive*.' She gave the word rabbit ears. 'I didn't want to tell you they were rubbish before, but now you're going to go and ruin your life, I might as well. They're boring. Seen it and heard it all before. Yawn.'

'You *bitch*.'

Beth flopped onto her back. 'Don't go, Jamie.'

'I'm going. And when I've got a deal, and a limo, and I'm playing Glastonbury, don't come whining to me for back-stage passes.'

He turned on his heel and stormed out of the cabin. He stood outside in the corridor. Switzerland was whizzing past in all its perfection, making him dizzy. He felt like crying. He didn't know what to think. He knew he was being an idiot, like Beth said, but he was angry.

He saw Stephanie coming down the corridor towards him. Her face was concerned. She saw he had his bag over his shoulder.

'Jamie,' she began.

'Save it,' he said rudely. 'You're all right. If you play your cards right, you'll probably get a ring on it by the end of the trip. You've got Dad right where you want him, haven't you?'

He didn't want to look at her face. He couldn't believe the bile that was coming out of his mouth. None of this was Stephanie's fault. But all he really wanted was his mum to be here. Back with his dad.

'Have you got money?' she asked, her voice very quiet and calm.

'Yep,' he said. 'That's one thing we're not short of in this family. But trust me, it doesn't make you happy. In case that's what you were thinking.'

He turned away from her. Tears were stinging his eyes. How could he have said that? Stephanie was just being kind.

The train plunged into the Arlberg tunnel. Jamie suddenly sensed everything close in on him. He felt claustrophobic, panicky, but there was no way out. He wanted to run, but there was nowhere to run to yet. Damn the lot of them. Damn Beth. Her words rang in his ears, and the confidence he had felt earlier drained away. The band was no good.

'Jamie . . .' Stephanie was talking to him, her voice gentle. He set his jaw and turned to face her. 'Listen. I know things are tough at the moment, but you don't know how lucky you are. When I was your age I didn't have any choice about what I could do with my life. We didn't have any money. It didn't even occur to my parents that I could have gone to university. I had to leave and get a job. It wasn't a career . . . just a job. It took me over ten years to realise that I could have a dream. And now I've got it, but it was tough. Very tough. No doors were opened for me, because I had nothing to prove my worth. No qualifications. No degree. So I know you think it's boring, and toeing the line, and uncool, but please – don't turn your back on the opportunity you've been given. I would have loved the chance to go to university. I'm telling you this as one who knows how tough it is without the advantage it gives you . . .'

She trailed off. Jamie was staring past her, a muscle in his cheek ticking, his fists clenched.

'You think I'm a spoilt brat,' he said eventually.

Stephanie hesitated. 'Yep,' she said. 'But you're allowed to be. You're eighteen years old. You've had a tough time lately. And we're all clichés, in our own way.'

He darted a glance at her. He didn't like being called a cliché.

'So – you could do the predictable thing and tell your dad to stuff it. Get off at Innsbruck. Mess your life up.'

He put his head on one side. 'Or?'

'Admit you were wrong?'

Jamie chewed the inside of his cheek as he thought about what Stephanie had said. Despite himself, he knew she was making sense. He respected her. He didn't like to admit it, but he probably respected her opinion more than Mum's. What had Mum ever done with her life, after all?

'Hey. Come here.' Stephanie held out her arms to give him a hug. 'You know what, the bad news is life doesn't get any easier. But you need to listen to the people around you who've got experience.'

The train came out of the tunnel and into the open countryside, and Jamie felt his spirits lift just a tiny bit. Bright blue sky and coruscating sun dazzled him. He blinked, to keep out the light. He wasn't going to cry. There was nothing to cry about.

He walked up the train and into the bar, where his dad was changing the lens on his camera. He flumped into the seat opposite him.

'I've been a dickhead,' he said.

Simon put his lens away carefully in its case. Then he put out a hand and touched Jamie's shoulder. Just for a second.

'Let's have a beer,' he said.

Stephanie stood in the doorway watching them. One crisis averted, she thought, at least for the time being.

Twenty-seven

At Innsbruck, the train stopped for half an hour to change engines. The sky was bright, the air was crisp and most of the passengers got off to stroll up and down the platform underneath the Olympic ski jump that towered above them.

Emmie had dressed for their arrival in Venice in an eau-de-nil tea dress. A wide-brimmed straw hat trimmed with a swathe of chiffon and a diamante brooch gave her the look of a romantic bohemian – Merchant Ivory meets Blooms-bury by way of Downton Abbey. She made everyone else look as if they hadn't bothered, thought Archie, with a touch of pride.

'Oh my God,' said Emmie. 'Don't look – at least, don't stare – but I swear that is Sylvie Chagall.'

Archie saw a diminutive blonde swathed in caramel cashmere and tobacco-brown suede trousers sitting on a bench, raising her face up to the sun.

He shook his head. 'Sylvie Chagall? Never heard of her.'

'You must have.'

'I'm totally clueless when it comes to celeb-spotting. Jay was always pointing people out when we were in London.' He indicated with his hand that it went straight over his head. 'So who is she?'

'She's a French film star. An icon. They've even named a handbag after her.'

Archie was flummoxed. 'Why would you want a handbag named after you?'

'You know, like a Hermès bag? A Birkin, or an Alexa?'

Archie struggled with the concept. 'I'd like a beer named after me, I suppose. Or maybe a sports car.'

Emmie was staring. 'It is definitely her. Oh my God, I would so love to go and talk to her. I love her films. You must have seen *Fascination*?'

'Nope.'

Emmie looked at him in astonishment. 'It was filmed in Venice. There was that famous scene, where she jumps off the bridge into the canal?' She pointed at him. 'I'm going to send you a box set of her films. You mustn't leave the house until you've watched every single one of them.' She burrowed in her bag and pulled out a piece of paper. 'I'm really sorry, but I'm going to ask for her autograph. I know it's a terrible thing to do, but she's one of my idols. And how often do you get the chance to meet one of your idols?'

Archie watched as Emmie strode up the platform and sat herself down on the bench next to the woman. He couldn't imagine asking for someone's autograph, not in a million years. But as he watched, he saw the woman laugh, and the two of them engaged in animated conversation. He had to admire Emmie's cheek. He'd never met anyone like her before – confident, but not aggressive. Positive, but not grating. Everything seemed so simple to her.

Five minutes later, she came back. She was bubbling with excitement.

'You won't believe it.'

'What?'

'She told me she loved my hat. I told her I'd made it, and that I was a milliner . . .'

She trailed off.

'And?'

'She wants me to make her a hat for her wedding. She's getting married, Archie. She wants *me* to make her a hat.'

She clasped her hands in front of her, her eyes shining.

'This could be my lucky break, Archie. It'll be in all the magazines. She's a legend. A legend, and she'll be wearing one of my hats.'

'That's pretty amazing.'

Emmie put her arms around his neck, drew him to her and whispered in his ear. 'She's marrying Riley. The photographer? They've been lovers for over fifty years, and he finally proposed to her last night, in the dining car next to ours. Isn't that just the most romantic thing you've ever heard?'

After Innsbruck, the train left the Alpine perfection of Switzerland and forged its way through Italy, passing through vineyards full of twisted, stumpy vines. The lush green pastures were replaced by rich red earth. Pink buildings with red roofs clung to the mountainside, ruled over by the square towers of the campaniles in each village.

The journey was slipping away. The passengers felt a mixture of regret that it was coming to an end, combined with the excitement of arriving in Venice. The restaurant cars were alive with buzz and chatter at lunchtime, as waiters brought them bream, and carpaccio of scallops, served with potato blinis as light as air and finger-lime caviar: tiny citrus pearls that burst in the mouth in an explosion of zest. Then raspberry macaroons, with Szechuan pepper ice-cream, a melting pool of unctuous spice.

Late in the afternoon, as the Orient Express drew closer to her final destination, an air of anticipation grew in the carriages. No one wanted to leave the cocoon of luxury they had grown used to, yet the glamour and allure of Venice were calling. Bags were packed; arrangements for travel were made. The barman distributed his final bills. Robert handed everyone back their passports and wished the inhabitants of his carriage all the best for the next leg of their adventure. He hated saying goodbye: he always felt as if he had made new friends.

He thought about everything that had gone on in his carriage over the past twenty-four hours. Riley's proposal to Sylvie. The man who had come to reclaim his sweetheart. The Stone family, reconciled. And the girl with the beautiful hats. What would happen to her? he wondered. He would probably never find out.

They all still had Venice to continue their stories, he thought. Venice was a city that made things happen. It always had an effect. Venice made people wake up and open their eyes. Robert could already sense her magic as they drew near, onto the causeway that crossed the lagoon, steel-blue water rippling in the afternoon sunlight, luring the newcomers like a siren, weaving her spell. Venice changed people. It made them see the future for what it was.

Twenty-eight

*I*t was astonishing, thought Adele later, how a seemingly successful and intelligent woman, who should have learned from her mistakes, could tell herself that something so intrinsically wrong was a good idea.

By February, Adele had convinced herself that she needed to go to Venice to replenish her stock – the gallery was doing surprisingly well. William needed no persuading. He was extremely proud of her.

'Whatever you need to do to continue your success,' he told her.

She was to go for nine days. She arranged for someone to sit in at the gallery in her absence – she had a small network of people who worked there on an ad hoc basis. If anyone wanted to buy a painting the prices were clear, or they could wait for her return.

She didn't think about the consequences of what she was going to do. All she could think about was having Jack to herself, in a foreign country, for several nights. Having his undivided attention. Seeing him, feeling him, smelling him again at Christmas had reawakened her desire. She now missed him so much she ached, every part of her, her mind and her body and her soul. She didn't chastise herself for undoing all

266

the hard work she had achieved, surviving without him for all that time.

They arranged to travel down to Venice on the Orient Express. That in itself made the trip an adventure. Adele had never slept on a train before: it seemed such a romantic notion. To get to the Orient Express, they had to meet in Paris. Jack was already there, as he had several meetings set up. Adele made her way on her own, down the coast by train, then over the Channel by ferry, and then on a train again. She'd never travelled so far alone; she'd never been abroad on her own. Excitement and anxiety jostled for supremacy in her stomach, meaning she couldn't face anything more substantial than a cup of strong coffee with plenty of sugar.

They were due to meet at the Gare de l'Est. The air was cold and full of mist. The Orient Express was waiting in the station, pulled by a steam engine, huge, majestic and determined. The station was busy, the air filled with foreign chatter as men and women swept back and forth, crossing her path while she searched for Jack. What would she do if he wasn't there? She felt very far from home and rather fearful. If he chose to abandon her, she would have no idea what to do. Get on the train regardless? Make her way back home?

As she began to panic, she asked herself what kind of fool arranges to meet a man who's not her husband at a foreign railway station? People were looking at her, and she felt vulnerable. She obviously had the air of someone who didn't have a clue what she was doing. It would only be a matter of time before some criminal gang closed in on her and she was swept off to be sold into slavery . . .

Someone brushed up against her and she jumped, her nerves shredded. She heard a familiar laugh; an arm wrapped itself around her, and warm lips brushed her ear. Lack of food, worry and relief made her head spin.

Within minutes Jack had arranged for the porter to take her luggage and had swept her on board. It was as if she had been transformed into royalty. They were shown to their cabin with much pomp and circumstance. Adele was swept away by the magic of it. As they waited for the train to leave the station, she stood by the window as Jack held her tighter than he had ever held her before.

'I've missed you,' he said, and she knew he didn't say those words lightly. It made her heart swell with love and longing.

The train journey was unforgettable. The feeling of freezing fog in her lungs when she leant out of the window, combined with the sharp scent of burning coal. The intermittent sound of the whistle as the train thundered along the track. The countryside flashing past; things she wanted to look at gone in an instant – farms, villages, churches, lakes, rivers, cattle. An endless supply of food and drink to their cabin, brought by the most charming white-gloved steward who couldn't do enough for them.

But most of all she adored having Jack to herself. There were other guests on board, of course, but they didn't know them, so it wasn't the usual social whirl, with people crowding round him to get his attention, and for once Jack didn't seem as desperate to forge new friendships as he usually did. He was content with her. She had him alone, all to herself, his undivided attention, and it was wonderful. Just Jack and Adele in their tiny cabin, tangled in each other's arms. Drinking calvados straight from a bottle he had stashed in his luggage – it made her splutter but she loved the fire it lit inside her. Writing love letters on the Orient Express notepaper – she tucked one under his pillow for him to find at bedtime and he laughed when he read it, then sent her one back. Sitting on the end of the bench looking out at the snow-capped Dolomites, his chin resting on her head as she lay back against him, gazing at the wisps of cloud. Cold fingers on warm skin; even warmer lips.

Their lovemaking was fierce and intense, much more so than ever before. During it, they were the only people in the world. He looked down at her, and she felt as if she had been taken to a higher plane. It made her sob, for she had no control. She had no idea that a woman could feel like this. Maybe other women didn't? Maybe it was just her? She certainly didn't know how she could carry on a normal life again.

The train arrived in Venice. Adele thought at first that the city was a hallucination, a mirage brought on by the intensity of the train journey and her emotional state, something her fevered imagination had conjured up. How could this be real, this breathtaking city floating on water, the softness of the stone almost dissolving into the sea, a miasma of turquoise and terracotta and ochre topped with a froth of white cloud?

The private boat they took from the station drew up to the Cipriani, which was on Giudecca, the island from where so many of the iconic views of Venice had been painted. Adele held onto Jack's hand and stepped onto the steps that led to the hotel reception. She felt like a princess, a goddess. The sun broke through the white clouds as she began to walk, bathing the hotel in a coral glow.

This was, she knew, the moment in her life when she was to be her happiest. Nothing else had or would ever come close.

*

She spent the days on her own while Jack had meetings, accompanying him on the boat that took guests over to the jetty by St Mark's Square, then exploring the city with a guidebook, entirely overwhelmed, convinced she had stepped into a fairytale. She made a half-hearted attempt to look for the stock that was supposed to be her alibi, but she was too entranced by the city and the romance of her situation to be able to concentrate. She felt as if she had been bewitched. Her usual businesslike aura evaporated and she wandered the streets almost in a daze, until the evenings when they met up and took the boat back to the hotel. Jack laughed at her passion, her enthusiasm for this tiny city.

'You're under its spell,' he told her. 'But it's not surprising. I've never met anyone who didn't fall in love with it. How could you not?'

On the last day they spent the morning at the hotel. They were due to take lunch with a business contact of Jack's. The Fantini family were marble merchants, and supplied many sculptors with stone, several of whom were Jack's protégés, so they had much to discuss.

They sat by the window looking out over the sparkling water. Adele looked up to see a slight figure moving through the dining room, her arms outstretched and a wide smile on her face. Jack jumped to his feet and was immediately enveloped in a theatrical embrace.

'Adele, this is Sabrina. Sabrina Fantini. They have sent their deadliest weapon to do business with me.' He was grinning from ear to ear.

Adele had never seen anyone so beautiful in her life.

Sabrina wore a dress of black silk taffeta, with a full skirt that showed off her tiny waist. Her dark hair was piled on top of her head, and her heels were high, yet she barely reached Jack's shoulder.

Sabrina turned to greet her, exuding the same warmth she had to Jack, holding her close.

'Adele. I've heard so much about you. Jack speaks of you all the time. And you are as beautiful as he described.'

Adele knew she was foolish to glow at these words, but she couldn't help it. To know that Jack had talked about her to someone else meant so much. She felt validated, more secure in her position.

Throughout lunch Sabrina entertained them, regaling them with behind-the-scenes gossip from the Biennale, the infamous art festival which had been held the year before, and tales of her extended family. Adele was riveted: it was all so alien to her, so glamorous, so far removed from her parochial existence. She couldn't keep her gaze off Sabrina. Her eyes, thick with liner and fringed with ridiculous lashes, flashed and sparkled as she spoke in a stream of heavily accented English interspersed with Italian exclamations. Adele gave up trying to understand what she was saying. Jack drank and listened and occasionally laughed.

Over coffee he excused himself for a moment. Adele felt awkward left alone with Sabrina, with no idea what to say or ask or do. But it was as if Sabrina had been waiting for this moment. She put a hand on her arm. Her fingers were the longest and most slender she had ever seen; the nails on the end dipped in blood-red lacquer.

'How did you manage it?' Her eyes gleamed with intrigue. 'You have tamed the infamous Jack Molloy.'

Adele was puzzled.

'I don't know what you mean.'

Sabrina laughed. 'You don't need to pretend. Four years ago I was sitting in that chair you are sitting in right now, hoping, praying . . .' she threw her hands up in a gesture of helplessness, rolling her eyes. 'Wanting him to look at me the way he looks at you. I didn't think he was capable of it . . .'

She trailed off, looking sad. Adele felt sick.

'You love him?' she asked, horrified.

'No. Loved. Loved.' Sabrina stroked her arm. 'You don't have to worry about me, carissima. I am no threat. I can see that.' She gave a twisted smile. 'Usually by now he would have come to find me. Lured me into his bed to have his wicked way. Not that I ever minded. But this time . . .'

She shook her head.

Adele was astonished. To think that Jack would pass over this exotic creature in favour of her? Unless Sabrina was playing a game of double bluff? But Adele didn't think so. She was quite genuine. There was no side to her. She was just being honest and frank about her feelings, in a way that Adele, with her small-town Shallowford mentality, wasn't used to.

Adele looked into Sabrina's eyes and she saw pain and longing that were only too familiar. She had seen those emotions in her own reflection so many times. She felt a sliver of fear enter her soul, even though, according to Sabrina, she had won the battle and captured Jack's heart, against the odds. She was taken back, back to the Irish girl's warning that night outside Simone's, the night she had become Jack's lover. The girl had warned her Jack was a monster, that he had no feelings for anyone, but Adele now knew for certain he did, that she had broken the spell. But what good had that done her? She couldn't fool herself any longer. She felt impending doom, perhaps because she knew this dream had to come to an end. She wanted to remain here forever, with her lover, but how could she?

She had responsibilities. She could hardly abandon the gallery now it was doing so well. The boys were due home in a week's time for the Easter holidays. She felt sad that the last time they had come home for half term they hadn't seemed to need her so much. They were getting so big, so independent. But she was still their mother. She had bought them chocolate rabbits in a chocolate shop off St Mark's Square the day before, only suddenly they seemed a bit babyish for them. It made her want to cry.

Adele picked up her coffee and drank. It was dark and bitter, like the feeling that was wrapping itself round her heart.

Later that afternoon the sun went from Venice. Jack went to see a dealer in the Dorsoduro and Adele continued her tour, but the warmth and colour had gone from the city. It was as if all the pigment had slipped from the stone and into the water, which became as muddy and dark as the water used to clean an artist's brush. The little streets felt gloomy and claustrophobic, the canals forbidding; the sky above her pressed down, grey and unkind.

The two of them were quiet during dinner, knowing they were going to leave the next day.

'We need to talk,' said Adele.

'No, we don't,' said Jack.

'We can't carry on like this forever.'

'Why not?'

Adele sighed. Yet again, it was all so simple for Jack. 'Because it's not fair. Because it's not real. We're stealing our happiness from other people.'

Jack took a swig of his brandy. He was frowning. 'I like it like this,' he said stubbornly.

'But don't you see? This has been perfect. It's never going to get any better. So we should walk away. We can't walk out on our marriages. Neither of us wants that.'

She knew this was true. Even if she was the love of Jack's life, Adele knew he would never leave his wife. Rosamund provided him with security. It was her money that allowed him to lead the life he did. Every risk he took, Rosamund soaked up the mistakes. She gave him the respectability he craved. And his family. His children.

And she couldn't deny it was the same for her. William provided her with security and respectability. And her wonderful boys. The life that she enjoyed ninety-nine per cent of the time, except for the stolen moments.

'But I love you,' said Jack. 'And I need you.'

The words she would once have given her life for.

'You know I'm right,' she whispered.

He swirled the brandy in his glass, his face dark, his brows knitted. Jack had never liked being told the truth. He only ever liked his version of events.

'This trip has been magical,' persisted Adele. 'Nothing could ever be as wonderful. Not as long as we live. We should both find the courage to walk away, and treasure the memory.'

He looked out of the window. Outside, the black sea was turbulent and threatening, the waves throwing themselves around carelessly.

'You've always been so much braver than I have,' he told her.

Adele took the glass from him and put it on the table. Then she took his hand.

'This is our last night together,' she said. 'I want to remember it forever.'

They went to bed, and Adele's tears fell on him as they made love, each one diamond bright. Once he was asleep, she lay awake all night watching him. When dawn came, she ran her fingers over his skin one last time. Then she dressed, quickly and quietly. She flung her things back into her case. She held her breath as the metal locks clicked, but he didn't even stir.

She didn't hover over him, or go to give him one last kiss. She didn't even look back. She couldn't bear to say goodbye. She knew if he looked at her, smiled at her, spoke to her, she would be lost. She picked up her case and her bag and opened the door. As she shut it behind her she closed her eyes and breathed in. She felt as if she had been turned inside out, her heart pulsing red and raw. She wasn't sure her legs had the strength to carry her. All she wanted to do was sink back into his arms but she knew she had to leave.

She ran down the stairs, out of the door, through the gardens, eerie in the half-light of dawn, and into reception where she found the night porter. He got her a boat without question. Perhaps they were used to heartbroken women fleeing the hotel at peculiar hours? The boatman loaded her case and took her hand to help her on board. The water was grey and choppy, the air dank. She was glad Venice was looking at its worst. She knew she would never come here again as long as she lived. Its blues and corals and silvers would remain locked in her mind, just a memory.

As the boat ploughed through the water, she wondered if Jack had woken yet; if the bed was still warm from where she had lain; if he would roll over into the ghost of her and breathe in her lingering scent. And what would happen when he realised she had gone?

She arrived at the station. She had hours to wait before there was any train suitable for her escape, but eventually she boarded one bound for Paris. She couldn't face food, or even coffee. Intermittent sleep brought no respite, only vivid nightmares in which she lost everything, not just Jack.

Forty-eight hours later, she stepped back into the house at Shallowford with a determined tread. William was delighted to see her, but concerned by her appearance. She was wan and gaunt with her secret grief, but it was only too easy to blame a rogue oyster.

'Poor Adele,' he fussed, removing her coat and steering her towards the fireside. 'I prescribe tea and crumpets immediately.'

She sat by the warmth of the flames. Five minutes later, William returned with a tray bearing a silver tea-pot, two china cups and a plate full of buttered crumpets. She had thought she was never going to be able to face food again, that her torpor had taken away her appetite forever, but as soon as she began to eat she realised how starving she was.

As she began her third crumpet, she looked up to see William watching her.

In that split second she knew that he knew. Yet his look didn't challenge her. He wasn't inviting a confrontation. His eyes were kind and concerned. He sensed her suffering and didn't want to compound it.

How much he knew she had no idea; whether he had proof or if it was just a husband's instinct. For a moment she felt a little sick – the tea, the heat of the fire, the devouring of the crumpets. She had the urge to dash from the room. Yet she realised that would be as good as a confession. She breathed in *deeply to quash her panic, looking around her, reminding herself that she was safe here. She was in her own home, with the curtains drawn, the fire blazing in the grate, the dog dozing at her feet. Tomorrow she would wake and she would know exactly where she was. Where she should be: with William. Jack would always be there, in the back of her mind. She would always have the memory of Venice. But William was her husband. He was good and kind and he would look after her. Soon, her boys would be home again for the holidays and they would be a family. That was all she should want. That should be enough for her.*

William stood up to put another log on the fire. As he passed the back of her chair, he put out a hand to stroke her head gently. It was a fleeting moment, but the comfort and reassurance, the understanding implicit in that tiny gesture made her realise: it was going to be all right. Life without Jack was going to be all right.

Venice

Twenty-nine

Coming out of the rather prosaic Santa Lucia train station and into the bright sunlight of Venice was rather like stepping through the wardrobe and into Narnia, only with water, not snow. Emmie blinked in astonishment at the expanse of jade green shimmering in front of her, and the crumbling buildings that bestrode the canal, and the hundreds of vessels jostling for position.

She had no idea what they were supposed to do next. It was chaos.

'I think we should get a vaporetto, and not a water-taxi,' Archie told her. He'd been assiduously studying his guide book over lunch. 'It's much more fun going native, and we don't want to be ripped off.'

'OK,' said Emmie, but she was a little bewildered. How on earth were you supposed to navigate your way amongst all this? There were crowds of people everywhere: tourists, students, travellers, all with baggage, maps, cameras, crowding round the vaporetto stop, waiting for the next waterbus to transport them along the Grand Canal and further into fairyland.

Everything looked so soft. There were no hard colours or surfaces, just corals and ochres and turquoise with a touch of grey. The walls looked as if they would crumble into dust at the slightest touch. The street signs seemed to hang precariously on the sides of buildings; gothic arched windows with stone mullions hinted at the mystery that lay behind them.

Archie grappled with his tourist guide.

'We need to get the number one. It'll take us right down the Grand Canal. Let me take those.'

He took her hat boxes from her, juggling them with his own bag. Emmie picked up her case and followed him over to the bus stop. The vaporetto swayed in the water next to the landing stage as they jostled on board with the rest of the hordes. The water slapped the sides of the boat and they were off, the prow pushing through the glassy surface of the canal, rays of afternoon sunshine bouncing off it.

Emmie's head swivelled from side to side as the journey progressed. She glimpsed bridges and balconies and balustrades; distressed wooden shutters and wrought-iron lamps and arched windows; mullions and exposed brick. Uneven, crumbling foundations surrounded doorways almost completely submerged in water. Gargoyles and lions' heads leered at her from their buttresses; flowers tumbled from window boxes; faded signs made promises, but of what she had no idea. When she saw a black gondola nonchalantly making its way up the canal in front of them, she nearly swooned.

'Oh my God,' she breathed to Archie. 'The gondolier's wearing a striped shirt and everything. It looks so *real* . . .'

Archie was beaming from ear to ear. He felt genuinely excited. After the stress of the past few weeks, it was such a relief to feel positive again. He slid an arm round Emmie's shoulders.

'Bloody amazing,' he shouted over all the noise.

They passed familiar landmarks, so famous from school-books and films: the Rialto Bridge, the Accademia, the church of Santa Maria della Salute, the Doge's Palace . . . Palazzi vied for supremacy with their rococo splendour, some almost ridiculously elaborate.

Eventually they alighted at the bottom of the Grand Canal by the Piazza San Marco, and quickly got swept up in the late-afternoon crowds as they tried to navigate their way past stalls selling Venetian masks and Pinocchio puppets and ice-cream. There was a frenetic urgency in the air that could have been alarming, had they not taken the time to slow down and remember they were in control of their destination.

Not On The Shelf had booked them in for two nights at a tiny hotel down a narrow street not far from the piazza. As soon as they walked in between the buildings off the main drag, there was an air of gracious calm. The hotel was family-run, with just a few bedrooms, but it was utterly charming. A courtyard at the back was filled with greenery spilling from terracotta pots, centred round a crumbling fountain topped with a naked cherub. Inside, the look was faded grandeur meets Venetian glamour: ornate mirrors and picture frames, plump sofas, marble floors and a sweeping staircase.

Archie's bedroom was ludicrously over-the-top. The bed was a profusion of dark-pink velvet with a gilded headboard and over it hung a chandelier that looked as if it might pull the ceiling down. As soon as the porter shut the door, he looked round, slightly flummoxed yet wanting to laugh at its unashamed opulence. He pulled a pair of jeans and a shirt out of his bag and got changed. They only had tonight and tomorrow in this extraordinary city, and he was determined to make the next twenty-four hours as unforgettable as he could for Emmie. He got the sense that her life was a lot tougher than she made out. That she struggled to survive financially while doing the thing she loved best. He admired her hugely for it. And he would quite cheerfully have strangled the swindling Charlie if he ever had the misfortune to meet him.

They met in the foyer. Emmie was dressed in black Capri pants and a red shirt knotted at the waist, a beret at a jaunty angle on her head. She looked like a different person in every outfit she wore, yet underneath she was resolutely Emmie, thought Archie. He had never met another girl who was quite so sure of who she was.

Simon had ordered a private water-taxi from the station. Their boat zipped past all the other water traffic and made its way across the wide lagoon with determination. As they approached the island of Giudecca, they went past the huge Molino Stucky mill, past the long parade of houses, shops and restaurants, then finally the classical Chiesa del Redentore, resplendent in white, its wide stone steps ready to welcome worshippers.

Just after that, the boat pulled alongside a landing stage, marked out with gold and black poles, and there in front of them was the Hotel Cipriani, painted its trademark pink. Simon took Stephanie's arm as they stepped onto dry land and into the lush gardens, filled with espaliered lemon trees and scented jasmine. They were greeted by uniformed staff, and their luggage was whisked away while they walked up the brick path to the reception area. There the manager greeted them warmly, then escorted them to Beth's and Jamie's rooms, in the main part of the hotel.

Stephanie gave Beth a hug.

'I'll come and see you later.'

'I'm fine,' said Beth. 'I'm going to take a bath. Don't worry.'

She gave a brave smile, and Stephanie's heart went out to her. She must be beside herself with worry. Stephanie wished she could do something to alleviate it, but until they knew for certain, she was helpless. She had to try and get away as quickly as she could, to put Beth out of her misery.

Then Stephanie and Simon were led through marble corridors, along a terracotta-tiled tunnel and through sweet-smelling hedges to the Palazzo Vendramin, the palace adjoining the hotel. As they were shown their suite, Stephanie almost had to pinch herself. She had never seen a hotel room like it. At one end, floor-to-ceiling windows fringed with silk curtains looked out over the gardens. At the other, a seven-foot bed, made up with crisp white linen, looked out over the lagoon.

She wandered about, touching everything in amazement: the chinoiserie desk stuffed with stationery, the mirrored dressing table, the little table set with a pristine cloth bearing an exquisite platter of pineapple and mango, raspberries and kiwi. The manager explained to them that there were two butlers at their disposal, any time of the day and night. They just had to phone up for them.

It was all Stephanie could do not to laugh. What on earth

would they do with two butlers? She couldn't even begin to imagine.

Simon, of course, seemed to take it all in his stride. This was the kind of service he was used to. When the manager had gone, she came and stood by the window, and they looked out across the water, which was turning from gold to deep blue, to the magnificent Doge's Palace.

'This is just amazing,' she whispered. 'I didn't think it could get any better.'

He turned to her.

'I wanted this trip to be special,' he told her.

She managed a smile. It was more than special, but it didn't take away the pressing problem. She turned away.

'I need to go to a chemist,' she told him over her shoulder, as casually as she could.

'I'm sure the hotel will have most things you need. And if not, the butler can get it for you.' Simon grinned.

'No. I need to go there myself.'

'Whatever for?'

Stephanie hated playing coy, but it was her only tactic.

'Never you mind. You shouldn't ask a lady that.'

'Oh.' Simon looked slightly nonplussed. 'OK. Well, I'll come over with you.'

'No. I'd rather go on my own, if you don't mind. It won't take me long.'

Simon hesitated for a moment, then nodded. 'OK. I'll go for a stroll round the gardens. Get the lie of the land.'

'Perfect.'

Stephanie felt relief. It had been easier to deflect him than she thought.

She went into the bathroom. She looked longingly at the

huge marble bath, and the gorgeous shower gels and body lotions just waiting to be indulged in, but there wasn't time. She went down to reception and asked the concierge for directions to the nearest chemist. Furnished with a map of Venice, she went back to the landing stage to catch the hotel courtesy boat across the water. The ridiculously handsome driver, suave in his sunglasses, gave her a hand on board, and five minutes later they were sweeping across the lagoon.

She didn't have time to admire her surroundings. The pontoon on the mainland soon came into view, and moments later she was helped out onto the quayside. She pulled her map out and scrutinised it. There were hundreds of tourists milling about in the evening sun and she found them disorientating. Eventually she managed to get her bearings.

She made her way through the narrow streets, searching the crumbling walls for the faded black letters denoting the street names. There was no time to stop and look in the shop windows, enticing though they looked: she glimpsed handbags in candy colours, chic linen dresses and elegant high heels. They would all have to wait. She elbowed her way through the crowds: everyone else seemed happy to stop in their tracks and window-shop. Didn't they realise she was in a hurry?

At last she found the pharmacy, and was relieved to find it was open. She pushed open the door and stepped inside. The smell was familiar: the universal faint trace of antiseptic, but the boxes and bottles surrounding her looked unfamiliar.

What on earth was the Italian for pregnancy-testing kit? In fact, now she came to think of it, did they even have them in Italy? Maybe they just went to the doctor to find out? Her Italian was non-existent. She knew the names of every kind of pasta, but that was about it. The pharmacist came out to help her, a middle-aged woman with glasses.

Stephanie mimed looking at a stick.

'Bambino . . .' she tried, then gave a thumbs up and a thumbs down.

The pharmacist looked puzzled.

Stephanie tried patting her stomach. 'Bambino?' she tried, again, then shrugged. She felt absolutely ridiculous, but was grateful there was no one else in the shop.

This time the pharmacist's eyes lit up.

'Aaaaah! Test di gravidanza?'

Stephanie nodded, hoping that this was indeed what she meant. Moments later the pharmacist handed her an oblong box. She looked at the packaging and decided, by the pictures, that she had cracked it.

'Grazie,' she said gratefully, and counted out the money.

The pharmacist smiled as she put it in a bag. 'Buona fortuna.'

She was wishing her good luck, Stephanie realised, obviously thinking it was for her. It was too complicated to explain, so she just smiled, took her change, and left the shop.

The sun was starting to set as she took the boat from the pontoon back to the hotel. She made her way as quickly as she could to Beth's room.

Beth was lying on her bed in the white hotel dressing gown.

Stephanie held out the bag.

'Let's get it over with,' she said. 'Then we can decide what to do.'

Beth took the bag wordlessly and disappeared into the bathroom. It was the longest three minutes of Stephanie's life. She sat on the bed, praying for it to be negative. The alternative almost didn't bear thinking about. There were so many ramifications for everyone. She resolved that she would do anything she could to support Beth and the baby, if it came down to it. She had a feeling Tanya wasn't the maternal type, let alone the sort to embrace being a granny sooner than expected.

Beth came out of the bathroom. She was drained of colour, her eyes dead. She looked so terribly young.

'Positive.'

'Oh, sweetheart,' said Stephanie, and her heart sank. How much easier it would have been if the test had been negative. Now there was nothing but heartache and difficult decisions ahead.

Beth dissolved into tears. 'What am I going to do?'

'It's going to be OK,' Stephanie promised her. 'Honestly, Beth. It's not the end of the world. I know it seems as if it is.'

'I'm having a baby,' said Beth. 'I don't know how to look after a baby.'

Stephanie held her by the shoulders.

'Listen to me,' she said. 'Whatever you decide to do, I am right by your side. I'll support you all the way. And I mean all the way. You're not alone in this, Beth.'

'There's no point in even having this conversation.' Beth sat down heavily on her bed. 'Dad won't let me have it.'

Stephanie frowned.

'Sweetheart, it's not his decision. He can't force you into anything you don't want to do. And anyway, I'm sure he wouldn't.'

'You don't know him.' Beth looked miserable. 'Look how mad he was with Jamie. He'd throw me out.'

'You don't really believe that, do you?'

Beth shrugged. 'All Jamie wanted to do was defer uni for another year. That's nothing compared to having a baby, is it?'

Stephanie took both of her hands in hers.

'I think your dad would surprise you.'

Beth looked at her. She had a funny expression on her face.

'You don't know why Mum left, do you?'

Somehow, Stephanie had a feeling she wasn't going to like the reason. 'I thought it was because she met Keith?'

Beth shook her head. 'No. That wasn't the real reason. The real reason was Dad made her have an abortion.'

'What?'

'Yep. Mum got pregnant, a couple of years ago. It was an accident. Dad made her get rid of it. That's why she left, not because of Keith. She couldn't get over what he'd made her do.'

Stephanie felt a chill wash over her. 'You must be wrong. Surely he'd never do anything like that?'

Would he? How well did she really know Simon, after all? They'd only been going out for three months.

'He did. He said the last thing they needed in their marriage was another baby, with all the stress and everything and the fact they weren't getting on, and it wasn't fair to bring it into the world.' Beth's eyes were swimming with tears. 'So what would he say to me?'

Stephanie needed time to think. This bombshell was too awful to take in, but in the meantime she needed to reassure Beth.

'I won't let him force you into anything you don't want to do. Trust me. It will be your decision. I'll make sure of that.'

She scooped her up in her arms and held her tight. Beth clung onto her.

'Will you tell him for me? Will you tell Dad? I'm just so scared.'

'Of course I will.'

Beth looked upset.

'But not until after the trip. I don't want to spoil it. You mustn't say anything to Dad until it's over. I'm so sorry. You've been so kind to me, and I've ended up ruining it all for you . . .'

'Of course you haven't.'

Stephanie couldn't imagine how Beth was feeling. She wished she could make it all right for her. She felt a rush of affection. Beth was being so brave and grown up, and unselfish. She could see she genuinely didn't want to ruin things for Stephanie.

'Listen. Why don't you get dressed? We'll go for an early supper and you can get a good night's sleep and it might all seem better in the morning.'

She knew she was just spouting platitudes, but there wasn't much else she could say or do.

Beth threw her arms around her neck again.

'I'm so glad you're with Dad,' she told her.

Stephanie didn't like to say that, in the light of what Beth had just told her, she was starting to get cold feet about her relationship with Simon.

The four of them had supper in Cip's. They decided they wanted a fairly low-key evening, so they chose this over the more formal Fortuny restaurant in the main hotel. Situated right by the water, overlooking the lagoon, Cip's had a relaxed, buzzy atmosphere, with the air of an upscale yacht club. They sat outside on the deck, warmed by heaters, as the water turned a deep navy-blue and the moon shone down on them. They ordered creamy mushroom risotto and Pinot Grigio, and if Simon wondered why Beth wasn't drinking hers, he didn't say anything.

Stephanie found she could barely eat, even though the risotto was the best she had ever tasted: creamy but firm and wonderfully rich. She didn't know if it was her doubts about Simon, or her fears for Beth, but suddenly her stomach was in knots. Everything seemed so fragile.

Simon, meanwhile, was entirely oblivious to any under-current, chattering to the waiters in his not-terribly-good-but-enthusiastic Italian. All evening Stephanie watched him, wondering. Had she only just scratched the surface of the man she had considered herself in love with?

In bed, Stephanie lay awake, worrying. She was as far away from Simon as she could be. She couldn't bear to be anywhere near him. Luckily, the bed was enormous, so she was a good three feet away. She feigned an upset stomach to excuse her distance, blaming the mushroom risotto. She just couldn't take in what Beth had told her about the termination. It made her go hot and cold just to think about it. Had he really forced Tanya into it? Surely you couldn't *make* your wife go through with something like that? Or had he just made it clear how very difficult he would make life if she didn't? Perhaps he'd threatened to withhold money? Money seemed to be very important to Tanya. Perhaps he'd bought her off?

She slipped out of bed and went to look out of the window. Everything was still and dark, except for the lamplights along the boulevard, and the silhouette of Venice across the water, lit by the moon.

She sighed. The revelation had changed her opinion of Simon totally. She knew he was strong and determined, and maybe a bit of a control freak – that was a parent's prerogative – but a bully? A bully whose actions she couldn't condone, not in a million years. For the first time since she had met Simon, she began to sympathise with Tanya. Had she lived under a reign of terror that she couldn't bear any longer? Was that why she had left?

There were too many unresolved issues, too many questions, a myriad of doubts. She wasn't sure what to do, but this wasn't what she had signed up for at all. She had wanted to be part of the family, for them all to work together as a unit and bring some stability and happiness back into the home. But now she questioned what her role would be. She wanted to be Simon's equal, his confidante, his lover – not the person who had to question his decisions and spring to the defence of his children when they did something he disapproved of.

'Steph!' The voice made her jump out of her skin. 'Are you OK? What are you doing?'

It was Simon, sitting up in bed, looking concerned.

Stephanie sighed. They might as well have the conversation now as over the breakfast table.

'I'm sorry, Simon, but I can't see how this is going to work.'

'What on earth do you mean?'

'I can't carry on with this relationship.'

Simon laughed, but it was a scared laugh. 'What are you talking about?'

He looked so convincing, sitting up in bed, bewildered. Not like a man who had ordered his wife to . . .

'You're not the person I thought you were. And I'm sorry, because I love you, and I love the kids.'

Simon got out of bed, walked over to a lamp and turned it on. The sudden light made her blink.

'Hang on a minute. I don't understand. What's changed, all of a sudden? What's all this about?'

He looked genuinely distressed. She supposed she owed him an explanation, a chance to defend himself. It was only fair.

'You made Tanya have a termination.' Even as she spoke the words, they made her shudder.

He looked at her in horror.

'Who told you that?' he demanded. 'Did she phone and tell you that? Or one of her helpful friends?'

'It doesn't matter who told me. Did you?'

He was staring at her.

'I can't believe you would think that of me, not even for a moment.'

Stephanie held her hands up in protest.

'Why not? I mean, you were happy to banish Jamie,

because he was about to do something you didn't approve of—'

'That's entirely different!'

'Is it? Isn't it just imposing your will on someone else? Without taking what they want into consideration?'

He flinched at this. His face seemed to crumple. He'd been caught out, thought Stephanie. Of course he didn't like it.

Simon stood up and walked to the window, and stared out for a few moments. When he turned back, Stephanie could see tears in his eyes. For a moment her indignation faltered. She'd expected bluster and fury.

'When Tanya told me she was pregnant, I was delighted.' His voice was low, calm. 'Shocked, of course. And a bit . . . you know, daunted by the prospect of doing it all over again. But in a funny kind of way I thought that perhaps a baby would do her good. Would do us all good. It would calm her down and give her something to think about apart from herself.' A tiny trace of bitterness crept in. 'It was Tanya who decided to get rid of the baby. She realised it was going to cramp her lifestyle far too much. She presented the termination to me as a fait accompli. *After* she'd been to the clinic. She said it was a woman's right to do whatever she liked and she didn't need my permission or my approval. I'll never forgive her for getting rid of our child. It was the final straw for me. That's what gave me the courage to finally divorce her. I couldn't live with someone who could be so . . . I can't even find the words.'

At this point, Simon's voice cracked. Stephanie stepped forward, but he held up his hand to stop her.

'I expect she now feels guilty about what she did. And in

true Tanya style, she's probably twisted everything round to make herself blameless and me look the guilty one. It's what she's best at. She's very convincing.' He looked at her. 'I suppose it was Beth who told you?'

Stephanie nodded.

'So Tanya even tried to poison my own daughter against me.' Simon looked at Stephanie in total disbelief. 'I don't deserve that, Stephanie. I only ever try to do my best for my family, and that means being tough on them sometimes. The thing is, Steph, when you're trying to protect people, sometimes you have to be the bad guy. Or seem like the bad guy. Because kids do things and make decisions that you know are going to hurt them. I don't know – some people think you should let them learn by their mistakes. But I just get terrified . . .' He buried his face in her neck, stroking her hair. 'That's why I was so glad I had you. To keep me on track. To balance me out. To remind me that tough love isn't always the answer.'

Stephanie held him tight. Oh God, she thought. What was he going to say about Beth? She was going to have to tell him now, before the trip was over, because you couldn't share confidences like this and not play all the cards. He wouldn't forgive her if she kept it quiet till they got back. And anyway, Beth shouldn't have to wait.

'Simon,' she said. 'There's something I have to tell you.'

His head jerked up.

'Beth's having a baby. She's pregnant.'

He stepped back from her. In the half-light she saw his expression – a mixture of horror and shock.

'Beth?' he said. 'How do you know? When did she tell you?'

'She told me yesterday. On the train.' Stephanie put her hands on his shoulders and looked at him. 'She did a test last night. She didn't want me to tell you until we got back home. She didn't want to spoil the trip.'

Simon stepped away. 'I need to talk to her.'

He walked towards the door, but Stephanie stopped him.

'Don't wake her now. She'll be fast asleep. Let her rest.' She put a hand on his wrist and pulled him round to face her. The anguish in his eyes was almost unbearable.

'She's just a baby herself,' he told her, and Stephanie saw tears. He looked away, angry. 'This is all my fault. Our fault. Mine and Tanya's. Of course something like this was going to happen—'

'No!' said Stephanie. 'You mustn't blame yourself. It was an accident. The sort of accident that happens all the time.'

He winced at her words, but seemed to accept them.

'Does Tanya know?'

'I don't think so.'

'She mustn't know. Not until we've sorted things out. I don't want her getting her claws into Beth. God knows what she'll do. She'll use this against me—'

Stephanie could see he was panicking. She put her arms around him, soothing him.

'Hey,' she said. 'It's going to be OK. We'll figure things out.'

He took in a juddering breath. His face was crumpled. 'My little girl . . .' His voice cracked. 'I need to see if she's all right.'

'It's still very early. Let's go back to sleep for a couple of hours. Then get the butlers to bring us some breakfast.' She smiled. 'We can talk it all through, then go down and see Beth. When you've had a chance to think about it.'

Simon looked at her. 'You amaze me,' he said. He passed a hand across his face wearily. 'I'm guessing she'll want to keep it. I know my Beth. That's what she'll want to do.' He managed a smile. 'At least, I hope that's what she'll want to do.'

Stephanie thought her heart was going to melt. She had heard all she wanted to hear. The words of a non-judgemental father who was going to support his daughter, despite how much it might hurt him, despite how much he might disapprove.

Thirty

Unlike Sylvie, Riley hated lie-ins. He woke at six and knew it would be several hours before she surfaced. She always had a mammoth sleep debt after filming, and he wasn't going to disturb her. He left her nestled amongst the goose-down and slipped off to the Rialto to stock up on food for the next few days.

He made his way over the Accademia Bridge and through the maze of canals that led to the famous markets. He knew the route like the back of his hand now. They were staying in the same apartment they always took: a piano nobile on the Grand Canal – a suite of rooms on the first floor of a fifteenth-century palazzo which took advantage of the fine views.

As he walked, he watched daily life emerge behind the scenes: two young boys with a football in an otherwise silent square, a woman hanging out the washing, two old men sharing cigarettes and banter before going their separate ways, tiny little dramas unfolding against the most exquisite backdrop, the players so nonchalant about the setting. This was the Venice Riley loved: the secret underbelly, while Sylvie preferred the drama and showmanship of the Venice on show for the public.

At the market, he moved like a native amongst the crowds of Venetians out to get the cream of the crops, chatting in Italian to the stallholders, some of whom knew him by sight if not repute. They were too busy to be star-struck, although over the years he had photographed most of them. Today, though, he was firmly off-duty. He bought zucchini still crested with their bright yellow flowers, and deep red tomatoes, as bulging and misshapen as a middle-aged woman in a too-tight frock. An upright bundle of white asparagus. Pea pods mottled green and purple and white and black. Tiny antediluvian spider crabs. Berries glistening crimson and burgundy and scarlet, plump with juice, which would be perfect for Sylvie's breakfast when she finally emerged.

He wandered back to the apartment laden with his pur-chases, delighted to see the sun fling the early-morning clouds to one side and work her magic on the city. He began to plan what they might do and then decided – they would do nothing. It was wonderful for both of them not to have a schedule to refer to, telling them where they were going, what they were doing, when they could eat, when they could breathe. And the wonderful thing about the apartment was that it was so far from reality they could both relax immediately, without the interim winding down that was often so difficult on a holiday. Of course, being on the train had helped. The Orient Express always took your troubles away, swept you off to a better place, wherever that might be.

When he got back he was surprised to see Sylvie was up, dressed in faded jeans and a white long-sleeved T-shirt. She'd opened the windows to let in the invigorating spring air and the translucent light, and was perched on a sill, sitting sideways with her knees drawn up, looking out at the canal, the vaporettos and motor launches and gondolas zig-zagging their way from side to side in an elaborately choreographed dance.

'Hey. Good morning.'

She looked over at him and smiled. 'I woke up and you were gone.'

'You know I can't sleep in. I got us some food.'

Riley put his shopping bags down in the small kitchen area. It was often the way in Venice – the main rooms were grand and spectacular, while the cooking facilities were insignificant. He supposed it was because people preferred to go out to eat. He walked back across the marble floor, past the huge U-shaped B and B Italia sofas that were a perfect foil for the frescoed walls and dramatic chandeliers. Hidden in a carved cabinet was a docking station. He put his iPod in.

Before this trip, he had made a compilation of all the songs that had meant something to him and Sylvie over the years. It had taken him hours to source and download them. Some of them had been long-forgotten, tucked away in the recesses of his mind, but as he had looked back, using photographs as an aide memoire, they had floated back to him. Pulling them out had been a bittersweet experience – a memory of a time long ago, but a memory nonetheless. No one could take that away from them. Not yet, anyway.

He pressed play. Music began to trickle out of the hidden speakers, filling the room yet somehow not dominating the space, as only the best sound systems can.

As Sylvie heard the music, she turned and smiled.

'Marianne Faithfull. "As Tears Go By",' she said. 'I had that crazy party, remember? Come As Your True Self.'

Riley smiled. 'You were half angel, half devil.'

He remembered it so clearly. Sylvie dressed in red, with horns and a tail and a pair of angel wings. He'd been in black and white – a photograph.

'We played this all night. Over and over.'

He took her hand and drew her off the windowsill. She smiled and settled into his arms. He put one hand on her waist and entwined his fingers in the one that bore the ring. As she lifted it, it gleamed, glittering in the sunlight. They began to move to the music. Every note, every beat, every word was ingrained in them. Nothing in the song had changed, just as nothing in them had changed, not really. From the outside, their appearances were different, but their souls, their beings, were just as they had ever been.

Had he made a mistake? wondered Riley. Should he have asked her to marry him on that sultry night, just as he'd been tempted? Something inside had told him the time wasn't right, but now he wondered what might have happened. Would they have had children? He didn't allow himself to imagine what they might have been like, their little Rileys/Sylvies. Or how different their lives might have been. Perhaps their relationship would have cracked altogether under the strain of their respective careers and the inevitable temptation. Few of the people they knew who had got together then still were. And that would have been a tragedy. Chances were, he wouldn't have had her here, now, in his arms.

No, thought Riley. He had been right to wait. As the last few chords of the song that had been theirs that summer faded way, he reflected that he might have had to wait almost a lifetime, but theirs was going to be the most perfect marriage.

Thirty-one

Simon and Stephanie decided that Stephanie would go
and talk to Beth first, and explain that Simon knew
about the baby. No matter how they played it, emotions
were going to run high, but Stephanie thought Beth would
panic if Simon confronted her straight away, no matter how
sympathetic he was.

In her room, Beth was worn out from sobbing all night.
'I didn't sleep,' she told Stephanie. 'I can't believe I've been
so stupid. I've always thought girls who got caught out were
so dumb. And after what happened to Mum . . .'

Stephanie sat on her unmade bed. She had to choose her
words carefully. Beth needed to know the truth, but she
didn't want to vilify Tanya any more than was necessary.

'You need to know something, Beth. Your dad didn't
force your mum into a termination,' Stephanie told her. 'I
think maybe your mum changed the story a little bit. She
was probably upset about what had happened.' She was
trying to be as tactful as she could.

'How could she do that?' demanded Beth. 'That's evil.'

'Maybe she felt bad about what she'd decided?' Stephanie
had no idea how Tanya could have been so manipulative,
but she didn't want to damage Beth's relationship with

her mother. She would need her over the next few months, no doubt. Stephanie hoped Tanya would be able to stop thinking about herself for once. 'People sometimes do silly things when they are sad or stressed.'

Beth nodded. 'I guess . . .'

'And listen – I told your dad this morning. About the baby. I couldn't keep it a secret from him. I hope you're not angry, but I thought it was for the best. And anyway, he wants you to know, whatever you decide, he'll support you.'

Beth swallowed. 'Where is he?'

'Waiting outside. He loves you very much, Beth.' Stephanie stroked the girl's cheek. 'Do you want to see him?'

Beth nodded. She couldn't speak. Stephanie walked over to the door, and opened it. Simon stood outside, anxious. She stepped aside to let him in.

Father and daughter walked into each other's arms, wordlessly. Stephanie felt a lump in her throat as she watched the two of them. She couldn't imagine what was going through Simon's mind as he held Beth. He must have been thinking back over the years, over all his hopes for her. Perhaps wishing things had turned out differently or blaming himself.

The door bounced open and Jamie stood in the doorway, grinning ebulliently. 'Hey you lot. What's going on? Are we going for breakfast or what?'

He looked round at all their faces. No one said anything. 'What is it?'

Beth made a wry face. 'I'm up the duff.'

Jamie stared at her. 'When?' he asked. Then, 'Whose is it?'

Beth hesitated. There was no point in lying or covering up. 'Connor's.'

'Connor's?' Jamie clenched his fists and stepped forward. 'I'll kill him,' he said.

'Don't,' said Beth. 'It wasn't like that. Don't blame Connor. It was my own stupid fault.'

'Does he know?'

'No.'

Pain and bewilderment flitted across Jamie's face. He walked over to his sister and held her in his arms.

'It'll be OK, Bethy,' he promised her. 'Won't it, Dad?'

Simon nodded, choked up, and embraced the two of them.

Families, thought Stephanie, weren't a tight unit that travelled on the same track. They ebbed and flowed. Each individual had their own issues and hang-ups and agenda. Sometimes they dovetailed and sometimes they clashed. Within that unit there were alliances and feuds and dis-agreements that were in a constant state of flux. Allegiances could swap in the blink of an eye. But it didn't mean they weren't as one underneath it all. That was how they func-tioned. Everyone had a role, but sometimes those roles changed, reversed, swapped, depending on the circumstances.

And Stephanie realised just what her role should be in the midst of this family. *She* should be the one to keep them on track. They'd been through such a lot, and each of them had suffered in their own way. The words from a Stevie Wonder song floated back to her. Something about keeping strong, and moving in the right direction. She could do that for them. She could be the voice of calm, an objective eye.

She stepped towards them. She stroked Beth's hair,

squeezed Jamie's bony shoulders, then slid her arm around Simon's waist.

They drew her into their circle, the three of them. And so they were four. She had become, in that moment, one of the family.

Thirty-two

'We've only got a day,' Emmie told Archie at breakfast the next morning in the courtyard of their hotel. 'So we need to make the most of it.'

'Well,' he said cheerfully. 'You choose where you want to go. I'm a cultural savage.'

'I think we should go to the Scuola Grande di San Rocco. To see the Tintorettos. Then maybe the Guggenheim? But I don't know. Do you prefer classical or modern art?'

'Um – pass. Neither are my chosen specialised subject. I'll go with the flow.'

Archie was the first to admit that he knew nothing about culture, but he was happy to be guided by Emmie. More than anything, it was her delight and pleasure in the small things that entranced him as they made their way around. An art shop, the window full of powdered pigment in colours more vibrant than any rainbow, deep and rich and powerful. A display of Murano chandeliers, ridiculously elaborate and over-the-top, the milky white twists of glass tipped with ruby red and emerald green. In the Campo San Barbara, in a tiny shop window by a little stone bridge, Emmie gasped at the eccentric paraphernalia – stuffed rabbits, marble skulls, antique dolls, a silver mousse mould in the shape of a salmon.

'I want to take it all home and put it in my studio!'

Archie couldn't see why anyone would give any of it house-room, but he was charmed by her enthusiasm.

He was, however, gratified to find that the Tintorettos blew his mind. He hadn't expected to be in such awe of their majesty – all the walls inside the Scuola hand-painted with a boldness and a sensitivity that made him want to cry. He had never felt that way about anything. He couldn't grasp how one man could achieve such perfection, and how, even though he was pretty sure he didn't believe in God, the depiction of both the Old and New Testaments could move him so profoundly. He gazed up at the ceilings: he saw savagery and rawness and tranquillity, all outlined in heavy gold.

'It's almost like a religious experience,' he said. 'I'm not used to that kind of thing.'

'I suppose that's the point of great art,' Emmie told him, pleased by his unexpected reaction. She'd supposed he would be bored within five minutes and would want to move on, but in fact it was she who became anxious to go.

'We can't stay here all day,' she said. 'We've got places to go, bridges to climb.'

'So where next?' he asked, clutching a paper bag full of postcards, and feeling humbled. He hadn't even been bothered to paint the wall behind the loo at home when he'd had the cistern replaced.

The Guggenheim confused him. He loved the simplicity of the art deco building, with its wide steps leading down to the Grand Canal, but he didn't really understand any of the art or find it attractive. He pored over a Willem de Kooning, entitled *Woman on a Beach*. He could vaguely make out a leg and a head, but apart from that it looked as if someone had chucked a load of paint on a canvas.

'I'm sure everyone says it,' he told Emmie. 'But I could do that.'

She just laughed.

'And I like things to look like what they are,' he grumbled. 'Give me the Tintorettos any day.'

Afterwards, they sat at a café drinking luminously orange Aperol spritzes. From her handbag, Emmie produced a sketchpad and a tin of coloured pencils. She began to draw.

'This is going to be my Venetian collection,' she told him. 'For next winter.'

She quickly drew a feathered turban in pleated Fortuny-style fabric, and a two-tone top hat in black and red, like the inside of a gondola. Archie sat in the afternoon sun and watched her sketch. He could feel the warmth of the sun on his skin as a dreamy contentment settled upon him and the liqueur-charged Prosecco bubbles worked their magic. For the first time in weeks, he was doing nothing, absolutely nothing, but relax. His mind began to wander. A few weeks ago, he would never have imagined himself sitting in a sun-drenched piazza with a girl like Emmie, a girl he would never have found otherwise . . .

'Just out of interest,' he said. 'What did Jay write about me on the entry form?'

Emmie put the finishing touches to a big bow on the side of the hat while she remembered.

'He said you were a scruff,' she said finally. 'But you scrubbed up well.'

'Cheek!'

'That you were quite shy, but actually, you quite liked a party. Once you got going.'

'True . . .'

Emmie put her head to one side while she remembered the rest. 'And that you valued loyalty over everything.'

Archie looked away. He didn't trust himself to speak. Those last few words reminded him so sharply of the friendship he'd had. And what he had lost. On the table, his hand clenched into a fist. He wasn't going to lose it. Not here, with Emmie, after such a lovely afternoon. Then he felt her fingers slide over his and squeeze them gently. She didn't say anything. She didn't even look at him, just carried on sketching with her other hand. But this time, he didn't pull away.

Thirty-three

Imogen woke to the sound of pealing bells and seagulls. For a moment, she thought she was dreaming. She was at the Cipriani, in Danny McVeigh's arms. It really didn't get any better than that. She wriggled as unobtrusively out of his embrace as she could, pulled on a T-shirt and picked up her phone to check her emails while she brushed her teeth in the bathroom.

There were three from Sabol and Oostermeyer. All with details of potential apartments attached. She clicked on them, then flicked off her phone with a sigh. She didn't want to look. Reality was starting to filter in, cutting through the fantasy. She felt an overwhelming sense of disquiet. Suddenly the thrill of Danny's romantic gesture and the euphoria of having him with her had faded, to be replaced by an anxiety she couldn't shift. The emails had reminded her of the commitment she had made, a commitment she could hardly go back on if she wanted to be taken seriously. You couldn't just accept jobs then turn them down five minutes later because your schoolgirl crush had swept you off your feet.

Or could you?

Troubled, she called room service and asked them to

send up breakfast. She'd have to have a serious conversation with Danny about their future and how he saw it. They hadn't talked about it at all on the train or during dinner last night at the hotel. Somehow the real world didn't seem relevant when you were on the Orient Express, or arriving in the glamour of Venice.

When breakfast arrived she took the tray over to the bed and shook Danny awake.

'Hey, girl of my dreams,' he smiled.

'We need to talk,' she replied.

'In my experience,' he said, 'that's never a good sign.'

Imogen fed him a slice of mango.

'I've still got to go to New York,' she told him, wiping the juice from his lips with her thumb. 'They're expecting me to go for discussions at the very least.'

'So. Nothing's changed then. Since your note.' Danny's tone was mild, but she sensed his anger.

'I don't know yet,' she told him. 'But you've got to understand. This is my career.'

'Well, I wasn't really brought up like that. So excuse me if I don't get it.'

'With the gallery closing, I've got to think about building a name for myself. So I can have choices. And money.'

'I've got money,' he said. 'If it's money you want, I'm pulling in shedloads. I can give you whatever you want.'

He didn't understand. Not at all.

'Let's talk about it when I get back from my meeting,' she told him. 'I don't want us to fall out over it.'

He didn't reply.

'Have I upset you?' she said.

'Nope,' he replied. 'Just put me in my place. Career first, me second.'

'No. I want both.'

'I only want you.'

He lay back on the pillows and shut his eyes.

'That's easy to say,' said Imogen. 'But it's not very practical.' She felt indignation rising. 'I wouldn't expect you to give up your business.'

He sat back up again. 'I'd give it up tomorrow. For you.'

'And then what would you do all day? And what would you do for money? Go back to your old ways?'

As soon as she heard her own words she was horrified, but he was being totally impractical.

'Sorry,' she said. 'I shouldn't have said that.'

'No.' He threw back the duvet and climbed out of bed. She lowered her eyes. She didn't want to look at him. 'Heaven forbid that I should forget I'm just a McVeigh.'

'Danny, I don't think that at all. I think you're amazing. You've . . .' Oh God. How could she say it without sounding patronising? He'd done very well for himself, all things considered? 'I love you,' she managed, eventually.

He slammed the bathroom door shut.

Imogen put her head in her hands. Was the difference between them always going to be a problem? Even though it wasn't such a great difference anymore? He was a success, she knew that, though he chose not to brag about it. But she could tell, by the things he had bought, and the things he aspired to, and the way she'd heard him talk on the phone. Why couldn't she give him the credit for that, instead of rubbing his nose in his past?

Because he wasn't playing fair either. He was sulking

because she had ambition, and he found that a threat. Well, her career was part of who she was and if he didn't like it . . .

Imogen walked over to the cupboard and started to choose what to wear. She'd go and see Jack Molloy. By the time she got back, Danny would have calmed down, she was sure of it.

The island of Giudecca was tiny, and a quick glance at a map told Imogen that the apartment where Jack Molloy lived was in one of the houses that lined the front and looked straight across the water at the Zattere. If you loved art, where else would you buy a house? It had to be the most painted view in the world.

She had put on a cream linen shirt-dress with a wide belt. She wanted to look businesslike, but not too austere. She left the hotel by the back entrance, by Cip's restaurant. People were already starting to gather for drinks on the deck, enjoying a cocktail or a glass of wine and drinking in the sunshine and the magnificent view, warmed by the heaters that took the edge off the spring chill.

Imogen turned left, walking down the wide boulevard that ran alongside the water's edge. The midday sun was bouncing off the puddles caused by a brief shower earlier on. A breeze was coming in off the lagoon. The boulevard was well paved, interspersed with wrought-iron lamps with pink glass shades that reflected the red stone of the houses.

As she crossed several bridges, she noticed that the canals on Giudecca seemed wider than those in Venice. It made it less claustrophobic, and the light had a special quality. She passed several restaurants with tables outside, each more enticing than the next, before finally coming to a halt in front of the building that housed Jack's apartment, perched next to a canal with a wooden bridge. It was pleasingly symmetrical and grand, with shuttered windows and balconies, yet faded in its grandeur, the terracotta plaster peeling away in places to reveal a paler stone underneath.

By the heavy arched front door, painted a murky green, was a display of round, brass bells with each owner's name engraved underneath. In the middle she saw his: Jack Molloy. It seemed determinedly English amidst the elaborate Italian names – although she remembered that in fact he was Irish American.

She rang the bell. After two minutes there was no answer. Imogen felt a twinge of disappointment.

And then the door opened. Standing in front of her was a girl of about twenty-three, in a T-shirt dress and flip-flops, dark hair in a ponytail on top of her head.

'Oh, I'm sorry,' said Imogen. 'I mean – *scusi* . . .' She couldn't think what to say.

The girl gave her a warm smile. 'It's OK. You must be Imogen. Jack asked me to come down and get you. He's not very good with the stairs these days, I'm afraid.' The girl stood to one side. 'I'm Petra, by the way. I'm his housekeeper.'

Imogen followed the girl through the gloom of the hallway. She could smell the cloying damp from the nearby canals, barely masked by a large vase of lilies on a table. It was deathly quiet in the building, as if no one at all lived here. Two flights up, the door to Jack's apartment was open.

'Come on through,' said Petra, and Imogen stepped inside.

Floor-to-ceiling windows looked out over the canal, and the greeny blue of the water was echoed on the walls in a powdery, soft paint. Heavy linen curtains were hooked back with thick ropes. Two cream sofas faced each other in the centre of the room, and in one of them reclined Jack Molloy. His thinning hair was swept back and a cigarette smouldered in his right hand. His clothes were shabby and threadbare, but had obviously been expensive, as they still held their colour and their shape: a navy-blue shirt and white trousers. His eyes were hooded: hooded and hungry, for information and company.

'Jack Molloy. Forgive me if I don't get up.' He extended a hand, and offered no excuse for his inability to stand. Maybe he didn't have one? Maybe he just didn't want to get out of what looked like a very comfortable sofa at his age?

She took his hand: it was cool and dry and his grip was firm. 'Hello. I'm Imogen.'

'So – one of the twins must be your father?'

'That's right. Tim.'

He looked at her. 'You're not terribly like Adele.'

Imogen couldn't help feeling she'd disappointed him, as if he had been expecting a doppelganger.

'Well, yes. I'm shorter. And rounder. And not so dark. Or elegant—'

'You seem perfectly delightful to me. I was just observing. It's a very long time since I saw her. Though I think perhaps . . . the colour of your eyes?'

Imogen felt awkward being scrutinised. His gaze was very piercing.

'So – you knew my grandmother when she was younger?'

Jack was silent for a moment.

316

'Yes. Yes, I knew her when she first started the gallery. I like to think I inspired her, in a way. Though she was very driven. She certainly didn't need me.'

'It's been a huge success. But you know we're selling it? It's too much for her now.'

'And you don't want to carry it on.' His tone sounded slightly accusing. Imogen wondered if Adele had sent her here so Jack could persuade her to stay on at the gallery. Yet her grandmother had been only too eager to push her out of the nest.

'I guess I want a new challenge,' she told him. 'The world doesn't start and finish in Shallowford.'

'I'm sure you'll be a success, whatever you do.'

'I'll certainly try my best.' Her eyes hadn't stopped roaming around the drawing room. There were some impressive paintings on the wall. Worth more than the building itself, she imagined. 'You've got some wonderful work here.'

'I have. But you've yet to see the best. Your birthday present, I believe.'

Imogen shrugged. 'I've got no idea what it is. Adele wouldn't tell me. Only the title. I don't know anything about it.' She paused. 'Or why you have it.'

'I've been its guardian since the day it was painted.'

'Why? Why couldn't she keep it?'

'It was . . . complicated.' Jack flashed a defiant look at her.

Imogen raised her eyebrows.

'Complicated how?' Imogen wondered for a moment if perhaps it was stolen. She was certain Adele would have

317

nothing to do with a stolen piece of art, but there was definitely a mystery.

Jack smiled. 'I commissioned it for her birthday.'

He held out his hand for Imogen to help him to his feet. There was no weight behind him, and she realised how frail he was. The strength of his personality was deceiving.

He beckoned her to follow him. 'It's in the dining room,' he told her.

He opened a heavy wooden door. Inside, the walls were painted deep red. A gate-legged table that sat twelve took up most of the room, with ornately carved chairs at each place, like miniature thrones. At the far end was a shoulder-high stone fireplace. Over it hung a painting.

The moment she saw it, Imogen gasped.

A woman was sprawled across a green velvet chaise longue, against which her skin looked startlingly white. Her hair was half up and half down; one hand was at her throat, the other rested on her thigh. The look in her eyes was sheer contentment. No one could be in any doubt that she had just been pleasured by her lover; the playful half-smile on her lips said it all. She was womanhood personified; to call it erotic would be crass.

Underneath, screwed to the frame, was a gilt plate engraved with four words. *The Inamorata – Reuben Zeale.*

Imogen put a hand to her chest. She could barely breathe. It was one of the most magnificent paintings she had ever seen in her life. It was pure, raw Reuben Zeale – the most brilliant example of everything he had been lauded for. It was as if the woman was in the room with her. She felt that if she touched her skin, it would feel warm. That if she spoke, the woman would speak back to her.

But that wasn't what was so shocking.

What had rendered her speechless was that the woman in the painting was Adele.

Imogen turned to look at Jack, for confirmation.

He was gazing at the painting, one hand resting on his stick. He had a faraway look in his eyes. She couldn't quite discern it. Regret? Adoration? Longing. It was longing.

Something clicked in her brain. The piece of the puzzle she had been missing leapt out at her.

'You were lovers,' she whispered.

He didn't answer for a moment.

'I still miss her,' he said. 'I was a fool. I should never have started anything, but I am too vain to be able to resist a challenge. I adored her, but I never let on, until the very end. I had my own rules, which I thought made me invincible and untouchable.' He paused. He seemed to slump. 'All it meant was I ended up losing someone I loved very much.'

'What happened?' she asked Jack.

'Oh, your grandmother had enough sense to realise that I wasn't worthwhile. And that your grandfather was ten times the man I was.'

Imogen thought about her grandparents. They had always been so close. She couldn't imagine her grandmother having an affair. But judging by the painting, she had been quite young. Not much older than Imogen herself.

'She knew,' said Jack, 'that I would never make her happy. She knew when to end it. At the moment when everything was perfect. It was the only thing to do. She is a very wise woman, Adele.'

Jack picked up his stick and nudged the frame slightly, to put the picture straight. Imogen looked at it again.

'Is it really by Reuben Zeale?' she asked, but she didn't need confirmation. She could tell by the confidence of the brushstrokes, the sheer quality, the power of the painting.

Jack nodded. 'One of his earliest works,' he told her. 'But I think you'll find it's very valuable.'

'What on earth am I going to do with it?' Imogen suddenly felt overawed by the responsibility.

Jack fixed her with a beady look. 'You're to use it, to your advantage,' he told her.

Imogen couldn't begin to imagine the impact this discovery was going to have.

'An undiscovered Reuben Zeale,' she said. 'The media will go mad.'

'And it's up to you, my dear, to play them.' His eyes were sparkling now. 'As you will.'

'They'll want to know who she is. Everyone will want to know. I can't imagine Adele will want people to find out the truth.'

'That's a conversation you need to have with her. But nobody needs to know the truth. I think it's probably best if we continue to protect the ones who would have been most hurt.'

Her grandfather, thought Imogen. Had he known? And Jack's wife? They were both dead, but that didn't mean the story could now be exploited. It would be disrespectful to both their memories.

She put a hand to her mouth, totally overwhelmed. The picture was dazzling, and deserved to be shared with the world, but it was also intensely personal.

'I don't know what to do with her,' she said. 'I don't know if I can cope with the responsibility. This is momentous.'

'If I know Adele,' said Jack, 'she wants you to use it as a tool. To help you.'

'I can't sell it,' exclaimed Imogen. 'I'd never sell it!'

'No, no,' said Jack. 'And you can be sure if that was your decision, I'd buy it back off you. I'd sell every painting I had just to keep *The Inamorata* in safe hands.'

He glared at her. Imogen was left in no doubt that he would do so.

'She's in safe hands,' she assured him. 'I can promise you that.'

'Good,' said Jack. 'And I trust Adele's judgement. She was extraordinary.'

He turned away from her suddenly. Imogen felt her heart go out to him. She sensed a deep emotion in him, emotion that had gone unexpressed for a lifetime. She didn't know what to do, whether to try and comfort him, or to leave him alone. She felt an urge to embrace him, but she had only just met him. She cleared her throat, but before she could speak, he turned back.

'Have lunch with me,' he said. 'Petra will cook. We'll eat in here. I want to enjoy her for the very last time.'

He turned and walked out of the room. Imogen was left alone. It was very silent. The air in the room was cold, and she shivered.

The Inamorata. A woman with whom one is in love.

She thought about Adele and Jack's story, and their secret. When she looked at the painting, she could see for herself just how much it had meant to Adele. For someone to make you look like that, it must have been a deep and enduring passion. The kind of passion most people didn't experience as long as they lived.

The kind of passion that inspired literature, music, poetry – and art. Zeale had pinned it down on the canvas with an unnerving precision. She thought of the reaction the painting was going to provoke if and when it was revealed to the world at large. She felt proud that her grandmother wanted her to have it. She would make sure it was recognised and given the honour it deserved, however that may be.

Before she left the dining room, she looked at *The Inamorata* once more. There was something else familiar about it. It wasn't that it was her grandmother. It wasn't the features so much as the feeling it evoked in her. She empathised totally, but she wasn't sure why.

And then suddenly, it became clear. She'd seen that look in her own eyes. In the mirror. After being with Danny.

Jack cheered up over lunch, as if the food Petra provided had fortified him and made him strong again. She brought in a huge white platter filled with bundles of baby asparagus tied up with pancetta, crostini chopped with chicken liver and figs with fennel and salami.

'I don't know what I'm going to do when Petra leaves,' he told Imogen. 'She's an art student, and she has a very nice room here in return for feeding me. But she graduates this summer.'

'There'll be plenty of other girls like me at the college. I'll put up an advert,' Petra told him. 'And I'll leave my recipes.'

'They won't be the same,' Jack insisted.

'You'll fall in love with the next one, just as you fell in love with me two minutes after Abigail left.' Petra clearly had the measure of Jack, but she was obviously very fond of him.

The main course was pork belly with fennel, the skin crisp, the meat melting. While they ate, Imogen filled Jack in on her plans for the future. He had lots of interesting ideas, and Imogen could see how useful he had been when Adele had started out. He was generous with his knowledge, and not many people were.

'So what is Adele going to do?'

'She won't retire completely. I know she won't. She'll always be there if I need her advice. She loves it too much. What on earth will she do with her time if she gives it up?'

Imogen was confident this was true.

She looked over at Jack, who was gazing into the middle distance, suddenly subdued. He realised he was being watched, and jerked his head back to look at her.

'I adored her, you know. She deserved so much better than me. I would never, ever have made her happy. I'm far too shallow and vain.'

'Don't worry,' Imogen told him. 'My grandfather made her happy. Very happy.'

For a moment she thought she had been too sharp with the old man. Her words seemed to sting him.

'In a different way,' she added softly. 'I'm sure you were very special to her.'

She wasn't condoning what they had done, but she thought she understood. You couldn't dictate whom you felt passionate about. She knew that well enough.

After lunch Jack seemed to fade very quickly. He fell asleep at the table, his head nodding onto his chest.

'This is normal,' said Petra. 'He'll go off to bed in a minute.' She took away his glass and shook him gently. 'Jack, I think Imogen is about to go.'

He woke, and looked up at her.

'If you ever fall in love,' he told her, his eyes bright, 'if you ever find true love, don't walk away. Whatever you do, don't walk away.'

He stood up and walked out of the room without a backward glance. Petra began to clear away the plates. She gave a long-suffering smile. 'He gets like that when he's tired,' she told Imogen. 'He'll be fine again later.'

Imogen didn't reply at first. Jack's words had fired themselves straight into her heart. Suddenly everything made sense and was starting to fall into place.

'I must go,' was all she managed, and grabbed her handbag. 'Thank you so much for a lovely lunch.'

She just hoped it wasn't too late.

Jack watched the girl from the drawing-room window as she walked back down the boulevard to the Cipriani. He sensed a courage in her, as well as a vulnerability, that took him back. It was over fifty years, but the realisation that he had lost someone he truly loved hit as sharply as it had that morning in the Cipriani, when he had woken to find Adele gone.

It had been the hardest lesson he had ever learnt. He never had another affair. He had remained faithful to Rosamund, knowing that no matter how hard he searched he would never fill the hole left by Adele. And gradually

Rosamund became enough for him, and he learned to appreciate the things that truly mattered in life, like their wonderful daughters, and their glorious home, and their friends. He became happier, away from the pressure he had once put upon himself to make meaningless conquests. It had taken a meaningful one to make him realise how futile it all was.

He walked into the room that served as his study. It looked out over the canal at the back of the house, and if he leaned out of the window he could just see the edge of the island and a glimpse of the blue lagoon beyond. The walls were lined with books, hundreds and hundreds of books on art: a valuable collection, many of them long out of print. Here it was that he had written his reviews, his theses and several of his own books, none of which had made him a fortune but had given him great pleasure.

And hundreds of letters. Letters that he had written but never had the courage to send, all to the same person. He kept them, nevertheless, because they were a record of his feelings, a reminder of every emotion that had washed through him, from hope to elation to despair, in the years that had passed since they had spent their final few days together on the island. It was why he had returned to Giudecca after Rosamund had died, because he felt closer to Adele here than anywhere.

He heard the plangent note of the Santa Maria ring out. Two o'clock.

He drew a sheet of notepaper towards him, picked up his pen and began to write, his striking italics stark on the page. He started it in the same way he had begun all the others, the ones he had never sent.

My dearest, darling Adele,

What a pleasure it was to have your wonderful granddaughter here. Not least because it was as if a little bit of you was in the room with me. She has your spirit, your grace and your dazzling eyes, the eyes I have never forgotten. My last memory of you is the tears in them as you kissed me, the night before you left. I want nothing more than to look into them again so I can wipe the traces of those tears away once and for all. If you would consider meeting, it would mean the world.

I can think of no better keeper for The Inamorata *than Imogen. And Reuben, I know, would have been pleased that it is in safe hands. It was always his favourite painting.*

Yours, forever and always
Jack

He put down his pen and looked at the letter. He felt drained. He had resisted the urge to beg. After all, he wanted Adele to come of her own accord, not because she felt obliged. He pressed a sheet of blotting paper carefully over his words, folded the letter into three and slid it inside an envelope, then addressed it. That was further than any of his other letters had ever got. They were still in a stack, in the bottom left-hand drawer of his desk. He supposed it had been cheaper than a therapist, the ritual outpouring he had indulged in.

With a sigh, he swivelled round in his chair to look to the back of the room, where an easel stood. On it was a painting.

Petra, he thought, was a talented girl. One of the better

students he had nurtured over the years. When he had asked her to copy *The Inamorata*, she hadn't blanched at the task. She had done an excellent job. Only the most expert of analysts, the most exacting of critics, would have spotted the slight lack of confidence in the strokes, the merest hesitancy. It might not have the controlled abandon of a genuine Zeale, but it would fool ninety-nine per cent of viewers.

Yet despite this, for Jack, the spirit of the painting wasn't there. It was too far removed from its subject. The source of the inspiration hadn't been in front of the painter. He remembered Reuben's words when he had handed over the painting once it was finished. 'I feel as if I have painted true love,' he told Jack. At the time, Jack hadn't really understood what Reuben meant. By the time he had realised, Adele had gone and all he had left of her was the painting.

And so *The Inamorata* had given him both comfort and pain over the years. A reminder of what he had had and what he had lost. Even now, Adele's eyes were upon him, shining with the mixture of adoration and desire that he hadn't appreciated until it was too late.

There was a tap on the door, then Petra slipped in with his afternoon cup of tea.

'Is everything all right?' she asked him, sensing his mood. She was used to his capricious nature, knew that he could slip from convivial to sombre in the blink of an eye.

'I . . . think I'm just tired,' Jack told her. He managed a weary smile. 'Perhaps one too many glasses of wine with lunch.'

She put the cup down on the desk in front of him. She saw the letter, and held out her hand.

'Would you like me to post that for you?'

Jack stared down at it. It would be far easier to slip it into the drawer with all the others. That way he wouldn't be left wondering. That way, he was in charge of his destiny. If he posted it, he would have the agony of waiting for a reply.

'Yes,' he said. 'Yes, please. That would be very kind.'

Imogen came out of Jack's apartment in a daze. Outside, the bright sunshine hit her, and the white of the Zattere opposite rose up before her like a mirage. The sky and the water and the buildings were outlined with a sharpness that matched the clarity in her mind. A flotilla of gondolas glided past, serene yet totally focused on their destination. That was, she realised, exactly how she felt. Serene but focused. Suddenly the future was clear.

She wondered how much Adele had known this was what she needed, and if she had been sent to Jack Molloy to learn to recognise love when she saw it? Adele was wise and intuitive. It wasn't beyond her to second-guess what Imogen had been going through. She would have known that a simple conversation wasn't enough. That Imogen had to work it out for herself.

Either way, she didn't care. She knew what she had to do. Danny had known better than her what they meant to each other, and hadn't been scared to acknowledge it, yet Imogen had backed away. What had she been so afraid of? Love, when it was pure and right and tangible, didn't need any justification or analysis. She always went with her gut when she bought a painting, so why hadn't she been able to accept what they had for what it was?

Did she have some deep-rooted fear that the bad boy and

328

the good girl couldn't have a fairytale ending? Just because the rest of Shallowford might be sceptical? If that was what she was so afraid of, then why hadn't she done what Nicky had done, and married someone predictably safe and dull and boring?

She hurried back along the cobbles to the hotel. She wondered what Danny had been doing while she was gone. She longed to touch him, and kiss him, and tell him what he had known all along. What he had already had the courage to declare, because he was a better person than she was. She burst into the room, the smile on her face wide, her eyes bright with anticipation.

It was empty. Still and silent. It was as if no one had ever been there. The bed was perfectly made up, the once-tangled sheets smoothed to perfection and covered over. Everything was in its place, as if the room was ready for the next influx of guests. There was no sign of Danny or his belongings. His clothes, his bag, were all gone.

She sat on the edge of the bed as the energy and hope drained out of her. She was too late. She had driven him away, with her prissy, middle-class career-obsessed life-plan that left no room for spontaneity or change or compromise. No wonder he'd scarpered. He was probably thinking he'd had a lucky escape. He was probably already in some back-street bacaro, chatting up a sultry Italian girl with fire in her eyes and passion in her soul, who didn't think she was better than she ought to be . . .

She let out a little scream as a figure stepped through the curtains of the balcony and into the room. She jumped up, her heart pounding.

329

It was Danny. He stood there, in his jeans and a tight T-shirt and bare feet, a cup in his hand.

'You frightened the life out of me!'

'Sorry. I was having a coffee on the balcony.'

'I thought you'd gone.'

'Course not.' He frowned.

'Where's all your stuff?'

He laughed. 'The butler came and unpacked it all. Everything's hung up in the cupboard. He's taken my jacket away to dry-clean it.'

Imogen didn't know whether to laugh or cry. She put her face in her hands.

'What's up?' He came and sat beside her. He put his arm round her. She melted into him. 'Didn't it go well, the meeting?'

She managed to nod. 'Yes, it was fine. It was . . . very interesting.'

She didn't really know where to begin. Her brain was still processing everything: her grandmother's affair, the fact that she would soon be in possession of a painting that would blow the art world's mind. It changed everything.

'Danny . . .'

'Yeah?'

'I'm not going to go to New York.'

Not a muscle in his face flickered.

'What about . . . your career?'

'I can still have that. I can work with Oostermeyer and Sabol, as a consultant. I've thought about it. I'm more use to them on this side of the Atlantic. I'm going to get a London office. Go to New York whenever I need to. Get some more clients.'

He was nodding, trying to keep up.

'Well,' he said finally. 'Good for you.'

His voice was flat. She took a deep breath.

'And I'm going to carry on living in Shallowford.' She wriggled round so she was looking straight into his eyes. 'With you . . . ?'

She couldn't judge his reaction. He was the master of the blank expression, his features inscrutable, his eyes giving nothing away.

He stared at her for a moment. 'I don't know about that. I'll have to think about it.'

She felt her heart deflate, and hope shrivel. It felt like a burst balloon inside her. She supposed she deserved nothing more. She couldn't expect him to drop everything and welcome her with open arms. Then she saw the corner of his mouth twitch. He was, she realised, trying desperately not to smile. He looked up at the ceiling, but there was laughter in his eyes as he finally spoke.

'I think Top Cat might have something to say about your demands on my attention. He gets very jealous, you know. He's not good at sharing. He'd be a nightmare to live with—'

His words were cut off as Imogen gave a shriek of indignation and pushed him back onto the bed. She scrambled on top of him and pinned his wrists down with a mischievous grin. She looked down at him and his face was alive with joy.

'Well, of course,' she told him. 'If you want your life to be ruled by a mangy ginger kitten, that's up to you.'

He slid his hands up her thighs, under her dress. 'Hell hath no fury like a kitten scorned.'

For a few moments they stared each other out. Then she felt his fingers slide under the lace of her knickers, touching the bare skin. She couldn't keep up the pretence a moment longer. She melted down into him.

Danny McVeigh. She was going to live with him, in his fairytale cottage. They would walk hand in hand through Shallowford, proud to be together. She shut her eyes, and in her mind's eye she conjured up her school exercise book, with its tattered red cover. And on the back page, in inky splats, was written, over and over, Imogen McVeigh. Imogen McVeigh. Imogen McVeigh.

Thirty-four

By late afternoon, Emmie and Archie were exhausted. An opportunistic gondolier bore down on them just at the moment when their resistance was weakest. Minutes later, they found themselves lying back on a mound of richly upholstered cushions, gliding through secret hidden canals, miles away from the touristy crowds they had experienced earlier.

'I sing for you?' asked the gondolier eagerly. 'I serenade you, yes? The happy couple?'

'Oh no,' said Archie hastily. 'I think you've got the wrong end of the pole. Ha ha.'

The gondolier frowned. Emmie looked down at her lap and smiled.

'It's free,' said the gondolier. 'No charge.'

'But we're not an item,' said Archie, pointing between him and Emmie. 'We're not a couple. Just friends. Amigos?' He frowned. 'No. That's Spanish. How do you say "friend" in Italian?'

'I don't know,' said Emmie.

'Friends?' said the gondolier. He shook his head. He didn't look remotely convinced. 'Not friends, no.' He pointed between the two of them. 'I can tell.'

Archie looked at Emmie. 'He won't be happy unless we let him sing.'

She shrugged. 'When in Venice . . .'

Archie turned back to the gondolier and gave him the thumbs up. 'Go for it, mate. Sing your heart out. Go for your life . . .'

The gondolier beamed and burst into joyful song. Emmie put her hand over her face, laughing with embarrassment. Archie chewed his thumbnail, his eyebrows raised, but he couldn't help grinning too. The two of them exchanged glances, both equally self-conscious but amused.

'We've been conned,' said Archie. 'I'll have to give him a mammoth tip now. We fell right into that one.'

That evening, it took Archie and Emmie a while to find a place to eat they both agreed on. Eventually they found one, opposite a gondola repair yard – a proper authentic Venetian bacaro which served cicheti, the Italian version of tapas. They sat for hours, grazing on bruschetta and bocconcini and fritto misto, then a huge bowl of risi e pisi, the house signature dish, which was translated as rice and peas but was so rich and creamy and melting that seemed too prosaic a title. At the end, they forced down panna cotta with blackberries, and the owner stuck a bottle of grappa on their table.

'Be rude not to,' said Archie, and poured them each a glass of the fiery liquid.

By the time they came out, the sun had long gone from the sky. Emmie hooked her arm through Archie's and they began to sway their way gently along the canal-side, languid with rich food.

Twenty minutes later they were hopelessly lost.

'I'm sure that bridge there leads into the square that leads to the other square that leads to the bridge near the hotel,' Emmie pointed vaguely.

'It looks just like every other bridge to me.'

Several very large raindrops began to fall.

'It's going to pour.'

'We'd better run.'

'We don't know where to run to!'

The sky opened and it seemed as if the entire contents of the lagoon was being emptied over their heads. They were surrounded by grey, infinite grey, the buildings closing in on them, the canal as black as squid ink beside them. There was no one in sight. Everyone had wisely vanished indoors. They opened their map but in seconds it was wet through and completely illegible. Archie took off his jumper and put it over Emmie's head, pulling her into a doorway. There was just enough of a portico to shelter them. Next to him, she trembled with cold. He looked down at her, her hair plastered against her head, her mascara running down her cheeks. He felt an extraordinary urge he had never really felt with anyone before. Not in this way.

He wanted, more than anything, to kiss her.

She was looking up at him. 'This is the wettest rain ever.'

He couldn't stop staring into her eyes. She drew back a little, disconcerted.

'Are you OK?' she asked.

No. No, he bloody wasn't. He'd been hit by a thunderbolt and he was going to do something very stupid if he wasn't careful. He turned away.

'Archie!'

'We might as well just make a run for it,' he said. 'We're soaking as it is.'

He stepped out from the doorway and into the deluge. Water was trickling down the back of his neck. He was freezing. Freezing outside – and in. His heart felt as cold as granite.

Emmie trotted beside him, anxious, trying to keep up, then her face lit up.

'There we are!' she said, pointing at a nearby passageway. 'It's this way. Definitely. I remember that fountain. We're not all that far after all.'

He didn't reply. She grabbed his hand, tugging him. 'Come on!' she urged him. 'You'll catch your death.'

Maybe, thought Archie, that would be the answer. A quick case of double pneumonia that would carry him off and put him out of his misery. Death in Venice. How very appropriate. He hurried along with her nonetheless, his chivalry overriding his despair. Emmie needed to get back – she needed to get warm and dry as quickly as she could.

When they got back to the hotel, Archie shot into his room. 'I'll see you in the morning,' he mumbled. 'I don't feel too great, to be honest.'

He didn't look at her before shutting the door. He sat down on the bed, dripping all over the eiderdown. He shivered. The sooner they got back to England, the better, he thought. Before he made a fool of himself.

Breakfast the next day was excruciating. Archie blamed his silence on the grappa.

'The stuff always gives me a headache,' he said, but his head felt fine. It was his heart that was in agony.

336

He ate as many of the sweet bread rolls with strawberry jam as he could, just to give himself something to do. Emmie pulled her roll apart and scattered the crumbs on the ground for the tiny birds to peck at. They had barely spoken. She was clearly puzzled by his mood, but he didn't know what to say to justify his gloom.

Now it was almost time to leave, he couldn't bear the thought of going back home. The idea of that wretched cottage and all the work that needed doing to it made his skin crawl. He didn't want to think about the farm, or the business. Or a life without Jay to phone him up and drag him down to the pub, or flip up to Twickenham to watch the rugby. But he didn't have any choice. He and Emmie would have to make their way to the airport straight after breakfast. No doubt they would say a stilted goodbye at Heathrow, and make an arrangement to meet for lunch that they wouldn't keep. And she would slip through his fingers and he would never see her again, and he would disappear back to the farm and become a recluse, just as Jay had predicted, because without Jay to galvanise him his social life would wither. And he would get duller and duller by the day, less like the person he wanted to be, and he would no longer feel the little bit of warmth Emmie had injected into his life, the little bit of optimism, the feeling that there was something more out there.

The airport was crowded, brimming with people reluctant to leave the splendour of the most ravishing city in the world and return to normality. To roads and traffic and prosaic bricks and mortar, to places where the sun didn't dance on the water and turn the buildings to gold. The magic evaporated as soon as they walked through the doors and began to look on the departure board for their check-in desk. Emmie was subdued and rather agitated, repeatedly checking for her ticket and passport and searching in her handbag. As she stood in the queue for the check-in she twisted her fingers round and round.

She looked up at him. Her eyes were wide and round. 'I don't want to go home,' she said suddenly. Then she blushed, and looked away.

Archie felt his throat tighten. He couldn't think. Everything was so confusing. And then he thought he heard a voice: that dry, bemused tone.

'For heaven's sake, Harbinson. Just get on with it.'

Archie felt his heart start to beat faster. 'What?' he whispered.

This time, he definitely heard the reply.

'Go for it. You're only here once. Trust me on that one.'

Archie dropped his bag on the floor and turned to Emmie. 'I don't want to go back either.' As the next passengers were checked in and their baggage disappeared into the black hole, the queue shuffled forward. 'So let's not.'

Emmie laughed. 'Wouldn't that be amazing? In our dreams.'

'It doesn't *have* to be in our dreams, though, does it? We could make it reality.'

Emmie looked at him, perplexed, as they reached the check-in desk. She put down her hat-boxes on the conveyor belt. The check-in girl smiled up at them. 'Can I have your passports, please?'

'Wait.' Archie stopped Emmie from handing her passport

over. She frowned. He put his hand on her arm. 'Let's go back. Let's go back to the hotel, Emmie.'

'I can't. I have to get back.'

'What for?'

'I've got hats to make. Appointments. Stuff to do . . .'

'Are you telling me one more week would really make a difference?' Archie demanded. 'I don't mean to be rude, Em, but it's only hats. Surely your customers won't mind. Come on. You only live once. If the past few weeks have taught me anything, it's that. *Carpe diem* and all that.'

Emmie bit her lip and looked away. Her cheeks were burning pink. 'I don't have that kind of money, Archie. You know that. I can't afford to stay on.'

'I've got the money.' He had no idea what it was going to cost, but he'd find the money if it killed him. 'We'll have the penthouse suite, if it's available.'

The people in the queue behind were getting restless. The check-in girl was looking irritated. 'Excuse me. Do you want to go on this flight or not?'

'No, we don't,' Archie told her. He picked up his and Emmie's bags and her hat-boxes from the conveyor belt. 'Come on.'

Emmie stared at him open-mouthed. 'We can't just . . . not go home. We can't . . .'

'Why not?' Archie felt filled with courage and determination. He could feel Jay cheering him on from above. He felt giddy with recklessness and spontaneity. And something else. A big burning ball of heat inside that was driving him on.

'You're mad.' She looked incredulous.

'I'm not mad,' retorted Archie. 'This is the best idea I have ever had in my life.'

'I haven't got enough clothes!' she protested.

'We can buy clothes.' Archie strode across the airport, Emmie half-running after him.

'I've got a dentist appointment on Tuesday,' she protested. 'And I need to pay my TV licence. And tax my car . . .'

'It doesn't matter. None of it matters. It will still all be there when you get back. What matters is living for the moment. For now.' He turned to her, laden with the luggage. 'I don't want to go back to the farm, and deal with a load of paperwork. I want to have an adventure. I want excitement. I want . . .'

He looked at her. He couldn't judge her expression. But he knew this was the moment.

'I want you,' he told her.

She stood very still. Archie looked down at the floor. It was the most impulsive thing he had ever done. The biggest risk he had ever taken. The sound of the crowds around him roared in his ears. The airport announcements babbled in the background, incoherent. He shut his eyes. He wished he could spirit himself away. Bloody Jay, he thought, egging him on.

'OK then.'

Her voice was so low and quiet he barely heard it. He opened his eyes.

'What?' he asked.

She nodded. 'Let's do it.'

She stepped forward. He dropped all the bags and the hat-boxes. She threw her arms around his neck.

'It's the craziest thing I've ever heard,' she told him.

'Who cares?' he asked. Around them passengers looked askance as he picked her up and whirled her round. Eventually he put her down and picked their luggage back up. She had to run to keep up as he strode out of the doors they had only recently come in through. Five minutes later, they waited for the waterbus to take them back to the city, hands entwined.

'Hey,' grinned Emmie. 'We need to email Patricia.'

'God, no, she'll only want photographs,' groaned Archie.

'It's only fair,' insisted Emmie. 'After all, if it wasn't for Not On The Shelf . . .'

She laid her head on his shoulder.

Archie didn't reply. It was nothing to do with Not On The Shelf. That had just been the conduit. He drew Emmie towards him, tucking her into him to protect her from the breeze that was blowing across the water. 'Thanks, mate,' he whispered, and imagined Jay up above, sitting on a cloud, a twenty-first-century Cupid, raising a glass to the two of them with a satisfied wink.

Later that afternoon, Riley drove the motorboat that came with the palazzo back from the island of Burano, where he and Sylvie had had lunch at their favourite fish restaurant. She'd also bought a bolt of the lace the island was famous for, and was uncharacteristically coy about it, tucking it away at the bottom of her bag.

'Don't ask questions,' she warned, pointing at him, and Riley grinned.

Just before the landing where their boat was moored, they drove under a tiny bridge. On top of it stood a couple, locked in an embrace, kissing as if they would never stop, completely unaware of anything else around them. Riley's heart skipped a beat as he recognised them. It was the couple from the waiting room. The ones who'd been subjected to that terrible photo shoot. The ones who'd wished themselves a million miles away.

'The hat girl,' said Sylvie, and smiled, keeping yet another secret for another day.

Riley killed the engine, grappled in his bag for his camera. He was a pro. He was ready in seconds. He framed them perfectly as the setting sun exploded into a ball of fire, gilding them in a pool of molten light.

'That,' he said to Sylvie as he clicked the shutter, 'is the money shot.'

Afterwards

Thirty-five

Adele had been working tirelessly all week, sorting out what she was going to take with her from Bridge House when she finally left.

Nicky had brought a couple from London to view the house, prior to it going on the market officially. They had fallen completely in love with it and made a more than generous offer. Compounded by the fact that they had given Adele as long as she liked to find somewhere else to move to, it had left her with little choice but to accept. They had been charming, with a lively young family as well as three teenagers from the man's previous marriage, so they were planning to use the coach house as separate accommodation for when they descended. Adele felt she would be leaving her home in good hands, and although she was wistful – of course she was – she had always been adept at knowing when it was time to move on.

It didn't matter to her, though, now she knew that Imogen was going to be all right. Her granddaughter had come back from Venice lit up from the inside. Adele had been a little shocked by her revelation, but once she had met Danny properly her fears were allayed. Adele, of anyone, could recognise true love. She could tell it from infatuation.

They were a team, outlining their plans to her, bubbling with excitement and enthusiasm, their sentences playing leapfrog with each other: Imogen was going to move into Woodbine Cottage, then open a consultancy in London, with a small office-cum-gallery. They had plans to develop a specialist art security consultancy too, pooling their skills and contacts.

And they were going to hold a huge opening party to reveal *The Inamorata* to the world at large: her unveiling would be the perfect way to garner publicity for the new businesses. The picture would remain the jewel in the crown at the gallery, never for sale, but enticing customers and the curious alike to come and view the lost Reuben Zeale masterpiece. The art world would be abuzz with speculation and intrigue.

Imogen had made sure her grandmother didn't mind being on display to the world in this way, but Adele had reassured her. After all, there was no one alive now who would recognise the model for *The Inamorata*. She felt certain that most of the people in Simone's who had been aware of her affair with Jack had passed on by now, and even if one of them was still alive, and recognised Adele, then so what? It proved nothing. Celebrating this work of art was more important than protecting her privacy; Adele felt sure of that. The affair had been a lifetime ago.

As she passed through the hallway with a pile of old paperbacks to run up to the charity shop, the post plopped onto the doormat. On top of the usual bills and catalogues sat a white envelope with spiky black writing and a foreign stamp. She stood staring at it for a moment. She remembered a letter from years ago, a letter in pale turquoise ink that had changed her life forever.

All she could hear was the ticking of the grandfather clock in time with her pulse. Eventually she set down the box and picked up the envelope. Suddenly she couldn't open it fast enough, hungry for the words.

The letter was brief. Adele, usually so composed, felt the breath squeezed from her body and the peppery sting of tears. She read it again, three times over, but there was no need to search for hidden meaning. It was all there, his heart, right there on the page. No games, no pretence.

She walked into the morning room. What she was about to do wasn't foolhardy or reckless. She had no choice. She couldn't go to her grave without seeing him again. Hearing his voice and feeling his touch. It wasn't a betrayal. She and William had shared a wonderful life together. Their love had been enduring and authentic. Once she'd left Venice, she hadn't let her affair with Jack taint their marriage a moment longer. William had slipped away knowing that Adele's love for him was strong and true. Her decision wasn't going to change that.

She picked up the telephone and dialled, almost without stopping to think. In fact, it was important that she didn't. If she started thinking about dates, commitments, details, she would never do it. There would always be a reason not to.

The phone was answered almost immediately. 'Venice Simplon Orient Express.'

'Hello,' she said. 'I'd like to book a ticket. A ticket to Venice, on your next available trip . . .'

If you have enjoyed

A Night on the Orient Express

turn the page to read some travel tips from
Veronica Henry, to inspire you to make
the journey for yourself . . .

What to pack

If *A Night on the Orient Express* has inspired you to venture on this iconic journey of a lifetime, here is some sartorial advice.

You will need three outfits – something dressy and glam for the grand departure, an evening frock and something smart but more casual for the second day when you arrive in Venice.

The Venice Simplon Orient Express departure lounge at Victoria is always a fashion parade, as everyone gathers in their finery. My best tip would be to imagine you are dressing for a daytime wedding. Of course, it depends on the weather, but a gorgeous yet classic dress is the perfect option, or a chic tailored suit. Be inspired by Diane von Furstenberg and Chanel, although you don't have to splash out on designer labels. There are plenty of high-street alternatives which look the part. High heels suit the occasion – now is not the time for comfy footwear. And a lovely coat if it's chilly – don't spoil the effect by donning your dog-walking jacket. If you are a hat person – or even if you aren't! – then this is definitely the moment to bring out the millinery. A hat always adds a sense of occasion, from a discreet felt fedora to an elaborate cartwheel topped with an

ostrich feather. For men, a smart suit or jacket and tie will suffice (isn't it always so much easier for men?).

Dinner in the evening is the perfect opportunity for showy opulence. Silk, satin, velvet – whatever your preference, it should be luxe and glamour all the way. If you have heirloom jewellery, now is the time to get it out of the safe. If not, just bling it on with some good costume jewellery. An updo will also make you feel the part. For men, black tie is the easiest option, but they won't be thrown off if they just go for a smart jacket.

The next day can be less dressy and more casual as the train travels down towards Venice, leaving you to curl up in your cabin with a good book or recline in the bar with a hot chocolate laced with brandy, followed by lunch. By now you will be feeling thoroughly relaxed, so maybe a slouchy jumper and trousers or a sweater dress would fit the bill. Remember, you will be making your way into Venice at the end of the day, so comfort is more of an issue. Jumping on a vaporetto in towering heels might not be such a good idea!

And please – don't forget to pay attention to your accessories, especially your luggage. It doesn't have to be vintage Louis Vuitton, but don't go stuffing your overnight things into your gym bag.

All in all, remember – you can't overdress on the Orient Express!

Five books inspired by trains

A train is the perfect setting for a writer, as your characters are captive and the sense of a journey is always inspirational.

The Little Engine that Could by Watty Piper
A delightful childhood tale, which teaches you that if you don't give up, you will succeed in the end.

The Railway Children by E. Nesbit
When they have to move to the depths of the countryside, the lives of three children are changed irrevocably by the nearby railway line.

Murder on the Orient Express by Agatha Christie
A classic – Hercule Poirot investigates when a man is found murdered in his cabin, and no one is beyond suspicion.

Anna Karenina by Leo Tolstoy
Anna catches her first sight of her lover-to-be, Vronsky, on the train – with tragic consequences.

The Slow Train to Milan by Lisa St Aubin de Terán
A bohemian journey through Italy is related by Lisa Veta and her eccentric older lover Caesar.

Five films set in Venice

Venice is adored by film-makers, understandably, and here are five of the most successful that have exploited the gloriousness of the location. They might whet your appetite for a visit.

Death in Venice
A composer becomes obsessed by a beautiful young boy as Venice is gripped by a cholera epidemic. Famous for its use of Mahler's Fifth Symphony.

Don't Look Now
A creepy, atmospheric thriller based on the Daphne du Maurier short story, this is emotional, erotically charged and unsettling.

The Tourist
A ridiculously enjoyable spy caper in which Venice and Angelina Jolie vie to be the most beautiful during the breathtaking action sequences.

Summertime
Katharine Hepburn plays a feisty spinster who falls in love for the first time in Venice – touching and ultimately heartbreaking.

Everyone Says I Love You
Woody Allen falls in love with Julia Roberts in Venice and tries to convince her he is the man of her dreams – with surprising consequences.

Pisi e risi

Pisi e risi is the archetypal Venetian recipe, served in count-less restaurants throughout the city, but simple to recreate at home and the perfect supper dish – children love it.

> 500 g frozen peas (do use fresh if you have them, but blanch them first)
> 1½ litres warm chicken stock (you can use a stock cube but fresh is nicer)
> 2 tbsp butter
> 50 g *cubetti di pancetta*
> 1 onion, finely chopped
> 225 g risotto rice
> 1 glass white wine
> Handful of fresh Parmesan, finely grated
> Handful of flat-leaf parsley, finely chopped
> Salt and pepper

Melt the butter in a heavy-bottomed pan, then fry the diced onion and pancetta together until the onions begin to soften. Add the rice, and stir until all the grains are coated in the butter and the oil is released by the pancetta. Pour in the wine and simmer gently, stirring until the rice has

absorbed the liquid. Continue doing this with ladles of stock – you need to pay attention and make sure the rice doesn't stick to the pan. Once the rice is cooked through but still firm, add the peas and a final ladle of stock and cook through. The risotto should still be quite runny, not dry. Add salt and pepper to taste, then throw in the handfuls of Parmesan and parsley, and serve in bowls.

The Inamorata

This cocktail is inspired by the painting Jack had commissioned of Adele, and by their final journey together taking in London, Paris and Venice.

25 ml lemon juice
50 ml London dry gin
25 ml Cointreau
Prosecco

Put the first three ingredients in a cocktail shaker and shake with some ice cubes. Strain into a flute, and top up with chilled Prosecco.

To be drunk lolling on a velvet chaise longue in a silken chemise. The author takes no responsibility for what happens afterwards.